The Bottled Bootlegger

A Doro Banyon Cozy Historical
Mystery-Book Five

D.S. Lang

Book Cover by Karen Phillips

Editing by Alyssa Colton

ISBN ebook: 978-1-962039-13-0

ISBN paperback: 978-1-962039-14-7

Chapter One

Dorothea Banyon leaned back in the passenger seat of Everett Mallow's Willys-Knight roadster. "It's been a lovely evening," she observed. And their first one out together. Certainly, more would follow.

"It sure has," Ev agreed as he drove out of Sylvania and west toward Michaw. "Now, we realize we can talk about more than crimes and sleuthing."

When Doro glanced at him, she only saw his profile in silhouette due to the darkness, but a lilt of laughter was in his voice. She lightly tapped his arm. "We've talked about other topics over the past year."

"We have, but investigations have taken a lot of our time." He focused on the road, but his voice still held pleasure. "Tonight was easy and fun and casual."

"It was," she agreed. Now that they were stepping out, Doro no longer felt conflicting emotions. Quite the contrary. Her fondness for Ev was growing and solidifying. As far as she could tell, he felt the same way. But this was their first formal date. Getting better acquainted was important, which meant they were a long way from courting, a more serious commitment than stepping out—much more serious. At least that was the prevailing sentiment among the other women of her acquaintance. Since she had never had a beau, Doro was not sure about the nuances of male-female relationships. Could their friendship—or whatever it was—fizzle at this stage? Possibly, she supposed. The idea held her joy in check. What should she say now? Uncertainty held her tongue.

After a few moments, Ev spoke. "Your grandmother called this morning and invited me to your birthday dinner. She said it's not a surprise." He hesitated for a heartbeat. "And you approved the guests."

His odd tone made Doro shift toward him. Now that they were outside town, the darkness completely hid his face, so gleaning the source of the change in his voice was impossible. Perhaps escorting her to her grandmother's home bothered him. Was it too much, too soon? Unsure, she made a general observation. "On the train trip home, Aggie and Gram brought up having a little party. They insisted I need to celebrate on the day, even though we had a special birthday dinner with my parents." Bittersweet recollections filled her mind as Doro thought about her summer in Colorado. Spending time with her mother and father had been wonderful, but she longed for the days when the entire family had been in Michaw, the days before consumption had forced Julia Banyon to leave Ohio for a more hospitable climate. When returning became impossible, Doro's father had followed. Since the three of them could not be together for most special occasions now, both of her parents wanted to mark any when they were. That had led to the early recognition of Doro's special day.

"You don't want to celebrate here?" Ev's query broke into Doro's reverie.

Again, he sounded odd—reluctant, uncertain, unwilling? Or was she reading too much into his tone and words? "I love festivities, but please don't feel like you have to come."

He shot her a quick glance before looking back at the road. "I'd love to be there as long as I'm not intruding."

Relief had Doro sinking back in the passenger seat. "You won't intrude. After all, we're..." Her voice trailed off. Should she say they were stepping out? They were. Weren't they? Did one time constitute really stepping out? Not for the first time, Doro's social inexperience with the opposite sex came to the fore. Most young women of twenty-six, which she would be in less than three weeks, were married. Doro had not even had a serious beau.

Several moments passed before Ev, his voice hushed and husky, spoke again. "You agreed to come out with me tonight, which signals the start of stepping out, doesn't it? I mean, we talked about it a little in Chicago and after you got home." He cleared his throat. "Sorry, I'm not exactly an old hand in social situations. I've always been busy with work."

Although his features were obscured, Doro could picture Ev in her mind as she had during her summer visit to Colorado and on the trip home—especially after she had been kidnapped by a killer. During that ordeal, Doro had thought long and hard about her future. With her life in jeopardy, she'd deliberated about Ev and a relationship with him, not her lifelong dream of becoming the Michaw College library director. But dreams could merge, couldn't they? That seemed more possible now than it had a few weeks ago.

"Doro? Did I misunderstand you?" Ev asked. "I don't want to push you into anything, so maybe I shouldn't have asked if the Board of Trustees' decision to employ married women made a difference to you. Maybe you felt like you had to come out tonight. Last winter, your reason for not wanting to see each other was your focus on your career. I thought now that you can keep your job and also..." He cleared his throat but said nothing more.

His assertion evoked a potent memory. The previous Christmas, Ev had expressed his interest in being more than friends and colleagues. He had wanted to step out and court. Citing Michaw College's ban on female faculty members marrying, Doro had turned him down by saying she did not plan to wed, so stepping out was not sensible. But he had obviously misconstrued her current silence, so Doro rushed to explain. "I'm glad you asked, because the change in policy makes a difference. A big one. I've never been out with any young man more than twice, because I thought marriage meant giving up my career. That's the only reason I didn't think we should see each other socially." Abruptly, she realized how her statement might sound. "Not that we're courting. We're just stepping out. That's all. We have to start..." Her voice trailed as Doro realized she was blathering.

"As you can tell, I have little experience with social niceties myself."

A low chuckle left him. "We're a good pair."

Warmth spread through Doro. "We are. Anyhow, I hope you'll come to my birthday celebration. My grandmother has a housekeeper, Mrs. Ogilvie, who is a wonderful cook, so there'll be plenty of good food. Either she or Aggie will bake a cake. Both are talented in the kitchen."

"You are, too."

Doro clucked her tongue. "Not really." The truth was that some of her efforts had been disastrous.

"Your sugar cookies and shortbread are excellent," Ev assured Doro. "Not that I think you should have to make treats for your own birthday."

Doro's pleasure increased. "Gramma Rose has an ice cream churn, so we'll make it fresh to go with the cake, and I'll make shortbread again soon."

"Great. It's my favorite cookie."

He had said as much during Michaw's May Days celebration, and Doro had not forgotten. Nor would she. A little indulgence especially for him would be a gracious gesture, which brought a question to her mind. "When is your birthday?" Ev had started his job at the college the previous October. In the time she had known him, he had not mentioned the special date. She hoped she hadn't missed it. Every birthday deserved to be remembered and feted.

"Three weeks after yours. I turned twenty-six right before I moved to Michaw."

Relief filled her. "Good. We'll have to celebrate your day, too."

A moment passed before he replied. "It's a nice thought, but not necessary. I haven't done anything special in years. Not since I was a kid, and my mom always made a cake and a special meal."

His statement brought sadness and determination. "But we'll see that you celebrate this year."

Again, time ensued ahead of his response. "All right, but don't go to a lot of trouble."

"It's no trouble. We can make it small, like mine." Doro's mind filled with ideas. "It'll be around the start of classes, so the weekend beforehand might work. We could have dinner at Gramma Rose's house with ice cream and cake. How does that sound?" She hoped she hadn't overstepped with her enthusiasm, but she wanted a party for him. Knowing he had not celebrated since childhood tugged at her heartstrings.

"Sounds fine," he said with a hint of humor in his voice. "First, we'll celebrate you."

His lighthearted tone lifted Doro's spirits even further. Any awkwardness fell away, and she felt more at ease than ever. For the next ten minutes, they chatted about nothing in particular, and she enjoyed every moment.

Their casual conversation ended when they turned off the road from Sylvania and headed into the homestretch. In a matter of minutes, they'd be back in Michaw. Farmhouses were scattered along the way, but one cottage—now visible—was of interest, so Doro was not surprised when he shifted into low gear. The old homestead had been under scrutiny from local lawmen for months. Ev, who served as the Michaw College campus security officer and the town deputy constable, was one of them.

"That's Wade's vehicle in front of the house," he said.

Doro craned her neck for a better look. The Packard definitely belonged to Wade Lammers, the local constable. "I wonder why he's here. Would Wade drive by at night?" Both lawmen monitored the suspected bootleggers living in the cottage, which made Wade's presence a cause for concern. Had something happened while she and Ev were in nearby Sylvania for a night of fun? Something bad?

"He might. I have come by late on occasion, but I'm going to find out why he stopped." Ev exited the vehicle. When Doro opened her door, he swiveled toward her. "Stay here. I don't like how this looks." His voice was low and grim.

Part of her, a big part, wanted to go along and see for herself what was happening. But she might be a distraction if she did, so Doro reluctantly agreed. "All right."

After nodding, Ev moved away to peek into Wade's Packard before he disappeared behind the house. For several minutes, Doro peered into the darkness. She saw nothing except a lamp burning in the cottage's side window. Not a single sound reached her ears, which increased her anxiety. As time stretched out, she grew more and more concerned. Where was Ev? And what about Wade?

Finally, unable to wait another moment, Doro got out and tiptoed toward the barn at the back of the property. When it came into view, she stopped in her tracks. The doors were wide open and light poured out. Silhouetted inside the building were Ev and Wade, both of whom were on their knees, studying something on the ground. But what? As Doro grew closer, she realized the form was a *who*, not a *what*. She rushed forward.

Abruptly, Ev looked up. "Didn't I say to stay in my vehicle?"

The question held an edge, which annoyed Doro. "You've been in here for a while, and I got worried."

Ev grimaced. "Worried or curious?"

A sound similar to a chuckle left Wade. "Hi, Doro. I hope you and Ev enjoyed dinner and the movie." He glanced at the body on the barn floor. "Sorry you have to witness this."

Doro followed the constable's gaze. "It's Mr. Fulton," she murmured.

"Yep," Wade said as he and Ev stood. Although three inches shorter than Ev, the town constable was ten pounds heavier, and it was all brawn. Ev was all lean muscle.

A host of facts rolled through Doro's mind. "Where is Mrs. Fulton?"

Wade shook his head. "No idea. She wasn't here when I arrived. I went in the house. No sign of her there, either."

An impending sense of doom blanketed Doro. "Mr. and Mrs. Fulton have been a cause for curiosity long before now." She and her best friend Agatha Darwine had first met the couple the previous December during a murder investigation. While not involved in the killing, the pair had long been suspected of helping their former employers, the Parsons, bootleg. Although Mr. Parson was dead, and his widow was long-gone, the older couple had stayed in the area, which gave rise to more speculation among townsfolk. As Doro studied Ev's expression, she considered their chance meeting in the Chicago train station. Less than a month ago, he had been with his old boss from the Prohibition Bureau, and she had been on her way home after spending the summer in Colorado. Ev and the senior Prohibition agent had been enroute to a meeting. While she had not asked about that discussion yet, Doro did now. "Since you were consulting with the Bureau about bootlegging runs going through or near here, I suppose you'll contact them."

He bowed his head and rubbed the back of his neck. When Ev looked back at Doro, his silver gaze glimmered. "I'm surprised you haven't asked me about my time in Chicago before now."

"I'm not actually asking you now," she pointed out in a cheery tone.

"But you'd like to know." Humor laced his tone and glittered in his gaze.

Admitting the truth seemed wise. "I would, although no matter what I ask, I'm sure you won't reveal everything."

Wade cleared his throat. "I'm going to look out back." With that, he slipped away.

Doro turned back to Ev, who gave a rueful smile. "Sorry, but I can't give all the details. As I told you in the train station, the Bureau has evidence of liquor being transported from Toledo to Chicago, which isn't surprising. We figured as much a while back. Now, it's a certainty. What concerned my old boss was the proximity of the distribution route to Michaw, and the possibility that someone here was involved."

"The route being Chicago Pike and the someone being Fulton." The main road was only fifteen miles south of town. Rumrunners could easily head out of Toledo and through or near Michaw on their way to the primary course, which would take them to Chicago.

"That's what we believe."

Doro's gaze strayed to Mr. Fulton's body. "The Fultons are known to the Bureau?"

Ev nodded. "The couple has been under federal scrutiny for rumrunning, and so was their former employer. But you're already aware of that."

"Mostly from town gossip," she replied. "Mr. Parson seemed like a slick character, but I only saw him in passing, and that was a few years back."

"Slick is a good word. From what I've heard, the Bureau was close to nabbing him when he died in an automobile accident. That was before I became a federal agent."

A troubling thought, one that had arisen in the past, hit Doro. "Was it really an accident?"

Ev put both hands out, palms up. "There's no solid evidence to say different, although there's plenty of suspicion."

For several moments, Doro mulled over the possibilities. "Now you're sure Parson's widow and the Fultons kept his business going." Townsfolk had gossiped about the likelihood, but gossip was not always valid.

"Yep, although she's been gone since last winter, Wade and I were confident Fulton continued the operation, and he paid dearly." Ev's attention returned to the body on the dirt floor.

"Why would his rumrunning partners kill him?" Doro asked.

Ev jerked a thumb toward an open door at the back of the barn. "It looks like booze was stored in there, but only a few bottles remain. Although we can't be sure what happened, there's a possibility that the Fultons were working with more than one group of gangsters to transport booze, which is a bad idea.

Loyalty is key to those guys. Betray them, and you're as good as dead. Or the Fultons might've been keeping some bottles to sell themselves. Also, dangerous. Only one thing is for sure, he wasn't killed for being a loyal partner."

A shiver rippled through Doro. "I suppose not," she murmured after scanning the body again. "I don't see a gunshot or knife wound."

"Mr. Fulton was hit over the head with a blunt instrument. Since there's a bottle next to him, that could be the weapon, but what most likely killed him is hitting his head on a corner of the wagon."

Doro's gaze veered to the intact bottle and back to the bootlegger, who was inches from the old conveyance. "So, it might not have been premeditated."

One of Ev's shoulders rose and fell. "Hard to say at this point. Beyond the evidence here, Mrs. Fulton and their vehicle are gone, but we need to see if anyone noticed her leaving and what time that would've been. Since this place is fairly isolated, that may not be easy."

Doro shifted from foot to foot. "Do you think she killed him?"

"Not at all. I doubt if she was capable of swinging a bottle hard enough to knock him down. Besides, we figure Fulton's killers hauled most of the liquor away." Ev gestured toward the barn door. "There are multiple footprints going from here outside."

Doro studied the tracks, which appeared to vary in size. "It looks like more than one person came and went."

"Yep, but exactly when isn't clear. Tonight, today, yesterday? Wade was careful to walk to the far side, and so was I. So much is left to uncover. It's only a guess that bootleggers came for a pickup tonight."

"But they'd be most likely to kill Mr. Fulton," Doro suggested.

"That's what Wade and I believe," Ev replied. "My old boss will have an opinion, but I'm guessing he'll feel the same way."

"Because of what he knows about liquor being transported along Chicago Pike."

"Exactly." He shoved his hands in his jacket pockets. "When Wade comes back, I'll take you home. I'm sorry our first evening out ended this way." Genuine regret roughened his voice.

Mixed feelings filled Doro. Her question reflected one of them. "Are you coming back?"

"Sure. We need to get Doc Silven out here and contact the county sheriff. Doc can come on his own, and I'll go to the office to make the calls. If Wade isn't in town by then, I'll come back tonight."

"What about Mrs. Fulton? Could she have been kidnapped?"

"I doubt it, since their vehicle is gone," Ev replied.

For a moment, Doro mulled over possibilities. "Since more than one person was here, one could've killed Mr. Fulton, and the other took Mrs. Fulton away in her car."

Ev rubbed his forehead. "It's something we need to consider. It's also possible, she left before the murder. Although that seems less likely. But Wade and I will check around. With luck, we'll find someone who saw her today. If not, looking for her will be another facet of the investigation."

"What will be another facet?" Wade asked as he stepped into the barn again.

"Locating Mrs. Fulton," Ev said, turning to the constable.

"Absolutely." After Wade glanced from Ev to Doro and back, his expression lost some of its tension.

"Did you find anything useful?" Ev asked.

Wade shook his head. "No good clues around the place, although we'll want to check the house and the storeroom more fully. Searching the storm cellar is a good idea, since I only gave it a cursory look. Before then, I'd like to get your old crew out here. At least your old boss. If you'll call the Bureau and Doc, I'll stay and make sure nothing gets disturbed. Silven's verdict on when Fulton died is important to me; it had to be within the last couple of hours."

"I doubt if he can pinpoint it more closely than that," Ev said. "I'll stop by the Silven place after I drop Doro off. Then, I'll head to the office and call Canton before coming back."

When she and Ev had crossed paths in the Chicago train station, Doro had met Lowery Canton, who was a senior Prohibition agent and Ev's former supervisor. The man had appeared polished and professional.

"Thanks, Ev. Sorry, this isn't the best way to end a night out," Wade said.

"It goes with our jobs," Ev replied.

The comment made Doro think of her best friend. "Does Aggie know you were called out here?"

Wade nodded before he and Ev exchanged a long look. "She does."

"What made you drive out?" Doro asked.

Wade shoved his hands in his pockets and fidgeted around. "Jug Barnes was coming back from Sylvania and saw Alf Waggoner's old jalopy parked a few miles from here. Then, when he passed the Fulton house, Jug saw a fancy LaSalle phaeton parked near the barn. Since he knows about bootlegging, he called me as soon as he got home. When the operator didn't locate me at the office or my house, she telephoned my ma's place. Aggie, the kids and I were there for dinner, so Jug came over," Wade replied.

"Because he didn't want to talk over the telephone line," Doro observed. The farmer had a reputation for being taciturn and wary.

A grin touched Wade's mouth. "That's right. No sense adding to the town gossip." His humor fled. "Although news of the murder will spread quickly."

"It will," Doro murmured.

Wade faced Doro. "If you would, please tell Aggie that it'll be late when I get home. I'll call her in the morning."

"Of course." Her best friend and the constable were getting more serious, so Aggie would undoubtedly be worried.

Ev turned to Wade. "A LaSalle phaeton is distinctive and expensive."

"It's definitely a luxury car," Wade added.

"But it's not the one you saw when you arrived," Ev said.

Doro shifted her gaze between the two lawmen. "Did you see a vehicle leaving, Wade?"

"Yep," the constable replied. "I saw one speeding out of the drive and heading east. That's all. I didn't see how many people were in it, let alone who it might be."

"But you're sure of the make, and it wasn't a LaSalle," Doro suggested, since Wade loved automobiles.

"It was a Cadillac roadster. Maroon with black fenders, a fold-down top, and running boards. I saw all that when my headlights hit it, and I've admired a similar car in a show-room," Wade replied. "But they're out of my price range and not a good choice for a family man."

For several moments, Doro considered the various vehicles in Michaw. "It doesn't sound familiar to me."

"Or to me," Wade agreed. "It's the first one I've seen outside a dealership."

"Same here," Ev added. "Not that I saw this one."

For a moment, Doro stared out the open barn door into the night. "So, there were two different vehicles here tonight.

"It seems so. A LaSalle phaeton and a Cadillac roadster," Wade replied. "Judging by what Jug said about when he was past here and when I arrived, it's not likely the two cars came together."

"That's my guess," Ev put in. "But they're both expensive automobiles."

"Which means both vehicles could belong to bootleg-gers," Doro commented.

A moment of silence preceded Ev's response. "Yep, it does."

"I'm afraid so," Wade murmured. "I don't want to rush you two off, but I'd like to get Doc out here and hear what your old boss thinks, Ev. The county sheriff, too. Then, come back here. I'd like to sort out any potential clues before I leave."

"Will do. See you in a while," Ev said to Wade before escorting Doro to his Willys-Knight roadster.

After they were both inside, she turned to Ev. "This may be a complicated case."

"It will be," he agreed.

Multiple questions flowed through her mind, and she asked the most pressing one. "Will you keep consulting with the Bureau?"

A long moment of silence filled the vehicle. "If I'm needed."

The answer was expected, but not wanted. Prohibition agents were all too often hurt, or worse. If Ev did more than consult...Doro let her thoughts trail off. "Will the Bureau take over the murder investigation?"

"It depends. Wade and I'll handle things for now. But if Lowery and his men uncover important details, they may take the lead. Right now, it's hard to say."

"It'll be an intriguing investigation." Doro did not ask to help, because she could anticipate Ev's reply and, when he spoke, his words were predictable.

"An astute observation. Of course, you're shrewd. Very shrewd."

Doro waited for a *but*. When it did not come, she went on. "You don't want me getting involved."

A chuckle left him. "Like I said, you're sharp." Several seconds of silence preceded his more somber statement. "No, I don't want you in the line of fire."

The last phrase made the free-floating anxiety inside her solidify. "Because bootleggers are dangerous." He had said as much more than once. Not that Doro disagreed. Rival gangs often battled each other, and they did not care who got in the way. Sometimes, they targeted lawmen. Would Ev stick to mere consulting? Or would he don a federal agent's badge again?

"They are," he agreed. "Even though Mrs. Fulton may be safe, we can't be sure. I don't want you in a vulnerable position, which you would be if you work on the case."

Although part of her wanted to argue, Doro saw the sense in Ev's concern. And it touched her. "I don't enjoy thinking of you in danger, either," she admitted.

His right hand gently clasped her left before returning his to the gearshift. "Glad to hear it."

"You won't be, will you?" Reassurance would be welcome.

Again, he hesitated before replying. "Like I said in Chicago, consulting isn't dangerous."

"And that's all you're doing," she said.

"That's right. I've got my hands full with being the deputy town constable and the campus security officer. My old boss knows that. Besides, he understands why I left the Bureau and why I won't go back."

"Because you promised your sister you'd find a safer job," Doro put in. The previous fall, Ev had told Doro about his reason for coming to Michaw. His younger sister, and only family, fretted about him.

"Yep. She doesn't need to constantly worry about me."

Now, more than ever, Doro understood his sibling's fears. "I don't want you to go back to the Bureau, either."

His fingers clasped hers again. "There's no need to worry about that. I'm happy here, and I plan to stay."

The warmth of his callused palm sent shivers through Doro. "Good."

"Wade and I will need to meet with Canton." As he shifted into a lower gear, Ev released Doro's hand. "He's apt to come to Michaw, but one of us may need to go into the city, since I'm not sure he can spare agents to look around here."

"You'd go," she said with a sense of certainty.

"Probably, because they know me. They already have some solid ideas about the Fultons' fellow bootleggers, and they may have suspects in mind, as far as the killer. The facts are troubling. Jug Barnes saw a LaSalle, but Wade witnessed a Cadillac leaving. He didn't see the LaSalle, and some time passed between when Jug drove by the Fultons' house and when Wade got out there."

As Doro gazed out the side of the car into the darkness, she considered the details. "The time gap means it's fifty-fifty that the visitors were from two different bootlegging operations."

Ev tapped one forefinger on the steering wheel. "You're right, which will make identifying the killer, or killers, more challenging. Fulton working with more than one gang was mentioned in Chicago. Like I said, if he was, that could've led to his murder. With luck, Wade and I might add to the evidence by digging around Michaw."

"Was Mr. Parson associating with multiple bootleggers?"

"We can't be sure, but he ran a speakeasy, which makes that likely."

Fresh anxiety gripped Doro. "I'm concerned about Mrs. Fulton. She and her husband shouldn't have been rumrunning, but they helped Aggie and me last winter after we were held hostage. Besides, no one deserves to be killed in cold blood."

"I agree, but it's not a rare occurrence among bootleggers." A long breath escaped him. "That's why I don't want you involved in this case. After being held by a murderer last December and kidnapped by another killer less than a month ago, I'd think you'd want to stay out of harm's way for a while."

"Actually, I was hoping to avoid murder cases for a long time. Except in books."

"I wish we both could, but that's not possible at present." He inhaled deeply. "I promise to give you a summary, once the killer is caught. Will that suffice?"

"You always say how astute I am." Even peripheral involvement was better than none at all. Would he agree to that? "Maybe you could share some details along the way."

Moments of silence passed before Ev responded. "That's not a bad idea, as long as you don't act on anything we discuss."

Relief had Doro slumping back in the passenger seat. "I already promised I wouldn't, and I won't." Although she did not want to sit idly by, Doro realized how dangerous digging into the activities of rumrunners might be. "Neither of us is likely to be deeply involved this time. At least not if the murderer is a bootlegger."

A moment passed before he spoke again. "Like I said, the Bureau may take over. That'd be a plus, since I'll need to prepare for the start of the school year, which is coming soon. Last year, I came several weeks into the fall term. Is it hectic those first days of classes?"

Although she sensed he was aiming for a calmer topic, Doro did not resist the change in conversation. "Absolutely," she replied, "although I wouldn't expect trouble. Just nervous freshmen, excited upperclassmen, and busy professors." After a moment, she voiced another part of the new academic year. "There's a home football game on that first Saturday, with a dance afterward."

"President Adams mentioned that, but I'm free to go to both, since I don't have to work." Ev replied. "If there's a problem, I'll act, of course."

"That's not likely," Doro told him. "There's never been trouble at campus events."

He cleared his throat. "Then, would you go with me to the game and the dance."

Pleasure chased other emotions away. "I'd love to," she replied without hesitation.

"Great. I was going to invite you to another movie, but I can't make solid plans until we wrap up this case or the leads go dry."

"I hope the case gets solved soon," she murmured.

After pulling to a stop in front of Wheaton Hall, Ev turned to Doro. Only his profile was clear. "So, do I. Wade and I will work on it, and so will Lowery and his men. The sheriff may, too." He shifted to face her. "You must have a lot to do preparing for a new school year."

"Not too much yet, but I want to work on my book. I got feedback from my parents and my grandmother while I was in Colorado."

"When do I get to read it?"

His question surprised but delighted her. "After I polish it. Maybe in a week or two."

"Good, since I may be tied up a lot of the next week, I imagine. We could get a big break, but I don't count on it. As for discussing elements of the case, please be patient."

"I'll wait to hear from you." With difficulty, because her curiosity was hard to throttle.

Ev nodded before exiting the automobile and helping Doro out. After walking her to the front door, he took her hand. "I enjoyed the evening, and I look forward to doing it again as soon as possible." He bent forward to brush her lips with his.

The featherlight kiss ended all too soon, and Ev was stepping away before Doro could react. Although smooching on the doorstep was not appropriate, she wanted to call him back. Instead, she murmured, "It was a lovely evening. Thank you."

He inclined his head. "I'll let your grandmother know I'm coming to your birthday celebration. The case should be closed by then. Even if it isn't, I can take a few hours off, so may I pick you up?"

"That would be wonderful. If we leave here about four o'clock, we'll have time to relax before dinner. Aggie, Wade, his children, and his mother will come, too, but in his vehicle. I planned to squeeze in with them, if you couldn't attend." Going with Ev was better. Much, much better.

"I'll see you before then, I'm sure. The next few days will be hectic, but I'll call when I can." With that, Ev hopped into the roadster and drove off.

As Doro watched the taillights disappear, she wondered how the next days would play out. Surely, Mr. Fulton's killer would be captured soon. But when? And how might she help without breaking her promise?

Chapter Two

With classes still three weeks away, Doro used the next several days to polish her mystery novel, but she also waited for word from Ev. When none came, her apprehension grew. Was he so busy that he didn't have a few extra minutes to telephone? Was his promise to talk over clues going by the wayside? Or was something else to blame for his silence?

Little Tee's presence was a solace, and Doro talked to the pup about her concerns more than once. Often, she chatted while they were out and about. The dog's response, turning her head from side-to-side with one ear up and the other down, always evoked chuckles from passersby. Walking Tee proved challenging, because she headed toward Ev's accommodation in the men's residence every time. Over the summer, he had moved from a garage attic at the college president's home to Melling Hall. Since Doro knew he wouldn't be there, she did not stop. According to Aggie, who telephoned daily while watching the

Lammers youngsters, both Ev and Wade were spending the bulk of their time investigating. Where and how remained a mystery.

Wednesday, she was about to fix a light lunch when a knock at her door interrupted. After finding Aggie in the hall, Doro ushered her friend inside. "Did you have fun with Wade's children?"

After flopping into a chair, Aggie nodded. "Yes, but three days with them wore me out. I don't know how Wade's mother does it. They're full of excitement and energy, which is great, but I'm glad Mrs. Lammers is back. She got them calmed down right away. I need to develop that skill." When Tee rushed over, Aggie bent down to pet the dog's head. As she did, a swath of her wavy auburn hair fell forward. Aggie hastily tucked it behind one ear, but it tried to escape again. "I bet you miss seeing Ev, little one."

Doro took a seat across from her friend. "She does, but she's splendid company for me."

Aggie lifted Tee into her lap, where the pup settled. "Dogs are wonderful. Wade's children want one, and they're trying to engage my help in convincing their father."

For a moment, Doro focused on her friend's relationship with the town constable. "Are you helping them?"

"I always wanted a dog myself, but Wade is hesitant because they need plenty of attention. All three children will be back in school soon, and sometimes he works long hours, so no one would be home with a pup. Tee goes with Ev as he makes rounds on campus, and you keep her when he's busy. That wouldn't be the situation for Wade's family." The pup yipped, as if in agreement.

"Things could change at the Lammers home in the near future," Doro suggested with a grin.

A slight smile played across Aggie's lips while pink rose to blot out the freckles on her face. "Not too near. We're courting. If we decide to marry, I'd wait until the school year ends next spring. It'd be an easier transition for all of us."

The remark made sense and had Doro thinking about her own future, although only briefly. "It was kind of you to watch the children while Mrs. Lammers visited her sister in Cleveland, especially since Wade has his hands full with the Fulton case." The two friends had only spoken in passing over the past few days, and Doro was eager to discover what Aggie learned about the murder. Wade must have shared some information, especially while Aggie watched his kids.

"He and Ev have been working nonstop, from what I gathered. Wade dropped by his mother's place in the evenings, but the children wanted his attention, so we didn't talk much."

Disappointment filled Doro. She wasn't aware it showed on her face until Aggie spoke again.

"Ev has been even busier than Wade," her friend said. "Because the Prohibition Bureau feels certain the murder was related to bootlegging, it's heavily involved. Of course, Ev's old boss is leaning on him to provide information about the Fultons. Actually, Agent Canton wants a lot more details."

"Leaning on him in what way? Relying on him or pressuring him?" Doro asked.

A wistful look covered Aggie's face. "Wade thinks it's some of both, with an emphasis on pressure."

"Is that his opinion or what Ev told him?"

A half-shrug moved one of Aggie's shoulders. "Since two Prohibition agents came to town with Agent Canton on Sunday, Wade and Ev have had few chances to speak privately. They've been going in different directions. I've only seen Ev once, and that was in passing. I ran an errand uptown and had the kids with me." Her expression softened. "Ev said he'll call you as soon as possible."

Torn between relief and doubt, Doro asked another question. "Is he really that busy?"

Aggie nodded. "All the lawmen are working long hours. The federal agents are looking into the liquor angle, for the most part. The sheriff's office is helping, as needed. From what I understand, the likely killer is part of a bootlegging gang. We haven't had a chance to chat, but does that mesh with what you saw Saturday night?"

"It does," Doro replied. "You heard now about the two vehicles."

"Wade mentioned seeing a Cadillac leave, and Jug Barnes witnessing a LaSalle at the Fulton place before that. It sounded like the two vehicles weren't there near the same time."

"From what we figured, that's true. Then, there's Alf Waggoner's jalopy being parked between Sylvania and Michaw."

Aggie's auburn brows rose a fraction. "Past experience has shown that not all bits and pieces are important."

"True," Doro agreed. "In this case, bootlegging and the murder seem closely intertwined, so I'd think the Bureau might end up taking over the entire investigation."

Aggie drew up one shoulder. "Right now, Wade is focusing on the murder while Ev is doing double-duty. He's the contact for both sides. Of course, he's investigating to get more details, too."

The picture painted by Aggie's words evoked concern. "Is he all right?"

"Other than being exhausted—Wade's description of Ev—he's well." Empathy filled Aggie's hazel gaze. "Be patient with him."

A chuckle escaped Doro. "Ev suggested the same thing when he dropped me off on Saturday night. He must've known he'd get involved in a lot of extra work, but I thought he'd call on Monday. Now, it's Wednesday." Her amusement disappeared. "I wonder exactly what he's doing." Despite Ev's insistence that he wouldn't go back to the Bureau, Doro speculated about his current role. Surely, Wade must know. Would he tell?

Aggie laid her hands on her lap. "Like I said, I only saw Ev briefly. This morning, I asked Wade where Ev is. He wasn't forthcoming with information. A lot of hemming and hawing about how they're both busy with the case and their other duties. As far as the investigation, it's not just finding the killer. They've been searching for Mrs. Fulton to no avail."

The woman's disappearance remained in the back of Doro's mind, although her friend's statement brought it to the forefront. "Neither of the Fultons got involved with local folks, despite living here for several years," Doro observed. "They came to Michaw from Toledo, but what neighborhood of the city, I don't know."

"According to Wade, no one has a good lead on that," Aggie replied. "They're still trying."

Trying was the perfect word for the situation. Doro's patience was definitely strained. Her normal eagerness to go sleuthing warred with her promise to Ev about not getting involved. "I've racked my brain to recall every tidbit about the Fultons, but we had little conversation with them last winter."

"True," Aggie agreed. "We were in a hurry to get to a safe place, and they were kind enough to take us."

While investigating a murder the previous Christmas, the two friends had been held captive by the killer. After escaping, they had run next door, where the Fultons offered to drive them to the home of Wade's mother. Mrs. Fulton had been especially solicitous, and her husband had been concerned as well. But the pair left after dropping off Doro and Aggie. "They were. And we ran into them at the Michaw May Days celebration."

"They provided some information, but that's as far as the conversation went last spring," Aggie said. "Even though it's a lot farther, I've heard they go to Sylvania to shop."

"I have, too," Doro agreed. Although the fifteen-minute drive was not burdensome, most Michaw residents bought groceries and such in town. A trip to nearby Sylvania was usually to see a movie, make a special purchase at one of the shops, or go to the train station. "I wonder if anyone there has seen Mrs. Fulton since Saturday."

"Wade talked to the Sylvania constable and some of the business owners. No one over there has seen her for a couple of weeks."

Doro chewed on her lower lip. "A while back, I asked Gramma Rose if she ever ran into the Fultons, and she hadn't."

A pensive expression blanketed Aggie's face. "Your grandmother knows everyone in Sylvania, so that means the Fultons didn't get acquainted there, either."

"Everyone knows everyone, just like in Michaw, but you're right. The two of them likely didn't get to know others because they didn't want people speculating about their illegal activities," Doro said.

"It's a lonely way to live," Aggie pointed out.

"Lonely but lucrative. And dangerous. The woman is either on the run or being held against her will." Doro swallowed convulsively. "Or dead."

Aggie clasped her hands and put them to her mouth. "Why would they kidnap her only to kill her later?"

"Maybe they thought she had important information?" Even as she spoke, Doro wondered how likely that was. "Whatever the reason for her disappearance, I hope we find out soon."

"So do I," Aggie agreed. "So do I."

෴

The two friends ate lunch before Aggie, pleading fatigue, headed to her own apartment. As soon as the door shut behind her friend, Doro went to the mirror and hall tree by her front door. She pulled her summer cloche—straw with a pink ribbon and matching silk flower—off its hook. As she put it on, Doro looked in the mirror and pulled a few locks of her brown hair out to frame her face. She told herself looking neat was important whether or not she encountered Ev, but her sea-blue eyes glittered with hope that he'd be in town. After straightening her hat, Doro grabbed her pocketbook, and hooked Tee's lead to her collar before heading out. A walk past the constable's office seemed like a good idea. Even if Ev was not there, Doro might learn something from the young clerk.

The August sun beat down with a vengeance, while humidity shimmered in the air. As she passed under the towering trees, Doro enjoyed the shade and let the little dog sniff, so she could have a respite, too. As they left campus, they were once again in the open. By the time she reached the middle of town, sweat beaded her back. As much as she loved Michaw, Doro fondly recalled the dry mountain air in Colorado Springs. Had it only been weeks since she had left her parents' lovely home? So much had happened in that time. Some were wonderful events, and some were not.

As Doro passed the door of the post office, she nearly ran into Jug Barnes. "Good morning."

"Morning, Dorothea."

The man, who had lived in Michaw for more than twenty years, was one of those who used Doro's whole name, much to her chagrin. "What brings you to town today? Isn't it a busy time on the farm?"

"Always busy, but I needed to pick up some mail." He shoved a thick envelope into his pocket. "Gotta get home."

As the tall, gaunt man turned away, Doro spoke again. "Just a moment."

His jaw tightened as he again faced her. "What? I got plenty to do."

Why had he made a special trip to town for an envelope? "I won't keep you, but I wondered about you seeing Alf Waggoner's jalopy on Saturday night."

A harrumph left Barnes. "Still sticking your nose into police matters, huh?"

Annoyance shot through Doro. "No. I've been invited to help." That wasn't quite accurate.

Barnes' dark gaze narrowed which deepened the lines fanning out from his eyes. "Is that so? Well, if you're involved, the constable will tell you what I told him. And that's not much." He put one forefinger to the brim of his sweat-stained hat, turned on his heel, and marched away. "Come on, Tee. We'll find out more about what he saw somehow." But how? Since Jug Barnes seemed an unlikely suspect, dropping the idea might be best.

As Doro and the little dog continued down Main Street, they encountered few other folks. No doubt the blistering noonday sun kept most inside, but Doro caught sight of a familiar figure outside the constable's office. "Hello, Colleen," she said to the clerk.

Colleen, a slender young blonde, smiled. "Doro, what brings you and Tee uptown on such a sweltering day?" As she spoke, she ruffled the dog's ears.

A look at Colleen revealed damp tendrils of hair clinging to her face and neck, while a flush colored her cheeks. Doro knew she must look much the same, since strands of her clipped bob stuck to her forehead. "I need to run a few errands, and Tee hates to be left behind," Doro replied, although that was not her primary purpose. "Why are you out-and-about?"

With one hand, Colleen wiped the moisture from her brow. "Running errands. I'd stay inside, if I could. At least the sun isn't beating on me there."

"Is the office uncomfortable?" Doro asked.

The girl frowned. "We have two fans, and they help a little. For the last hour, I've been going here-and-there for Wade. I stopped at the diner to pick up lunch, but I need to hurry back because Ev is in the office alone. He was waiting for a call, and he may have to leave again soon."

The comment opened an avenue for Doro to pose a question before going into the building. "Have he and Wade spent much time in the station this week?"

Colleen shook her head. "Hardly at all, especially Ev. Today is the first I've seen him since last week."

The information supported Aggie's belief, which relieved Doro. Ev wasn't going back on his promise to discuss the case with her, and perhaps he really hadn't had time to telephone her. "They both have their hands full," she said by way of a casual comment.

"They do," Colleen agreed. "Are you stopping in?"

"I could," Doro replied.

"Good. Ev will be happy to see you."

The clerk went inside and Doro, buoyed by the last remark, followed. Her gaze immediately rested on the desk in the corner of the large room. Last fall, only Wade had had a place to work. Finally, Ev had gotten his own space. Now, his head bowed, he was studying sheaves of paper spread across the surface. When the door closed behind the two young women, he looked up.

Even from across the room, the dark smudges beneath his eyes were impossible to miss.

"Doro. What a surprise," he said.

"I ran into Colleen outside, and she suggested I stop by." That wasn't exactly right, but he need not know. Doro did not want to look needy. Or pushy.

Tee yanked hard on her lead, which brought a grin to Ev's face. "And you brought my favorite four-legged girl, sweet Tee."

At the sound of her name, the dog yipped merrily. Doro bent to release her. Watching Tee's delight at seeing Ev warmed Doro's heart and, when he kneeled in front of the pup and let her lick his face, the warmth grew. "She's missed you," Doro observed.

Ev's gaze rose to meet hers. "The last few days have been hectic."

"So, I've heard," Doro replied. Her tone sounded critical, which she had not meant. Maybe Ev didn't notice, but Colleen must have.

The clerk lifted the bag in her hand. "I got my lunch, so I'll eat in the back room. If you need me, call out." With that, the girl hurried off.

Unsure if she should apologize for her tartness or leave, Doro shuffled nervously. "I guess she doesn't want to chat after all." Another side-step, since they had not planned to talk.

Ev stood up and gestured to the chair by his desk. "We could chat."

"If you're not too busy."

He ran one hand over his face. "I've got a few minutes, maybe a little longer. I've been on the go ever since I dropped you off

Saturday night. I think about calling every day, but by the time I get a chance, it's after midnight."

The admissions lessened her hesitation, and Doro crossed the space between them. Tee looked from one to the other before coming to Doro's side. When Ev again gestured to the chair, she sat down while he returned to his own seat. As he organized the papers into neat piles, she studied his face. The dark shadows were more pronounced up close, and his eyes were red-rimmed and bloodshot. Thinking back to the previous fall, Doro remembered he had looked as exhausted. Then, he had started his job at the college early, due to a murder on campus, while continuing his work as a Prohibition agent. Another memory leaped to mind: Ev had been shot in a speakeasy raid during the week he had done double-duty. Almost immediately, Doro chastised herself. He was solving a murder, not chasing down bootleggers. "Aggie said you and Wade have been working nearly nonstop," she observed in a casual tone.

His weary gaze met hers. "We have." A rueful smile lifted his lips. "My days have been packed, like I said. Telephoning after midnight wouldn't be popular with the other residents of Wheaton Hall or the local operator."

Not to mention that it would cause gossip, but Doro withheld the comment. "It's unlikely any of us would hear the telephone ring, since it's in the main hall near the front door."

He drove his fingers through his dark hair. "Yeah. I wasn't thinking."

"Because you're tired."

"I can't deny that." Although he slumped back in the chair, Ev offered a weary grin. "I'm glad you stopped by."

The words sent her spirit soaring. "I had to come uptown, and I ran into Colleen. Which I said already." When the pleasure left his expression, Doro stopped abruptly. Warmth rose in her cheeks. "That's not quite true."

His dark brows rose. "What is the truth?"

Only a scant hesitation preceded her reply. "I wanted to see you."

Another smile, a brighter one, ensued. "I've wanted to see you, too."

For several moments, Doro savored the bond between them. "Any special reason?"

A chuckle left him. "Do I need one?"

Joy lifted her spirit. "No, not at all."

"Since you're being forthright, I will be, too. I thought about throwing pebbles against your window at the women's residence hall." He paused for a moment. "If I had, would you have come down?"

"Yes." The word was out before Doro considered the wisdom of voicing her feelings. She was about to tack on some excuse, but Ev spoke first.

"Good to know." A grin tugged at one corner of his mouth. "But I won't do it. As a deputy constable and the campus security officer, I have to maintain decorum."

Doro smiled in return, but his observations evoked dismay, too. "You're also a consultant to the Prohibition Bureau."

His silver gaze fell to the desktop. "Mostly, Wade and I are working on the murder case. If we learn anything related to bootlegging, I report it to my old boss. As far as the bootlegging part, Lowery gives me what they have, which isn't a lot. I wish we knew more, because townsfolk are upset. Although the couple was aloof, no one likes him being murdered or Mrs. Fulton disappearing. It's worrisome and puts everyone on edge."

"That's true on campus, too. Some faculty members aren't back yet, and no students are, but I worry about the murder not being solved before the term begins. A little concern will turn into real apprehension then. As for Mrs. Fulton, do you have any inkling of where she headed. Or, if she's even safe?" She and Aggie had speculated, but Doro—wanting to learn Ev's opinion—withheld their exchange.

"On your train trip home, you solved a killing in short order," Ev commented. "Your other cases were cracked in less than three weeks. But, as an amateur sleuth and mystery novel fan, you're aware that's not always true."

"I am, but they weren't solely my cases. And suspects were limited on the train," Doro pointed out. "The same was true with the three cases you and I worked."

His lips quirked. "We partnered on two investigations. During the one in May, I was mostly flat on my back."

To Doro, Ev's humility was one of his best points. "You and Wade shared your insights, which helped Aggie and me a lot." In May, the two lawmen had been laid low after being poisoned during a town baking contest.

"You two would've figured it out on your own," he assured her. "But you're right about the number of suspects being a major factor."

"How many do you have?"

He swept back a short shock of hair. "There's no set number at this point. Lowery and his men have been looking at a couple of gangs who may run liquor between Toledo and Chicago. The supposition is that the Fultons worked with both of them, so agents are focusing on those two operations, and trying to find Mrs. Fulton."

Dismay filled Doro. "They don't have any ideas where she is?"

"No. Lowery found out where they lived before coming to Michaw. Agents searched the area, but no one in the neighborhood has seen either of them for months." He shrugged. "Or no one wanted to admit it."

His comment was food for thought. "Do bootleggers operate out of that neighborhood?"

"Big-time gangsters don't live there, but some of their minions do. Lots of people earn extra dough by transporting booze or being messengers. They don't cooperate with the law, because they don't want trouble."

"From the police or from gangsters," she suggested.

"Exactly, and the repercussions from bootleggers are always worse."

Ev need not expand on the observation. Not when Mr. Fulton's murder was vivid evidence of the fact. Although rumrunning was common, Doro possessed only superficial information about the actual goings-on. "How many gangs are in this area?"

"Several in Toledo," Ev replied. "We've already talked about Mr. Parson, Fultons' old employer, being a bootlegger. He owned one speakeasy and might've been in a couple more. The couple kept working with his associates from what I know. But we aren't sure about all of the man's rumrunning connections."

Something in his tone bothered Doro. "Agent Canton must realize who they are, especially if they're still running speakeasies."

Ev released a long breath. "He wants more solid evidence, which he's trying to get now. We need to know how many bootleggers did business with the Fultons. There are loose threads hanging, but Lowery hasn't pulled the right one yet. Maybe soon, though."

"Weren't the agents able to help with details about the Fultons and rumrunning? Surely, someone has seen him, or both of them, in the city over the past months and even years. Wouldn't knowing which speakeasies he visited help?" As Ev drummed his fingers on the chair arms for what seemed like endless moments, Doro's frustration grew. "You don't want to tell me, despite your promises the other night."

Ev's head fell forward for a moment. Then, he met Doro's gaze. "It's not that. We have so little information, and it's frustrating, but I'll start with the most pertinent possibility. Mrs. Fulton's vehicle was found near a speakeasy in Toledo. She might've voluntarily left it there...or she might've been taken against her will, which seems as likely to me. I can't see her leaving the car."

For a moment, Doro considered the idea. "I don't understand it, either. The agents must've combed the area looking for her."

"They did, and they raided that speakeasy. No sign of her, and Cal Zee—the one who runs the gang—wasn't there. He's got another place in the city, a nicer one, and he spends a little time on the lakeshore."

Doro's eyes widened. "Do you think they took her out there?"

His shoulders rose and fell. "Maybe so. Or maybe she's staying at his other business. It has two floors of rooms above the bar. The Bureau couldn't raid both places at the same time, due to lack of manpower. Now, raiding the second one would be useless. If she was there, she won't be now. And it's just as likely that another gang took her. Or that she's out on her own."

While his last comments were valid, Doro locked on his knowledge of a particular speakeasy. "And you have details about this building because..." She let her voice trail off as her mind raced with possibilities.

Several seconds of silence preceded his reply. "Because I've been in it."

"On a raid?" Doro asked.

"Nope. Just scouting around last summer."

"Undercover."

A soft sigh left him. "I didn't show my badge. A couple of us went in and looked the place over. That was shortly before I took the job here."

Doro thought back to the previous fall when Ev had arrived at Michaw College. "Is it the bar you raided last October?"

He shook his head. "No. It's never been raided, but it caters to a better crowd than most places. Periodically, the big boss shuts down the liquor operation. The fancy place stays open. Then, there's music and food, but only soft drinks. Eventually, the speakeasy gets going again." Ev folded his arms across his lean waist but did not meet her gaze.

Was he being evasive, or was she too suspicious? Doro was not certain, but she sensed Ev was not disclosing the details of last summer's trip to the speakeasy. Asking outright was unlikely to glean more information, so she focused on her anxiety for the widow. "Is there a chance Mrs. Fulton will be brought back to the city?"

"There's a chance she never left, and it's possible she wasn't kidnapped. We don't know." Ev bent over to scratch Tee's ears.

Briefly, Doro considered the situation. "Wouldn't there be some sign of her having been kept at the speakeasy?"

"Maybe. Maybe not."

Again, his response was vague, so Doro revisited the crux of the case. "You're all set on the motive being Fulton working with two or more different bootleggers?"

"Pretty much. Loyalty is a big deal with that crowd. Another related idea is that Fulton was filching a few bottles from every shipment."

"Oh, my," Doro mumbled. "That seems foolish." Ev had mentioned it the night of the killing.

"It's downright stupid. If he worked with two bootlegging gangs and stole booze from both, he signed his own death warrant."

Bile rose in Doro's throat, and she swallowed hard to force it down. "And possibly his wife's, too."

"Yep," Ev agreed.

When he did not say more, Doro asked a question lingering in the back of her mind. "Are they sending someone in undercover?"

His lips twitched. "Is that something you read in one of your mystery novels?"

Answering a question with a question triggered Doro's suspicion, but Ev looked calm and casual. Maybe he really wondered about her curiosity. "It seems like a good way to learn more, and Prohibition agents go undercover. You did."

"Only a couple of times, but you might be correct. I haven't heard the possibility mentioned. Right now, Wade and I are focused on finding Mr. Fulton's killer, since the murder was committed in our jurisdiction."

The statement did not quite mesh with Ev being the liaison to the Bureau, but Doro let it slide. "Maybe Mrs. Fulton was kidnapped at the house, so that'd be your concern, too."

"Maybe is the key word. Because her car was found in Toledo, the city police are involved. The sheriff will help us out here, too. If necessary."

Briefly, Doro studied his expression. "What's your gut feeling? Do you think she's all right?" The question, which never left her mind, had to be voiced again.

One of his shoulders rose and fell. "I hope so."

Anxiety knotted Doro's insides. "I hate to think of her being harmed or killed."

"So do I." He paused for a moment. "It's also possible she abandoned the car and left town by train."

Doro's brow furrowed. "Was it close to the station?"

He shook his head. "No, but she could've gotten a taxi. The Toledo Police are checking the cab companies to see if one of their drivers picked her up."

Doro slumped back in her chair. "I wonder where she might go. Other than the Fultons helping Aggie and me the night of our kidnapping and seeing them at the May Days celebration, I didn't talk to them much."

"I wish I knew."

The telephone ringing interrupted the conversation, and Ev rushed to answer. Although Doro listened intently, she gleaned little from his terse responses. When he hung up, Ev leaned back in his chair. "That was Lowery Canton. He's got a little new information and wants me to come into the city for a meeting. As soon as Wade is back, I'll leave. I may stay overnight at Lowery's place, so don't be alarmed if you don't see me tomorrow."

"Would you stay longer than one night?"

His silver gaze moved away from hers. "I might be there a little longer."

Ev's words and actions sent suspicion flowing over Doro. Part of her wanted to quiz him, which would be both futile and foolish, since he had already said sharing every detail was out of the question. Using the greatest restraint, she nodded. "Understandable. I'll see you when you get back and have a few free minutes." For a moment, she considered bringing up her encounter with Jug Barnes but let it slide. The farmer's dismissal of Doro as an amateur sleuth was hardly unusual. Plenty of townsfolk found it a cause for derision or amusement.

A look of surprise briefly crossed his face. Then, Ev nodded. "I'll call when I'm in town again."

Slightly satisfied, Doro got to her feet. "I should run a couple of errands. Take care of yourself, Ev."

He smiled. "I will. I definitely will."

Despite his good-humored reassurance, Doro—Tee trotting at her side—left the office with doubt and dismay plaguing her. Ev had shared some details, but he had also evaded questions. Why?

Chapter Three

Late that night, hope hit Doro when another Wheaton Hall resident tapped on her door late to say she had a telephone call. "Who is it?" she asked.

The woman shook her head. "I don't know. Our operator is on the line, so she can connect you to the woman right away. I'm headed to my rooms, so please turn off the lights downstairs. It's nearly midnight, and everyone else is already tucked in."

Dismay smothered optimism. A woman, not Ev, was on the line. "All right. Thank you." Before leaving her apartment, Doro turned to Tee. "I won't be long." The little dog's response was to curl deeper into the sofa cushions.

After hurrying to the telephone in the front hall, Doro picked up the dangling earpiece and turned to face the wall unit. "Hello."

"A long-distance call for you, Doro. I'm going off-duty and to bed momentarily, so if you get cut off, it may be a few minutes before I get back in here. The board will sound, of course, but it's been a long day and I'll go right to sleep," the operator said.

"Get your rest," Doro said.

"Thanks, I hope to," the operator responded before continuing. "Professor Banyon is on the line, so go ahead, ma'am."

"Thanks," Doro murmured. Moments passed before a female voice, soft and thready, sounded.

"Dorothea Banyon?"

The question, and it was a query, seemed odd. Whoever was on the line had made a call to her, and the operator had verified the connection. Why ask for confirmation? "Yes, it's Doro Banyon. To whom am I speaking?"

A period of silence before the woman replied. "I need to be careful. I asked, and your operator goes off-duty at midnight. The one here is busier, so they shouldn't be listening."

"Operators don't usually eavesdrop," Doro said, but why worry about that? Who was this woman? Why was she contacting Doro in the middle of the night? An idea popped up. "Mrs. Fulton? Is that you?"

"It is."

Relief collided with curiosity. "Are you all right?"

"For now, I am," the older woman replied.

"Where are you? The police can help you."

"I have to be careful."

The repeated refrain reinforced the woman's fear. Since Doro did not want Mrs. Fulton to hang up, she offered reassurance. "I'll do whatever I can for you."

"Thank you." Although the voice remained tremulous, a thread of relief ran through it. "You've solved crimes, so you're probably working on my husband's murder."

The widow's last statement evoked trepidation and curiosity inside Doro. Mrs. Fulton sounded sure her spouse had been murdered. "Did you witness it?"

"No, but I..." Mrs. Fulton's ragged voice trailed off. "I can't talk about the details now."

Although she wanted to press for more, Doro did not wish to upset the poor woman. "I'm so sorry that happened." What else should she say? She was interested in the case, but she was not actually involved in the investigation. Passing information on would help, so Doro asked a question. "Were you at your house on Saturday night?"

"I was inside," the woman replied in the same shaky whisper. "We were expecting a pickup of liquor. It'd come from Canada through Detroit and was going to Chicago."

"And gangsters were picking it up," Doro said for clarification.

"Minions were supposed to come, which is usual," Mrs. Fulton said. "But it didn't turn out to be usual. A fancy automobile pulled in ahead of the pickup time. Although I didn't recognize it, my husband did. He was upset right off and told me to hide until they left. I already had bags packed."

"Why were you packed?" Doro asked.

A sigh sounded. "I'd wanted us to get out of bootlegging for a long while. We finally had enough money to go wherever we wanted, which we were set to do as soon as this last batch was picked up."

"I'm so sorry." Doro hesitated only a heartbeat before asking a pertinent question. "Were you working with more than one bunch of gangsters?"

"We were. My husband said it'd help us get funds faster, and he assured me that all would be fine. But it wasn't." Her voice broke on the last phrase. "A terrible idea."

Again, sympathy for the woman rose inside Doro, but the best way to help was to gather critical details. "What kind of car was it?"

"I don't know vehicles well, but it was sort of blue, I think. Four doors. A good size car. Fancy, not like I'd seen before."

A fancy blue automobile described the LaSalle phaeton, so Doro made a mental note. "Descriptions of the men would help."

"They drove to the back, so I could see their heads, but not their faces. All three wore hats."

Disappointment dogged Doro despite learning that a trio had been in the first car. "The lawmen need leads. Can you give me names or descriptions of men who came to your home in the past?"

"I don't want to say more on the telephone."

Frustration filled Doro, but she offered an alternative. "You and I could meet. You choose a place and time, and I'll be there." For a long moment, Doro thought the other woman had hung up. Then, Mrs. Fulton responded.

"There's a small café on Chicago Pike right outside Toledo. On the west side of town." The widow added more specific directions. "I could be there tomorrow morning about ten o'clock."

"I'll be there," Doro assured her.

"Please don't bring any lawmen with you. I won't come in until I'm sure you're alone."

Conflicting feelings battered Doro. A solo encounter with the woman could be dangerous. What if she wasn't telling the truth? Common sense dictated Doro's next words. "Would you mind if I bring my friend Aggie? You met her last Christmas, remember?"

"Of course, I remember. I suppose it's fine for her to come. Just no lawmen. Not even Lammers and Mallow."

Misgivings edged into Doro's mind, but she had to agree or risk having the widow back out. "See you tomorrow."

The widow's reply was to hang up. Doro moved more slowly because her misgivings persisted. Should she call Ev? For a long moment, she considered the possibility and decided not to, because he would insist on going with her or meeting Mrs. Fulton by himself. And that would not work.

※

Early the next morning, Doro headed to Aggie's apartment and explained the situation. She finished with, "Will you go along?"

"Of course," her friend agreed. "Maybe we should tell Ev and Wade, though."

Since Doro had already considered and dismissed the idea, she shook her head. "If we do, one of them will want to come. Then, Mrs. Fulton will disappear. She told me a little on the telephone, but she'll only share more in person. Besides, Ev may not be back from Toledo."

Aggie moved restlessly, changing her stance as her weight shifted. "We'll tell them what we find out, right?"

"Certainly," Doro replied. For a fleeting moment, her conscience was tweaked. She had promised Ev not to investigate on her own, but what alternative was there? None, if they wanted to get information from Mrs. Fulton. Besides, it wasn't like she and Aggie were meeting a gangster. Besides, a diner was a public place.

"I'd like to call Wade. I won't say where we're going or what we're doing, but we usually talk in the morning."

A finger of envy traced Doro's spine. She and Ev had not gotten to that stage yet. With luck, no more crimes would interrupt the progress of their relationship. But who could say? In less than a year, Doro had helped to crack four cases, and a fifth was now on tap. Ev was open to her involvement, or at least her observation, and that was big.

The two friends descended the stairs, where Doro waited in the reception area while Aggie called Wade. Her friend returned within moments.

"Colleen is alone in the office. Wade is at an automobile accident outside town, and Ev won't be in until this afternoon."

Relief filled Doro, who had not been sure Aggie wouldn't have inadvertently let something slip to her beau. "Let's get going. I don't want to be late."

Moments later, they climbed into Doro's sleek Essex roadster and headed out of Michaw. During the thirty-minute drive, they discussed their approach with Mrs. Fulton. Both agreed that taking turns asking questions, and staying casual and upbeat, was the best strategy because it was the one they usually used.

When they neared the diner, Doro slowed down. "There's not much around here. A service station across the way, a church, and a few houses. It seems like an odd place for a restaurant, even though this highway is well-traveled. And the building doesn't look too old."

Aggie peered out the side window. "I'd feel better if there were cars at the church."

"Thursday morning at ten o'clock wouldn't be a busy time," Doro reasoned, but she did not deny her own anxiety. "The location would be ideal for rumrunners to gather going in and out of the city."

"My thought, too."

"At least there are some vehicles at the station." After parking her roadster next to the diner, she and Aggie entered and found a booth at the back. Only two other customers, an elderly couple, were inside. The waitress, tall and plump, brought menus and left after Doro said they would order when their friend came. After ten minutes passed, Doro got restless. "I hope Mrs. Fulton shows up."

"We got here early," Aggie said. "Let's give her time."

"We will," Doro replied, before being distracted by the waitress who returned with coffee, although neither young woman had ordered any.

"Figured you'd want a beverage," the woman said. "How about some water? Or juice?"

"No thank you." Doro tried to look past the big blonde, but found her view blocked when the lady shifted to one side. Craning her neck to see around the waitress did not help, because the woman moved again. "We're fine. You can come back when our friend is here."

The waitress failed to leave. "Just want to make sure you have what you want, in case I get busy."

After another glance around the restaurant, where only the older couple remained, Doro offered a smile. "We don't mind waiting, if you don't."

"No, we certainly don't," Aggie agreed.

What Doro minded was not being able to see the door and, maybe Mrs. Fulton not seeing them when she arrived. Within moments, the latter proved to be of no concern. A woman, wearing a hat pulled low on her head, stopped beside the waitress, who nodded. "Sit down, ma'am. Your friends have been waiting. I can take your orders now."

Doro expected Mrs. Fulton to want a menu, but she quickly asked for coffee and toast. Doro and Aggie also asked for toast, and the waitress slipped away. The widow shifted from one foot to the other as her gaze darted around the diner. Clad in a dove gray dress with a knee-length skirt, she was raw-boned and rangy. Since last winter, the woman had lost weight and, if the smudges under her eyes were any indication, she was not sleeping well. But who could blame her? "Please take a chair."

The widow's response was to sit facing Doro with her back to the room. After an exchange of greetings among the three, Mrs. Fulton plucked at her collar. "I can't stay long."

"You don't need to," Aggie assured her. "But you have some details to share in person."

A statement seemed less intrusive than a question, so Doro was glad her friend chose that option. When the other woman did not immediately reply, Doro made an attempt. "On the telephone, you mentioned bootlegging. How did you get involved? Through the Parsons?"

Mrs. Fulton shrugged. "Not exactly. At least not right off. We owned a bar in Toledo. John didn't have a trade, since he'd worked at the saloon since we were kids. We weren't able to buy it until after we'd been married for years. Mrs. Parson's father, she was Miss Snow back then, owned the place for thirty years or more."

"John was your husband?" Doro asked, realizing she had never heard the man's first name.

Tears pooled in Mrs. Fulton's eyes. "Yes," she whispered. "He was a fine husband."

"I'm sure he was," Aggie murmured.

After offering a similar sentiment, Doro asked for clarification about the sequence of events. "Her father sold you the bar prior to Ohio going dry?"

The widow nodded. "Yep. It was real nice, not low-class. Miss Snow came in often, which is how she met her husband. She was a bit of a wild girl. Anyhow, after we bought the place, she worked there. He was a customer. Before and after it was legal to sell liquor. After Prohibition, he came to us with an offer."

Doro thought back to what they had learned about Mrs. Parson the previous Christmas. As soon as she had arrived in Michaw, the woman had said she was from a wealthy family. Later, the story came into question. Now, it seemed like a complete fabrication. "Was Mr. Snow well-to-do?"

"Heavens no," Mrs. Fulton replied. "He did all right with the saloon, but wealthy? Not in that class."

Since that was not an important point, Doro returned back to the case. "After Prohibition, Mr. Parson offered you and your husband a chance to work with him bootlegging?"

"Pretty much. We couldn't make a go of our place without liquor, so he bought it from us. He'd already proposed to Miss Snow, and we moved to Michaw when they married," the older woman said. "I was nervous about bootlegging from the start, but we needed money coming in, so I agreed."

Desperation underscored the widow's comments, and Doro's heart constricted with empathy. "Many saloonkeepers must've found themselves in similar straits."

"They did, and a lot of them kept their saloons going. Better to break the law than to go hungry. Some sold out. Others switched to candy shops and made a lot less," Mrs. Fulton replied.

"A few evidently switched to speakeasies," Doro put in.

"But not usually in the same place, although the candy stores and coffee shops are sometimes fronts." Mrs. Fulton stopped talking when the waitress brought their food and resumed when the woman left. "It wasn't so bad until the gangsters got involved. That ruined plenty of honest folks."

Selling booze was not exactly honest, not since Prohibition, but Doro let the point slide by. "So, you and your husband worked with Mr. Parson. Rumors flew around Michaw for years about him rumrunning."

"He wasn't manufacturing or distributing booze. It was all for his own places, but it's how he got involved with the Kesler brothers in Toledo. Mrs. Parson sold out to some other gangsters about a year ago. The Zee- Yarrow gang, but my husband kept running liquor for them."

Doro pulled a notepad and pencil out to jot down the name. "And both gangs have speakeasies?"

"They do. We were at a couple of places recently," the widow said.

Aggie leaned forward. "You went along with your husband?"

A little shuddering breath left Mrs. Fulton. "I did, because we were looking to leave the area, like I told you. I wanted to make sure John didn't agree to storing or transporting more liquor." She shot a glance over her shoulder before grasping her coffee cup with both hands. "We had old friends in Toledo and saw them that night, too. The husband is also involved in bootlegging, mostly running booze across Lake Erie from Canada." Her voice became so low, it was barely audible. "He's a good man. Just fallen on hard times like lots of others."

"Did he also work with the Kesler brothers?" Aggie asked. "Or with the other gang?"

Mrs. Fulton shook her head. "Abe first worked for Zee and Yarrow. That's how we got involved with them. The Parsons mostly did business with the Keslers at the start. Well, with their father." Regret lined the woman's face.

Needing clarification, Doro asked another question. "Your husband was first involved with the Keslers through Mr. Parson. But he also worked with the Zee-Yarrow gang because of a friend?"

"That's right," the widow replied. "Abe, our friend, quit working with them, but John continued to store and run booze for both gangs."

Doro wanted to know more about the friends. "Are you staying with your friends?"

"They feel real bad about what happened to John," the widow said.

The response did not completely answer the question. Should she ask again or pose more queries? Doro took a bite of her toast and let the widow eat a little, too. When Mrs. Fulton had another sip of coffee, Doro went back to interviewing her. "You've met the Keslers and Zee and Yarrow."

The woman nodded. "I have. The two gangs are always at odds, so I don't know why John stayed working for both. He kept it secret because gangsters like them don't like being double-crossed, but it coulda come out somehow. I don't know." She laid her cup down. "I'm getting away within the next few days, but I want my husband's killers caught."

"Of course you do," Aggie added. "We do, too."

"Yes, we do," Doro agreed, "and so do Constable Lammers and Officer Mallow. It'd help them so much if they knew where the Keslers and the Zee-Yarrow gang operate." Even as she spoke, Doro wondered if Ev already had an inkling. After all, he had been to more than one speakeasy as a Prohibition agent, and he was talking regularly with his old boss.

Mrs. Fulton gripped her cup more tightly. "I can give you the address of Zee and Yarrow's speakeasies."

Doro pushed her notepad toward the woman, who jotted down names and places before handing the items back. "I'm not familiar with the streets in Toledo. Are these places down-town?"

"Mostly, yes," the widow said.

"What about the Keslers' places?" Aggie inquired. "Ev and Wade will want details about them, too."

The older woman glanced down at her half-eaten toast. For a long moment, Doro did not think the widow would respond.

Finally, she said, "I don't know as much about them."

Since that comment did not mesh with what Mrs. Fulton had already revealed, Doro looked at Aggie to get her friend's reaction. Aggie looked as perplexed as Doro felt. The older woman was not revealing everything she knew. Doro felt sure of that, but could they get the entire truth out of her?

"But you've met them?" Aggie asked.

The widow drank more coffee. "In passing."

"Where are their speakeasies?" Doro posed the question.

Mrs. Fulton glanced at Doro and back at her coffee before giving some street names. "Speakeasies are sometimes hard to find."

"Which is understandable," Doro observed. "The bootleg-gers wouldn't want their bars to be obvious to the police."

"No, they wouldn't," Aggie said before turning to Mrs. Fulton. "You mentioned Miami Street. That's on the east side of the river."

The older woman stared at her. "How do you know that?"

Aggie smiled. "I grew up in Toledo, so I'm familiar with the area. Is the speakeasy next to the river?"

A look of chagrin crossed Mrs. Fulton's face before she replied. "Close."

"Which would make it easy to receive and send liquor," Doro murmured.

"It certainly would," Aggie agreed. When Mrs. Fulton made no comment, Aggie directed a question at her. "Did the Kesler brothers or Zee and Yarrow ever come to your house?" Aggie asked.

"Never Zee or Yarrow," the woman quickly replied. "They sent their henchmen, sometimes with errand boys."

Alf Waggoner immediately came to Doro's mind, but she wanted to carefully weave his name in. "Do you know any of their names?"

Mrs. Fulton swallowed convulsively. "Some."

"If you told us, that would help the lawmen pinpoint your husband's killer," Aggie suggested in a soothing voice.

The widow looked around the restaurant. Briefly, her gaze seemed to stop but, before Doro could see her focus, Mrs. Fulton looked directly at her. "Patrick Sweebe is part of the Zee-Yarrow gang. He's often at the nice bar as a waiter, but he's really muscle for them. Maybe even a hitman. He stopped by our place more than once. Handsome and charming on the surface. Rough underneath. I hear his two brothers are the same."

"His brothers work for this gang?" Aggie asked.

"They run liquor to Chicago. Sometimes, they store it at the family homestead farther out Chicago Pike, just a few miles south and west of Michaw, I think. I'm not really sure. It could be at another location," the widow said.

Doro did not like the idea of more booze being stored so close to her hometown, but was that related to the murder? Although they were getting more information, nothing pinpointed a clear-cut lead to follow. When she and Aggie exchanged a long look, Doro noted her friend felt a similar frustration. "Ev and Wade must know something about the Sweebes." Not that the family had ever been mentioned by either of them. "So, this Patrick came to your place. Was he alone?"

"No, he always brought someone to help load the booze. Often, a couple of fellows, but he never introduced them, and I didn't see them up close. Only him." Mrs. Fulton ate some of her toast. "The Kesler boys did some of their own work, especially Phil. He's rougher looking than Patrick and not as smooth-mannered."

"What does he look like?" Aggie asked.

"Medium height and muscular build. Brown hair. Always came to our place with a couple of youngsters to do the hauling," Mrs. Fulton replied.

"Was it his car you saw on Saturday night?" Aggie posed the question.

For a moment, the widow stared into her coffee cup. "Nope."

"But you don't know cars well," Doro pointed out.

The woman's eyes went wide before she grimaced. "I know big, fancy ones from the sporty kind the young ones like."

"Phil Kesler is young?" Doro inquired.

"Twenty-one or so, I s'pose," Mrs. Fulton said. "He drove real fast. I can say that much."

"What color was his vehicle?" Aggie asked.

"Red. Bright red like a fire truck." Mrs. Fulton picked up her cup and took a long swallow of coffee.

While she jotted more notes, Doro considered what they now knew and what they still needed to know. "Two different automobiles were seen at your house on Saturday night. One was a two-tone blue LaSalle phaeton, which may be the one you saw, and the other was a burgundy Cadillac roadster."

Mrs. Fulton licked her lips. "I told you that I'm not familiar with car makes and models."

Frustration filled Doro, because she had a sixth sense that the widow was not being forthright. Was it out of fear or guilt? Knowing which might lead to a solution. "You didn't want to say much on the telephone, but what did you do after the vehicle drove in?"

The widow took a long swallow of coffee. "John told me to lay low until he came back, so I did."

"For how long?" Aggie inquired.

The widow made a dismissive gesture. "I dunno. It seemed like a long while, but I was afraid to come out."

"That's understandable, but the men didn't come in the house to look for you?" Doro asked.

Several moments passed before Mrs. Fulton spoke. "I kept hiding for a time." She cast a glance over her shoulder and stopped talking when the waitress came to their table.

"Can I get you ladies anything else?" the woman asked. "What about you, ma'am? Toast and coffee aren't much, and you look like you need more meat on your bones."

Mrs. Fulton focused on the table. "No, I'm all right."

The widow's demeanor bothered Doro, although she could not pinpoint why. A glance at the waitress's face only increased her anxiety because the woman's smile did not reach her eyes. The pair acted familiar with one another. Was Mrs. Fulton a regular customer? If so, wouldn't they use names? "We're all set. Thank you, though."

A minute's hesitation preceded the waitress's response. "Fine. Signal, if you want more." Then, she spun on her heel and strode away.

Mrs. Fulton put her napkin on the table. "I need to get going."

"Just a moment," Doro hurried to put in. Although she had wanted to be subtle, she asked a pointed question. "We heard Alf Waggoner does odd jobs for you. Was he at your place on Saturday?"

A puzzled expression covered the widow's face. "I can't imagine that boy being involved in my husband's murder. They got along real good. John was like a father to him." A wry smile tugged at one corner of her mouth. "Maybe more like a grandfather, cuz of our ages."

Since the Fultons must be in their late fifties, that rang true. "Did Alf help with bootlegging?" Doro made the query.

All amusement left Mrs. Fulton's face. "He did. Like us, the Waggoners needed money. The father died in France, which left the family struggling. No idea why the man joined the army. Foolishness."

Once again Doro's sympathies were engaged, but so were her suspicions. Why had the youngster's vehicle been seen between Sylvania and Michaw the night of the murder? Unsure about providing the information before learning more, she asked another question. "Was Alf at your place earlier on Saturday?"

"He was there in the morning, but I didn't talk with him. Alf and John went to the barn as soon as the boy drove in," Mrs. Fulton said.

"Did you see what they were doing?" Aggie asked.

"I was busy packing, so I didn't notice. Alf was there about an hour," the widow said.

Doro absorbed the information with interest. Sixty minutes was plenty of time to move crates of booze, but she wanted Mrs. Fulton's reaction to the suggestion. "Long enough to load or unload liquor?" When the woman did not immediately respond, Doro pressed on. "I was at your house on Saturday night, and I know almost all the booze in the barn storeroom was gone. Did your husband and Alf take it some place? Or was it still there that evening?" Knowing for sure would help.

The older woman looked toward the front of the restaurant, where the waitress stood staring at them. Mrs. Fulton put one hand to her mouth and spoke in an indistinct murmur. "They took part of it someplace. John wouldn't tell me, but he was getting a good sum of money for it." With one hand, she wiped at her eyes. "He gave that cash to me, which is why I can get away from this area. But I wish he was going with me."

When her voice broke on the last few words, both Doro and Aggie offered their sympathies. "Whoever killed him will be brought to justice," Doro promised. "But you're sure about Alf?"

"Why are you asking again?" Mrs. Fulton inquired, clearly put out.

"His jalopy was out on the road between Sylvania and Michaw that night. He must've left it and been picked up."

The woman got to her feet. "I don't know about that, and I need to leave." With that, she rushed toward the front door.

"She's in a hurry," Aggie observed.

"She sure is. Being nervous about the bootleggers finding her could be the reason." The urge to follow the widow had Doro on her feet, but their waitress came down the narrow aisle and blocked her path.

"Here's your check, ladies," the woman said as she slapped a slip of paper on the table. "Want more coffee?"

Both Doro and Aggie declined the offer. "No, we'll get going," Doro said, still trying to see Mrs. Fulton as she left.

"Pay at the front." The blonde shifted so that she was close to the table, too close for Doro to move toward the door.

By the time the waitress moved and the two friends got to the cash register, Mrs. Fulton was long-gone while Doro was left wondering how she had gotten to the diner and where she was heading now.

Chapter Four

Neither young woman spoke until they were on the highway again. During the few moments of quiet, Doro mentally reviewed Mrs. Fulton's information and actions. "I didn't see where Mrs. Fulton went. I would've liked to see if she headed toward Toledo."

"Neither did I," Aggie murmured. "The waitress blocked my view."

"Mine, too. She sure hurried to get in the way."

"When you jumped up, she might've thought we were skipping out on the bill," Aggie suggested.

"Maybe so, but you were still seated. Besides, she kept us from seeing the front door when Mrs. Fulton arrived, too." Although Doro could not pinpoint what bothered her about the woman's action, she tucked the concern into the back of her mind and made a more general comment. "We learned details, but nothing to point us in one direction. What did you think?"

"Much the same, but Ev might know more after being in Toledo. Piecing what the Prohibition Bureau has, together with what Mrs. Fulton said should help."

"True, but I guess I was hoping for a smoking gun."

A chuckle left Aggie. "A Sherlock Holmes term."

Doro laughed along with her. "It is. And a good phrase. Unfortunately, most mysteries don't have one. At least not early on. As for Ev learning more, I hope he's back."

Aggie shifted to look at Doro. "You sound troubled. Why?"

After gathering her thoughts and feelings, Doro posed a coherent response. Or at least as coherent as she could make it, since she had not yet coped with Ev's latest activities. "You know Ev went to Chicago as a consultant. Now, he's busy working with the Bureau, and he's gone to Toledo to meet with his old boss instead of Agent Canton coming to Michaw. I can't help but wonder about Ev maybe going undercover to investigate the bootleggers."

"Where would he go? As of last night, they didn't have enough leads to send an undercover agent to a certain saloon. Nothing we learned would point to one gang or the other, and he can't be in two places at once."

"True, but they might know something critical by now," Doro murmured.

"It's unlikely Agent Canton knows everything Mrs. Fulton told us, and her clues were helpful," Aggie pointed out.

Her friend's assertion was true. "They were."

Aggie laid a hand on Doro's arm. "Ev might be at the constable's office when we get back. If he isn't, worrying now won't do any good."

"Gramma Rose likes to say *wait to worry*."

"One of her favorite sayings, and I've heard it from her often."

After laughing along with Aggie, Doro took the conversation in a different direction. "She'll miss having you stay with her next summer."

Aggie folded her hands in her lap. "You sound very sure I won't be."

"You and Wade are courting. By the time school ends in May, you'll be on your way to the altar." When Aggie did not immediately reply, Doro shot a fleeting glance at her. "Nothing has happened, has it?"

"No, of course not. There's no need to rush to the altar."

"That surprises me. Wade wants to marry, and you mentioned marrying after the school year ends. And you care for each other."

"We do." Aggie paused for a long moment. "Before Gramma Rose and I left to spend time with you in Colorado, I wrote to my brother and told him about stepping out with Wade. His reply was waiting for me when we got back. I haven't said anything to Wade. Or you, because I had to think about it."

Her friend's tone disturbed Doro. "Your brother doesn't want you to marry?"

"He does. He just doesn't approve of Wade."

Disbelief filled Doro. "What? Wade is a fine person. A wonderful son and father. A good constable. Didn't you tell your brother all that?"

"I did. I also told him about the age difference. My brother says Wade is too old for me, and I shouldn't be raising some other woman's children. I should have my own."

Since Aggie adored her brother, Doro was careful with her response. "I didn't think the fifteen years mattered to you."

"They don't. Not at all. And I love Wade's children," Aggie replied.

"They seem to love you in return, so why the hesitance? Your brother and his family are in France, which means he doesn't know Wade." Aggie's brother had stayed in the country after the Armistice because he had fallen in love with a Frenchwoman. In the eleven years following the Great War, he hadn't come home to see his little sister at all. While Doro realized traveling from Brittany to Ohio would be challenging with youngsters, and probably costly, she thought he should be more concerned about his sister's happiness. And Wade made Aggie happy. That was clear to anyone who saw them together.

"My brother's response upset me. I thought he'd be excited for me." Aggie released a pent-up breath. "He's my only family now."

The hint of hurt in Aggie's voice twisted Doro's heart. "He should be happy. He should be supportive." When Aggie didn't reply, Doro continued. "You aren't changing your mind because of your brother, are you?"

"No, but it bothered me more than it should."

"That's understandable. From what you've said, the two of you were always close."

"We were. Now, he lives so far away, and his wife writes more often than he does. I still love him dearly, but he shouldn't have a say in who I marry."

"I agree. Have you written back?"

"Not yet. I'm still mulling over how to word my letter."

Doro chuckled. "You're an English professor and a poet, so you'll come up with something brilliant."

"As long as it makes my brother drop his objections, I'll be thrilled." A wistful note softened Aggie's voice as she gazed out the window.

After a sidelong glance at her friend, Doro concentrated on driving. For the rest of the trip, they reviewed Mrs. Fulton's revelations and went over how to present the information to the two lawmen in their lives. Doro still fretted over Ev's activities, but she withheld her concern. With luck, his vehicle would be in front of the constable's office. As they drove into the south side of Michaw, where the college sat, Doro suggested picking up Tee. Aggie agreed, so Doro scurried to her rooms to scoop up the little dog.

When they got into the car, Tee plopped on Aggie's lap. "She's happy to come along," the other young woman said as she petted the pup.

"Always," Doro murmured, but her mind remained on Ev. As she pulled to a stop on Main Street and saw no sign of his vehicle, Doro felt another stab of apprehension. Maybe he had walked to the station. She hoped so. Still being in Toledo might mean deeper involvement with the Bureau.

After exiting the car, the two friends headed to the office with Tee trotting along on her lead. Relief filled Doro when they stepped inside. Ev was already seated with Wade at a desk in the back corner. Both men stood as Doro and Aggie entered.

Tee yipped and pulled forward, so Doro unclipped her leash. The little dog darted toward Ev, who went down on one knee to greet her. While Ev scratched Tee's ears, she licked his face. Seeing them together warmed Doro's heart. "Tee missed you."

Ev glanced up. "I missed her, too, but she was in excellent hands, and I was only gone overnight."

"True," Doro murmured before exchanging greetings with Wade, who acknowledged her before focusing on Aggie.

"You both look tired," her friend observed as she looked from Ev to Wade.

"And we will until this case is closed," Wade replied. "But Ev is putting in more hours than I am."

Doro turned her attention to Ev. Dark smudges shadowed his eyes. "When did you get back from Toledo?"

"This morning," he replied. "I stopped by Wheaton Hall, but one of your fellow residents said you and Aggie left around nine o'clock. She didn't know where you went."

When Doro looked at Aggie, her friend nodded. "We're here because we got some important information about the Fultons and bootlegging."

Both men sat up straighter. "How and from who?" Wade asked.

"I'd like to hear that answer, too," Ev, his expression tense, chipped in.

Getting straight to the point seemed wise, so Doro was forthright. "Mrs. Fulton called me late last night and asked me to meet her. Aggie didn't know until this morning, but she agreed to go along."

"I wasn't back then, but you could've told Wade." Ev's tone was clipped and cool.

Aggie turned to her beau. "When I telephoned the office around nine, you were at the scene of an accident."

The constable nodded. "Colleen told me about your call as soon as I got back, although she didn't have a message from you."

"I didn't want to give away details. We had to meet Mrs. Fulton at a neutral location and couldn't delay, so I didn't have time to call again."

Wade gave a slight nod. "That makes sense."

Ev kept petting Tee but focused on Doro. "She didn't want you to tell Wade and me, I suppose."

His comment, straightforward and without annoyance, summed up the issue, so Doro nodded and said, "You're right. She wouldn't meet if a lawman came along. She even waited for us to go in before she came. Since the diner was just outside Toledo with few other businesses nearby, she would've seen who was coming and left without meeting us."

He drove his fingers through his dark hair. "The woman has good cause to be afraid, although not of Wade or me."

"She doesn't fear you two," Doro said. "She's nervous and upset. Her plan is to get as far away as possible, as soon as possible."

Ev shifted forward in his chair. "When is she leaving?"

"Within the next few days," Doro replied. "She doesn't want to talk with any lawmen. Maybe she's worried about being charged."

Dismay clouded Ev's eyes. "She wouldn't be. Not when she's providing information. Besides, it sounds like the woman was only peripherally involved."

"And she wanted her husband to stop much sooner than he did," Aggie put in.

Wade drummed his fingers on the desk. "He should've taken her advice. If he had, he'd be alive now."

Sadness dictated Doro's response. "Probably so, but they needed money." She continued by explaining that the Fultons lost their saloon when Ohio went dry, their connections to the Parsons, and why Alf Waggoner had gotten involved.

"Did she seem angry about Prohibition or say that's why she doesn't want the law involved?" Ev asked.

The question was food for thought. Did the woman hold resentment? Doro was not sure and indicated as much. "She didn't say so, but it's possible. Losing a business due to a change in the law has to be hard to bear."

"I'm sure," Ev agreed. "As for the kid, Wade knows more about Alf than I do."

A grim expression darkened Wade's face. "Alf has been doing odd jobs for years. I should've realized he needed more work long before now. The family has it rough."

"You were working on the railroad for years, and you have your hands full now," Aggie pointed out. "Besides, you can't take care of everyone."

"Thanks, but if the kid wasn't involved in the murder, I'll see what we can do to help him and his family," Wade replied.

"According to Mrs. Fulton, Alf wasn't at their home that evening, although he was there earlier in the day," Aggie put in.

After Tee laid down, Ev leaned back in his chair. "Did you tell her about his car being spotted that night?"

"We did," Doro told him before summarizing what the widow had said about the boy.

A rough breath left Ev. "I'd like to talk with him."

"Good idea," Wade said. "He must know as much as Mrs. Fulton, but what else did she say?"

"Quite a lot," Doro said, before outlining a few points from the conversation.

Ev released a low whistle. "What she said connects with some of what Lowery told me. Wade and I had just started talking when you two came in."

Anticipation had Doro moving to the edge of her chair. Surely, the men planned on sharing the news. When neither spoke again, Doro did. "What did he say?"

Only a moment passed before Ev responded. "The Bureau knows about the Zee-Yarrow gang and the Keslers. Lowery mentioned both gangs to me in connection to Fulton. Now, I can tell him one of the two is likely to be involved with the killing."

"Right," Wade added. "If Fulton only worked with the Kesler brothers and Zee and Yarrow, it's unlikely other bootleggers came out and killed him."

Doro nodded. "That makes sense."

"After we talk, I'll call Lowery," Ev said. "He needs to know you met with Mrs. Fulton, and he may have questions for you."

"We're happy to answer them," Doro replied. And maybe get answers, too.

"Of course," Aggie agreed. "But why don't we give you more details right now. Doro took notes."

Ev grinned as he again focused on Doro. "Like any accomplished amateur sleuth would."

Pleasure, at his good humor and the compliment, rippled through Doro. She pulled her notepad out.

"Why don't you jot down what I just said. Then, we'll have everything in one place," Ev suggested.

"A fine idea," Doro agreed. If she kept all the notes, she and Aggie would most likely stay involved in the case—unless Agent Canton wanted them out, but that remained to be seen.

"I thought so," Ev replied. "Another good idea might be to have Lowery come out here to talk. I don't want to say too much on the telephone. The Michaw operator isn't in league with bootleggers, but it's impossible to know about others down the line."

"If he could meet with us today, it would help," Wade said.

Ev stood up. "I'll put a call in now instead of later."

While waiting for the connection to go through, Ev stood at the counter and the others engaged in casual conversation. Doro also tried listening to Ev's end of the telephone exchange, but she gained little information that way.

After hanging up, Ev returned to the group. "Lowery will be here in an hour. He's interested in what you learned, but he wants to talk with the agents in the office about digging more into the Zee-Yarrow gang and the Keslers, too."

Chapter Five

With an hour to wait, Doro returned Tee to her apartment. After providing fresh water, she headed back to Main Street. Aggie, who had run errands, was already at the constable's office when Doro stepped inside.

"Lowery should be here soon, but sit down," Wade, who was just coming out of the back room, said.

Ev, seated at his desk, agreed. "It won't be long."

And it wasn't. Ten minutes later, the wiry man arrived. The memory of meeting the agent in Chicago sprang to Doro's mind, as did the same impression. Although short, Canton exuded strength and determination. His neat three-piece suit, starched white shirt, and crisp bow tie marked him as *all business.*

"How nice to see you again, Professor Banyon," Canton said.

"It's lovely to see you, too," Doro replied, despite not quite believing the man's assertion.

After the group exchanged greetings, Doro sat next to Aggie, while Canton took a chair next to Wade's desk, and Ev pulled his chair over.

"So, you two talked with Mrs. Fulton," the agent said. Neither his voice nor his expression hinted at his mindset.

"We did," Doro agreed.

A slight smile played across Canton's mouth. "I'd like to speak with the woman, but Ev said you don't know where she is or how to contact her."

"That's right," Doro agreed. "She wants no contact with lawmen. She's afraid. Most likely of being arrested or of being killed by the same men who murdered her husband."

"I can't blame her on the second point, but I'd move heaven and earth to keep the woman safe." A harsh breath left the agent. "I talked with several of my agents before leaving the office, so they're at work now. Zee and Yarrow have been under scrutiny for a while. Same with the Keslers. We'll hone in on both gangs, though. Before, we couldn't be sure that Fulton wasn't working with multiple gangsters. Narrowing it to two groups is useful."

"What about the Sweebes?" Doro asked.

"The family home is only a few hundred yards south of Chicago Pike," Canton said.

"Which makes it a perfect place for booze to be stored for short times," Ev observed.

"Like at the Fulton place?" Aggie asked.

"Similar, although we suspect the Sweebes only work for Zee and Yarrow. Mostly, Patrick, since his brothers make runs to Chicago," Canton replied.

"Mrs. Fulton mentioned them," Aggie put in. "Patrick, in particular."

"Interesting," the federal agent said.

The noncommittal statement provoked Doro's next query. "Why have two storage places so close together?"

Canton fiddled with his tie. "From what we've learned over the years, bootleggers don't like to keep all of their product in one place. Too risky. Their competitors might find out and target them, and we lawmen are looking for hidden booze if it's related to a big gang. I don't want my men investigating every suspected bootlegging accomplice. In fact, if either gang was small, we wouldn't spend time on them. We have too much to do with violent gangsters and their speakeasies right now. Fulton's murder isn't the only killing I've heard about, although it's the most recent."

The comments reinforced the dangers associated with investigating rumrunners. "Mrs. Fulton said Patrick Sweebe has a pleasant manner but can be dangerous," Doro put in. "He may be a hitman, according to her."

Canton nodded. "We know Patrick is muscle for the Zee-Yarrow gang. As to his demeanor, I haven't met the man." The agent's attention went to Ev, who had no response.

After studying Ev for a moment, Doro wondered why he didn't comment. If anything, he acted like he had not heard Agent Canton. Did he know Patrick Sweebe?

Wade's voice broke into her thoughts. "I've heard that his family is involved in bootlegging. That's about all I know for sure." While he spoke, Wade also glanced at Ev, who quickly looked away.

Their interaction, fleeting as it was, gave Doro pause. Did they know more than they were saying? Or was she concocting things? The latter was as possible as the former, because Doro had a vivid imagination. Time would tell if she was feeling insightful or imaginative, but wanting Canton's reaction, she said, "Mrs. Fulton said Patrick Sweebe is in one of their speakeasies at times."

"True. He's usually in their private room. We think it's primarily to spy on customers," Canton said. "Just in case one is a federal agent."

The remark reinforced Doro's concern about Ev playing such a role. After a glance at him, she voiced an observation—one that might evoke Canton's plans. "Do you have someone undercover in either bootlegging gang?"

Canton's dark eyes sparkled with mirth. "I couldn't tell you, if I did."

The answer did not bother Doro, but Ev's reaction—a tightening of his jaw—did. Had he and Canton discussed him going undercover? Since neither would admit that, she pushed it to the back of her mind. "I see."

"But I can tell you that both gangs are dangerous," the agent said. "Zee and Yarrow sent some of their men to shoot up one of Keslers' speakeasies a couple weeks ago. They've been rivals ever since the Kesler boys' father came down from Detroit. This latest conflict upped the ante."

"And put Fulton in more danger," Ev observed.

"His wife wanted to leave the area sooner, but he was set on making more money," Aggie put in.

"He should've listened to her," Canton said. "The Sweebes are tough customers. Knowing Patrick went to see the Fultons on more than one occasion is disturbing. I wish we had names for the other visitors, although the description of the vehicle helps, since it matches one seen on Saturday night."

His assessment had Doro revealing another point from Mrs. Fulton. "Alf Waggoner, a boy who lives out toward Lyons, did odd jobs for the Fultons, including running liquor. She said he was at their house early on Saturday but not later."

Canton set his jaw. "Ev and Wade told me about the kid's jalopy being seen, and I talked with the witness, Jug Barnes. The Waggoners don't have a telephone, and I don't have enough men to have one run out there on a possible goose chase." His gaze went from Wade to Ev. "I spoke with the mayor over their way, since they don't currently have a constable, and he saw Mrs. Waggoner yesterday. She's concerned about the boy's whereabouts, because he was last home on Saturday morning. Other than that, she was close-mouthed about the kid."

"Maybe she knows he's working with bootleggers," Ev said.

"At the very least, she suspects it," Canton agreed.

Anxiety knotted Doro's insides. What if Alf had also been killed? The possibility seemed all too real.

"I'd go out to the Waggoner place, but I want to stay around town, as much as I can," Wade replied. "While it's doubtful any of the gangsters will come back and cause trouble, I'd like to be vigilant."

"I understand," Canton replied.

Ev leaned forward. "I'll drive out there." He glanced at Doro. "Maybe you could come along. Mrs. Waggoner might be more talkative with you there. It'll be casual, since they don't live in this jurisdiction. I won't mentioned consulting with the Bureau, unless I have to."

Doro's heart leaped with joy. Before she could agree, Canton spoke again.

"Normally, I wouldn't countenance a civilian getting involved." He grimaced. "But it's too late to keep you out, and Ev is right. The mother might be more open with you."

Her spirit soaring, Doro agreed. "I think so, and Alf has sisters. They might talk with me, too."

"A good point," Aggie put in.

Doro smiled at her friend, who was always supportive. Aggie grinned back. When Ev caught Doro's gaze, his lips twitched. Despite previous misgivings about her involvement, he seemed happy to have her help now.

"All right. Talk to the Waggoners," Canton said before turning to Wade. "Their mayor said he hasn't been in the position long. Like in most small towns, it's part-time only, but there's a retired sheriff over that way who might have information about the Sweebes and others involved in rum-running."

"Roy Taylor," Wade said.

"He's been retired for a while, hasn't he?" Doro asked.

"About three years, but he was the sheriff in the adjacent county for years," Wade explained. "I mentioned him to Lowery the other day, and again to Ev, just before you two came in. Roy was a big help to me when I first took this job, and he may be able to tell you more about Alf Waggoner and the Sweebes, too. Same with anyone else involved in bootlegging."

Wade's explanation made sense, causing Doro to nod in understanding. "He should be an excellent source of information."

"Talking with Taylor isn't a problem, but be careful when you go to the Waggoner place." Canton looked at Doro before continuing. "Catching killers can be tricky, but going after bootleggers is more difficult. Much more difficult."

"More difficult or more dangerous?" Doro asked, because she did not care for his imperious tone. The affable man she'd met in the Chicago train station bore only a physical resemblance to this one. His demeanor was different, and she understood how he handled a team of federal agents. With brusque command and unswerving certainty.

Canton released a chuckle. "You've come right to the point, Professor."

"Ev is the one who made the point," she replied. "In fact, he's made it several times. I've assured him I don't plan to dig around on my own or with Aggie. Meeting with Mrs. Fulton was safe enough."

"That's right," her friend agreed. "We met Mrs. Fulton only because she refused to talk with any lawmen."

Again, Wade offered his support. "Understandable."

The senior agent nodded. "If that wasn't the case, I wouldn't be here or including you in this discussion."

His last statement had both Doro and Aggie frowning. While her friend remained silent, Doro did not. "Discussions often prove helpful in going over clues and suspects, especially when everyone involved has some level of experience. Don't you agree, Agent Canton?"

A grin took years off his face and officiousness from his demeanor. "I do, Professor Banyon, which is why we're all chatting now."

Something that sounded suspiciously like a suppressed laugh left Ev. However, when Doro glanced at him, his features were carefully composed. Only his gaze glittered with repressed amusement.

After a temporary lull, Doro spoke again. Multiple questions crowded her mind, but she tried one most likely to get an answer first. "Is there a lawman in the Sweebes' area?"

The federal agent gripped his chair arms. "Yep, and a couple of my men have spoken with him. He doesn't know much about bootleggers going through his town or locals working with them, but he's only been on the job for a couple of months, and he isn't from this area."

Canton's response was not illuminating, so Doro moved to another point. "Mrs. Fulton wasn't clear about the men who came the night of the murder."

"Did you believe she couldn't see them, or is she too afraid to tell everything?" Canton asked.

She and Aggie exchanged a long glance before Doro focused on the agent. "It's hard to say for sure."

"I agree," her friend said. "She might know more and be scared to say so."

Canton released a pent-up breath. "Identifying the men who went into the barn with Fulton is of top importance. Of course, I'd also like to know about the vehicle you saw leaving the Fulton place, Wade. It isn't the one that Mrs. Fulton described."

Wade braced his elbows on his desk. "No, it wasn't the same one, but it matches the description Jug Barnes provided."

"And the blue LaSalle was there first." Agent Canton made the observation.

"That's right," Wade confirmed.

The senior agent's jaw tightened. "It has to belong to one of the Zee-Yarrow boys or one of the Kesler brothers. Both gangs are fighting for control of operations in Toledo. The two groups are bitter enemies, who want to eliminate the competition any way they can."

His words confirmed earlier revelations and evoked fresh apprehension in Doro. Could the violence spill over into small towns like Michaw and Sylvania? She hoped not. "And they're both running booze along Chicago Pike?"

Canton put his elbows on his knees and clasped his hands. "It appears so, and knowing Fulton stored liquor for them is a major piece of evidence."

"This case is getting more complicated," Aggie murmured.

Lowery Canton's expression had Doro wondering if there were additional complications. "Do you think any of the Keslers ever visited the Fultons?"

The agent's only reaction was a quick, slight widening of his eyes. "What makes you ask that?"

At the other end of the sofa, a low chuckle escaped Ev. Doro shot a sidelong glance at him, but he had averted his face. For a long moment, she waited for him to weigh in. When Ev did not, Canton addressed her again.

"I must be missing something," the agent said in a clipped tone.

Ev cleared his throat. "Doro doesn't enjoy having one of her questions answered with another question." Although his mirth was muted, it was evident.

She lifted her chin a fraction. "It's an evasive strategy."

"Really?" Canton spoke the one word in a taut tone. "You realize I don't have to answer questions, don't you?"

The man's change in demeanor might have upset Doro if she was one of his agents, but she wasn't. And Ev was only working for the Bureau on a temporary basis, or so he claimed. With determination, she brushed that idea aside and went back to matters at hand. "Mrs. Fulton gave vague descriptions of the men who went to the barn with her husband the night of his murder. She only saw them in silhouette, and she hid before they got out of the car."

Canton's features lost some of their severity. "I see. What about seeing other bootleggers before Saturday night?"

"She told us that Zee and Yarrow never came out, but Phillip Kesler had," Doro replied. "According to Mrs. Fulton, he's the only one of the brothers who did." She provided a description.

Canton leaned back in the chair and folded his arms across his waist. "That fits him. He's the youngest brother." He paused for a moment. "He works with their errand boys and runners. Sometimes, he goes to Chicago or Detroit himself."

Wade released a low whistle. "Is he involved with the Purple Gang?"

Even in a small town like Michaw, that gang was known as the most powerful and most dangerous one in Detroit. Were they planning to move into Toledo? If so, what would it mean for lawmen in the area? As anxiety filled Doro, she looked at the three men in the room. What would it mean for them? Most especially, would Ev be affected?

"Not that I've heard," Canton replied.

While the agent spoke, Doro considered the implications. A glance around the room revealed the rest of the group was also engaged in silent contemplation.

"We need to find out a lot more," Ev said before turning to his boss. "What other steps are you planning now that we have details from Mrs. Fulton?"

Canton folded his arms across his chest. "Let's see what my agents discover today, and what you and the professor discover. The Toledo police chief will let me know when he has news, since his department is also aware of the Zee-Yarrow gang and the Keslers. Both operations have given him plenty of trouble." Canton turned to Ev. "We can talk again later or tomorrow."

"All right," Ev agreed.

"I definitely want to find out more about Patrick Sweebe and his family, and about Alf," Canton said. "I doubt if the Sweebes are also working for the Keslers, since Patrick's an integral part of the Zee-Yarrow gang. Young Alf might've done jobs for the brothers, though. As for the cars, I'll handle it from my side, but you could gather information here."

"I'll make more calls," Wade murmured. "The vehicle I saw turned south at the crossroad, but east-west routes intersect that route in several places before it crosses the Chicago Pike. Any of those highways could be used to get back to Toledo."

"Or even to Chicago," Ev put in.

"I'll try to find out if anyone has seen Alf's old beat-up jalopy since Saturday," Wade said.

"Whatever you find out will help," Canton said. "With Fulton working for two bootleggers, we've still got plenty of suspects. Even though one of the gang bosses likely ordered the murder, we'll arrest everyone involved."

Ev thrust his legs out in front of him. "We'll run down as many leads as we get. Do you have anyone undercover with the Keslers?"

Doro leaned forward to hear if the senior agent would respond. When he did, she listened with interest.

Canton pursed his lips. "We haven't been successful, although we've tried. The best we've been able to do is have an agent be a regular customer there. As a cover only. He may have some details for us. I couldn't reach him this morning, but he'll be in the office later today." The agent turned to Doro. "If Mrs. Fulton calls you again, I'd like to know."

"Of course, but she still won't want lawmen involved," Doro replied.

"That's understandable. Although I'd like to question her, you'd learn more," Canton said, "so, go ahead and talk."

"Doro doesn't need to do our jobs for us," Ev said, in a stilted tone. "She's already doing far more than enough to solve the case."

Ev's outburst surprised Doro. "Agent Canton didn't say anything about me getting deeply involved. In fact, he's made it clear he doesn't like amateurs in the mix."

A muscle twitched in Ev's jaw as he ground his teeth. "You don't know him as well as I do."

"Ev, you make me sound like I'm conniving," Canton said with a smirk.

"Do I?" Ev asked. "If so, it's because you can be."

As she looked from Ev to his boss and back, Doro wondered how he had gotten pulled into not only consulting but maybe more. Had Canton connived to achieve those ends? Most likely that was the case.

"All to a good end," Canton said. "Besides, the professor is right. I haven't asked her to do a thing, except let me know about any calls from Fulton's widow. I merely agreed about her going with you to talk to Taylor and the Waggoners."

Ev nodded. "Wade and I can pass details along to you."

"I'll clarify myself. I don't expect or want Professor Banyon or Professor Darwine in danger. If they meet the woman again, we'll have lawmen around," Ev's old boss said.

Some of Ev's tension drained away, and he leaned back in his chair. "And I'll be one of them."

"You will." Canton looked at his watch. "Any other important information, Professor Banyon? Like what direction Mrs. Fulton took when she left the diner?"

Doro drew out a lingering concern. "We didn't see Mrs. Fulton come and go out the front door. Parking is in back of the diner, but there's a church across the street and a service station nearby. She might've left a vehicle in any of those places, so I got up to follow her. Then, the waitress blocked my way."

"Blocked your way?" Ev asked. "You didn't mention that."

"Aggie thought the woman feared we were leaving without paying," Doro explained.

Wade turned to Aggie. "Did you get up when Doro did?"

"No," Aggie replied, "but the waitress seemed uneasy. I figured she worried about us skipping out."

"It's possible," the constable agreed.

"It's also possible Mrs. Fulton slipped some money to the waitress and asked her to keep you two from following her," Ev suggested.

Canton nodded. "That could be. She didn't want any coppers coming to the meeting, and she might've worried you'd tell us what she's driving or what direction she headed."

Briefly, Doro considered the ideas, which seemed sound. Even so, doubts nagged at her. "The waitress interfered with our view of the door after we arrived, too."

"She was an imposing figure," Aggie added.

Since her friend was not bothered by the waitress's behavior, Doro let it drop. "I'd still like to know which way Mrs. Fulton headed."

"As would I," Canton put in. "Anything else new?"

"Something Doro and Aggie told us before you got here was about the Fultons running a saloon before Ohio went dry," Wade told Canton.

The federal agent turned to the two young women. "I've heard about that. What did she tell you? Does she hold a grudge against the law?"

"That's hard to say," Doro replied. "They were in a bad place financially, which is why Mr. Fulton kept working for bootleggers."

"True of a few former saloonkeepers," Canton muttered. "Can't really blame them."

"She mentioned speakeasies being hard to find," Aggie observed. "She also said some are nice and others aren't."

"All true," Ev agreed. "Zee and Yarrow run two nice saloons, but one is fancy. The Keslers have one speakeasy that's classy, so they serve the good stuff there. The other place is a blind pig, a lower-class establishment where the liquor is probably bathtub gin."

"Do they really make alcohol in bathtubs?" Aggie asked, her hazel eyes bright with interest.

"Sometimes," Ev replied. "A bathtub tap is high enough to fit tall bottles under it. Sink faucets aren't."

Aggie's hazel eyes went wide. "Fascinating."

Doro already knew the origin of the term, and she was not fascinated. She was suspicious as she narrowed her gaze on Ev. When he had mentioned details earlier, she had not considered the implications. Now, she did. "And you know about all these bars, how liquor is made, and what type is sold in different places because..." Her voice, with a note of sarcasm, trailed off.

He had the good grace to look chagrined. After a moment, he held up his right hand, as if in surrender. "I've been in all four places."

"Recently?" Doro asked. A muffled chuckle left Wade, and Aggie's gaze brimmed with cheer. Doro scowled at each of them in turn. Ev making the rounds of various speakeasies was a cause for concern, not merriment. When he failed to reply, she pushed the point. "Well, was it lately?"

"Not really," Ev murmured, but he did not meet her gaze.

Doro opened her mouth to pursue the topic, but Canton interrupted.

"Did Mrs. Fulton supply details about her friends? The ones you mentioned in your summary," the agent asked Doro and Aggie.

Doro glanced at her notes before replying. "The friend's husband also works with bootleggers. She didn't want to give names or places, except for saying the man works for the Keslers now and brings liquor across Lake Erie."

Canton put both hands to his forehead. "From Canada."

"Yes," Doro agreed.

"Then, he's supplying the better speakeasies," Ev said. "The stuff coming down from there is legally produced."

"I wish you would've been able to follow her, because that man may have important information," Canton said.

"Duly appointed lawmen can get those details," Ev said, his tone sharp.

"Not if Mrs. Fulton wants to meet with Aggie and me again," Doro pointed out. While she did not want to argue with Ev, Doro hated being reined in. Something he should know by now. She had promised to be circumspect.

Canton looked at his watch. "I need to get back to the office, so I'd like to briefly review our plan for the rest of today. Ev and Professor Banyon will go to the Waggoner home and talk to the retired sheriff. Constable Lammers will make some calls." He glanced at Aggie. "Perhaps, you'd be good enough to take notes for him. I've seen his handwriting."

Everyone chuckled, which broke the tension. Aggie grinned. "I'm happy to help."

The federal agent rose. "I'll call around four with what I find out, as long as it's not confidential. If it needs to be kept under wraps, I'll ask you to drive into the city again, Ev."

"Sure thing," Ev replied.

Doro's first thought was to wonder if she could go along. Perhaps, Ev wouldn't need to take another trip into the city. But he needed to answer her question with specificity. Exactly when and why had he been to four speakeasies?

Canton turned to Doro. "If you hear from Mrs. Fulton again, please let me know immediately. Ev can tell you how to contact me at the office and at home. No matter what time of the day or night, I want to hear."

For several moments, Doro reviewed the possibilities. "She was scared, so I think she'll hide out or maybe she's already gone."

The agent looked glum. "I hope not. She could hold the key and not realize it yet." Canton cleared his throat. "I believe this is a good time for me to leave. Good luck, Ev." Then he said his farewells and left.

Doro again focused on Ev. "You haven't answered me about your trips to bars."

Since Ev remained silent, Wade responded. "He was checking the places out before leaving for Chicago."

Annoyance crept through Doro. "So, Zee and Yarrow were in your sights before Mr. Fulton was killed. The Keslers probably were, too." No wonder Lowery Canton made his escape. He didn't want to hear how Ev wiggled out of being honest. She glanced at Wade and back to Ev. "Which is where you were before going to Chicago and what caused Wade to be concerned."

A trace of color climbed into Ev's lean cheeks, but he held her gaze. "Only a few days before you and I ran into each other in Chicago, Lowery wanted to see me in his office, which I told Wade. I expected to be back the same night, but two agents were on another big case, so Lowery asked me to check out some places. I couldn't call Wade for fear of an operator overhearing."

"Once I found him, I understood," the constable assured Doro.

Aggie perched on the edge of her chair, braced her elbows on the desk, and leaned forward. "What I understand is that you went into Toledo, tracked down Agent Canton, and went to more than one speakeasy looking for Ev." She sounded annoyed.

As Wade's face suffused with color, he cleared his throat. "It wasn't exactly like that."

Aggie's lips flattened. "But it was almost like that, and I wonder how you both got into the places."

Amusement and admiration filled Doro. Her friend felt as annoyed as she did.

Wade put up both hands, palms toward Aggie. "All right. All right. Lowery let me know where Ev was heading, and I went to the same places. But we weren't there at the same times. As for gaining entrance, the Bureau has a couple of fellows who keep them up to date on passwords."

When Ev said no more, exasperation prodded Doro again. Why hadn't he told her about his forays before now? Was it such a secret? Was he hiding something else? "So, going to these places had to make you both suspect the Keslers or the Zee-Yarrow gang might be involved in the Fulton murder almost immediately. Why wouldn't you tell us?" The question hung heavily in the air for long moments. Wade drummed his fingers on the desk, and Ev averted his face. Doro felt her patience slipping away. "Why?"

"We were hoping to keep the two of you from being noticed by either side, especially since a few bootleggers have been at the Fulton place. None came into town, but you two are both curious," Ev explained. "And there was a chance Fulton was working with other gangs, too."

Annoyance filled Doro. "You mean I'm nosey. But I wasn't driving out to the Fultons and looking around. Not ever."

Ev released a pent-up breath. "It was an abundance of caution. Knowing rumrunners were so close to town bothered us. Of course, neither Wade nor I figured on Fulton being killed, although maybe we should have."

"Not even Lowery saw that as a possibility," Wade pointed out.

"Which doesn't explain not hinting at what you suspected," Doro said.

Ev leaned back in his chair. "All right. I'll be completely forthright. Canton didn't want me confiding in anyone except Wade, and I agreed." For a moment, he looked straight at Doro. "In my defense, when I consulted with the Bureau, I didn't think you and I would be involved in any way going forward. Not after your departure in May."

Guilt pricked at Doro when she recalled how she'd left abruptly with only a day's warning to him. At that point, anything other than a casual friendship as co-workers seemed out of the question. Three months away and being kidnapped by a killer had changed her mind. But he wouldn't have known that before he started consulting with the Prohibition Bureau. Although Ev could have shared the information since then, Doro relented. "I won't argue with that observation."

Something remarkably like amusement flickered in his silver gaze. "Good." After a moment, Ev continued. "I could've explained before I saw Lowery, but I honestly thought I'd be back in short order. I'm sorry for not being more open. Am I forgiven?"

His sincere statements and his contrite expression combined to overcome the last of Doro's dismay. "You are."

"Thank you," Ev replied with a wink.

"What about me, Aggie?" Wade asked. "I'm sorry I didn't reveal everything, but I didn't think I should break my word to Ev."

A soft sigh left Aggie. "Understandable, and I forgive you."

The grin splitting Wade's face lit up the room. "Thanks."

Colleen coming in the front door drew everyone's attention. For a moment, the girl looked taken aback. "I wasn't expecting all of you."

"We were having a meeting," Wade said, "and I'm glad you're back. None of us has had time to chat with townsfolk lately, but you get around. Anything of interest being discussed?"

She shoved her hands into her skirt pockets and shifted from one foot to the other. "There's some gossip. Folks don't like agents coming around." The clerk looked at Ev. "I'm not one of them."

Ev's mouth softened into a slight smile. "Who was talking about federal agents being in town?"

"Some men in the diner were talking about Mr. Fulton being killed," Colleen replied. "It's possible they had dealings with Mr. Fulton, though. According to them, a man shouldn't get arrested for drinking liquor."

"They aren't alone in that opinion," Ev observed, "but Prohibition agents don't go after drinkers. Unless people are caught in a speakeasy raid, they don't have to worry. Even then, they aren't held for long."

"I see," Colleen murmured. "I don't know much about any of that. When I worked for Mrs. Parson, I stayed in my room after supper and didn't go back downstairs until the next morning."

The observation reminded Doro of Colleen's eagerness to escape the Parson home last winter. At the time, the girl had insisted she knew nothing about what the Fultons and Mrs. Parson did, but was that really true? "Back in December, you mentioned being told to stay upstairs at night."

Colleen went pale. "I only went down once for a snack, but I got told not to do it again."

"And you saw nothing odd around the place, right?" Doro asked.

The clerk wrapped her arms around her waist. "Not really, only Mr. Fulton going out late at night. Sometimes, he got back at dawn, so I stayed in the attic until sunrise," Colleen replied. "His missus was nicer, but the mister could talk tough. That's why I was so glad to get this job and a room at Mrs. Lammers' boardinghouse." Her gaze rested on Wade. "Your ma is such a nice lady."

"She enjoys having you as a boarder," Wade assured the girl. "You're perfectly safe there."

When Colleen's shoulders sagged, Doro realized the young clerk had been tense. Probably due to the murder. "You haven't talked with the Fultons lately, have you? They seldom come into town."

"No, I haven't, and I'm glad we don't cross paths," Colleen said. She shifted restlessly. "But since he was murdered, I been wondering if the killer might realize I worked with the Fultons before."

"That's highly unlikely," Wade said. "You weren't involved in bootlegging and, as far as we know, no rumrunners actually came to the Parson place."

"They didn't when I was there," Colleen hurried to say.

"Then, there's nothing to worry about," Doro added. "Nothing at all." At least there wasn't unless someone else in town had details about bootlegging. Were local men merely upset about their booze supply being cut off? Or were they somehow involved in the trade and watching federal agents intending to report their movements to rumrunners? Either was possible. "Who were the men talking about the agents?"

"Mr. Beavers and Mr. Townsend," the girl replied.

Relief filled Doro. The pair were older gentlemen who enjoyed spirits and had complained about Ohio going dry. "That's not surprising."

"No, it isn't," Wade agreed. "They're dead set against Prohibition and have been for years. Not only that, they'd be curious about why three men in suits were at the Fulton place."

"Do they live out there?" Ev asked.

"Beavers does," Wade replied before smiling at Colleen. "They're good men, but they don't like Prohibition agents because they enjoy an occasional nip. It's nothing to worry about, though."

"Good. Now, I should get back to work," Colleen said.

"You've helped us a lot lately and been in the office alone often," Wade told her. "Go ahead and take the rest of the day off."

"Thank you," the young clerk replied.

The door had barely closed behind the girl when Ev spoke. "She seems worried about the Fultons' contacts knowing about her, but there shouldn't be a problem. We've discussed Parson and his involvement, but he died a few years back, and his wife is no longer around."

"I understand Colleen being worried. She's a young girl who's all alone. And she was treated poorly at the Parson house," Doro said. "She's working hard to better herself. Working here has helped." The girl's grammar and vocabulary had improved, and she wasn't as shy, either. "Colleen never mentioned seeing strangers at the place."

"No, she never did," Aggie agreed. "Being on your own at a young age isn't easy."

Doro knew her friend was thinking about the years after her parents died and her brother stayed in France. "You haven't been by yourself for nearly a decade." As soon as she had met Aggie, Doro had welcomed her as a sister, and the rest of her family had done the same.

"And you never will be again," Wade assured her.

"I know," Aggie murmured.

Although the exchange was brief, it telegraphed a world of love. Doro's heart swelled with joy for her friend before doubt surfaced. Maybe she should write to Aggie's brother and extoll Wade's virtues. But not until after the case was cracked. She moved the conversation back to the present. "Colleen has all of us, and your mother, Wade."

He tore his attention from Aggie. "I'll stop by the boarding-house later, just to ease her mind."

"I can do that," Aggie said. "That way, you can make your calls."

He nodded his agreement.

"And we'll get on the road," Doro put in.

Chapter Six

Since Doro's Essex roadster was in front of the constable's office, they took her vehicle for their two visits. The retired sheriff's home was closer, so they planned to stop there before going on to the Waggoner place. Doro felt confident that Roy Taylor would have useful information. She was less positive that young Alf's family would share details. Or that they knew where the boy was.

After getting out of town, she asked Ev what he thought about solving the case within the next week or two. If it was not solved before classes resumed, helping would become difficult, due to time constraints. When he did not answer, she glanced at him, only to find him dozing peacefully. Since catching up on sleep was more important than talking, she drove on in silence.

Fifteen minutes later, Ev roused. He rubbed his eyes and sat up. "Sorry."

"You needed some rest, although it wasn't much."

He glanced around and gestured to a white-frame two-story cottage on the right side of the road. "This should be the place."

Doro carefully steered her car off the road and on to the dirt path that ran alongside the house and on to a shed, a chicken coop, and a barn. As they pulled to a stop, a man came into view. Tall and muscular with gray hair and a matching mustache, he turned toward them. "That looks like Sheriff Taylor. I've only seen him a few times and not recently, but he looks much the same except his hair and mustache used to be dark brown."

A chuckle left Ev. "You'll probably say that about me, if I live to be his age."

As she pulled to a stop, Doro shot a sidelong glance at Ev. "If you don't go back to the Bureau, you'll probably live at least as long as he has."

His features softened. "I'm not going back."

Despite his casual expression, the assertion was not altogether reassuring. "You've promised to help them with this case."

"I'm helping right now, and so are you," he pointed out.

"True," she agreed with a grin. "Since you and the sheriff are both lawmen, although he's retired, you'll ask him most of the questions, right?" They had not discussed how to proceed, but Doro figured Ev would take the lead.

He shook his head. "Not necessarily, but I can start by asking about the Sweebes. He should have details about them. Chime in whenever you have questions."

The conversation died on the vine when the older man stopped on Ev's side of the car and leaned down to look inside. "Good day." His voice was gruff, but his expression was open.

"You're the college security officer and Wade Lammers' deputy, right?"

As Ev climbed out of the vehicle, he extended his hand. "That's right, sir. I'm Everett Mallow. This is Professor Dorothea Banyon," he added when she joined them.

The older man tipped his hat to her. "You grew up in Michaw, and now you're a librarian over at the college."

"Yes, I am," Doro replied.

"And a pretty good armchair detective from what I hear," the retired sheriff said.

When Ev's lips twitched, Doro repressed her own grin. Last fall, when they had worked together on a case, their first, he had promoted her from armchair detective to amateur sleuth, reasoning that the former solved mysteries from the comfort of home while the latter went out to investigate. "I've done a bit of sleuthing."

"Doro has done a lot of detective work and done it successfully," Ev put in. "She's a top-notch investigator. As good as any man I know."

A speculative gleam lit Taylor's brown eyes. "Great to have a solid partner in these matters. I didn't have many big cases, but my wife always listened and gave sound advice. She's inside baking bread. Some may be ready to eat, and there's a pot of soup on the stove along with coffee. Come on in, and we'll chat."

After the group entered the back door, Taylor called out. "Ma, we've got company."

A petite, round woman in her sixties turned toward them with a smile. Clad in a flowered cotton housedress and full apron, she looked every inch the typical housewife. Appearances could be misleading, which must be true in this case. If Mrs. Taylor had consulted on her husband's investigations, she was far from average—and so was he. Many lawmen, maybe most, would not ask their spouses for help on cases.

"Welcome," Mrs. Taylor said. "Two loaves of bread are right out of the oven. I'll slice it after it cools a bit. I've got homemade grape jelly and fresh-churned butter. Soup and coffee, too."

The combined aromas of fresh bread and hot coffee made Doro's mouth water. Since she had only picked at her toast, she was starving. "Thank you. That all sounds wonderful."

"I should've already introduced our guests," the retired sheriff said before doing just that.

Once greetings were exchanged, Mrs. Taylor urged Doro and Ev to take seats at the table. As they did, Sheriff Taylor kissed his wife on the cheek. In response, she patted his arm. Watching the pair, memories surged through Doro. Gramma Rose and Grampa Ben had been the same way, and her parents were, too. Her gaze slipped to Ev. When she found his attention on her, Doro felt heat rise into her cheeks. Would they have moments like this? It was too soon to know for sure, and the moment was broken when Mrs. Taylor turned to them with a question.

"Do you like peaches? We have several trees. Roy picked a few earlier, and I made a pie. It'll be ready in a half-hour," the older woman said.

"Homemade bread and fresh-baked pie. Real treats," Ev said with enthusiasm.

A wide grin covered Mrs. Taylor's face. "There's a pot of bean soup simmering. That would round out lunch."

"That's very kind of you," Doro said, "but we didn't expect a meal."

"No, we didn't," Ev agreed. "Just pie would be fine for me."

Doro could not repress a chuckle. "Officer Mallow has a sweet tooth."

Color rose high on his cheeks. "I won't deny it."

"So do I, son," the older man said. "Both our boys did, too."

Mrs. Taylor's smile disappeared. "They did, but I don't get to spoil them with treats anymore. They joined the army to fight in the Great War. One met a British nurse and lives in London. The other settled in New York City when he got home. He'd met a couple of fellows from there, and they convinced him it was livelier than rural Ohio."

"Because it is," her husband said with a chuckle. "We've visited him, and he gets home now and then." Taylor poured two cups of coffee and put them in front of Doro and Ev. After getting some for himself, he joined them at the table. "Wade called after you left his office to say you have questions for me, so we might as well get started."

Ev withdrew a pencil and notepad from his jacket pocket and handed them to Doro. "Your writing is neater than mine."

"It is," she agreed with a grin. His answering smile made her heart flutter, and she lowered her gaze to hide her emotions.

Ev cleared his throat and addressed the sheriff. "You know the Sweebe family?"

"Real well," Taylor replied. "All the menfolk have been in trouble over the years. Some minor issues and some big ones. I retired a couple years back, but after Prohibition began. I monitored them at that time. There was talk about them running booze from Detroit and Lake Erie to points south and west."

"All the men in the family?" Ev asked.

Taylor nodded. "Yep. The grandfather, old Nate, didn't actually transport the stuff, from what I know, but he had to realize his son and grandsons were doing it. Two of the kids go to Chicago often. Another is with a bunch in Toledo, which is the main reason you're here, right?"

"That's right," Ev agreed. "What do you think about Patrick Sweebe?"

While they were talking, Mrs. Taylor put a tureen of soup on the table and bowls at four places. She returned with bread, butter, and jelly before serving everyone. Doro and Ev offered their thanks, and her husband rose to help her into a chair before sitting again himself. The small caring gesture touched Doro's heart.

After a moment, Sheriff Taylor replied to Ev. "I haven't seen the boy for more than a year. When I last did, a glance at him said he's making good money at whatever he's doing. Expensive automobile and fancy duds. I'm thinking he's working for a major bootlegging operation. Am I right?"

"You are," Ev replied before providing a thumbnail sketch of the Zee-Yarrow gang. "What kind of vehicle is he driving?"

"A Packard roadster. Two-seater with a soft top," the older man replied.

Disappointment assailed Doro. Neither of the automobiles seen at the murder scene fit that description.

"I'll do whatever I can to help the two of you," the retired sheriff said. "I never went after folks making booze for themselves, but I don't like gangsters coming out here. Stopping them on Chicago Pike would be impossible. However, they don't need to set up shop in this county. I hope we can prevent that."

"So do I," Ev murmured. "You mentioned a grandfather and his son."

Taylor immediately picked up the thread of conversation. "The son is Patrick's father. He's laid up with gout, so not involved. The grandfather died a few years ago. Patrick has two brothers, who I already mentioned."

There was a hesitation before Ev spoke again. "I suppose Wade told you about me having been with the Prohibition Bureau before taking the job at Michaw College."

"He did," Taylor replied. "He also said you were working with them now."

"I left the Bureau last fall. My current role with them is temporary." Ev's tone was steady and strong, which gave validity to his assertion.

"How long were you with the Bureau?" the retired sheriff asked.

"A couple of years," Ev replied. "I took the job originally because violence from bootlegging got bad in Detroit. I was a beat cop and saw plenty of crime related to rumrunning."

"It's that way all over big cities," Taylor agreed. "But you'd had enough?"

Ev ran one hand over his face. "My younger sister wanted me to quit because she was constantly worried. Since it felt like the Bureau was in an uphill battle, I agreed. But bootlegging in and around Michaw bothered me enough to get involved again.

Earlier in the month, I supplied my old boss and some other agents with information. Being the college security officer and a town deputy constable are my jobs now, and I like both of them. I enjoy living in a small town and getting to know the people there."

Relief filled Doro. She picked up her utensil and dipped it into the fragrant soup. When Ev shot her a sidelong glance, she smiled. No need for him to realize she was still fretting.

"A wise decision if you want a normal life," Taylor said. "But I don't have to tell you that."

"No, sir," Ev agreed. "I like it in Michaw, and I plan to stay."

Mrs. Taylor, a smile on her face, looked from Doro to Ev. "You've established roots there."

"Yes, ma'am," he replied, "and I hope to establish more."

His reply sent warmth through Doro and, when she glanced at him, she saw the sincerity in his gaze. After a moment, she looked back at the notepad and tried to concentrate on the case. The sheriff's next statement helped in that effort.

"Getting back to young Patrick," Taylor said. "Gossip is that he occasionally makes runs to Detroit and Chicago, but is mostly in Toledo. He got into more than a few fist fights as a kid, and I hear he helps as an enforcer for Zee and Yarrow."

After a bite of bread, Ev responded. "He does, although Patrick acts as a speakeasy waiter, too. He came to the Fulton house a few times. That's from Mrs. Fulton."

Taylor's steel gray eyebrows rose a fraction. "Interesting. When did you talk with her?"

"I didn't," Ev said. "Doro and her best friend did."

Doro hurriedly explained. "My friend and I knew the Fultons a little, and Mrs. Fulton called me. She wouldn't talk with a lawman, so we didn't have much choice. We had to meet her alone or not get any information. She's terrified her husband's killers will find her."

"The woman is in a pickle," the retired sheriff said.

"She surely is," his wife agreed. "Poor thing. Her husband murdered, and bootleggers may be looking for her."

"If they think she can identify them, they are," Taylor agreed.

"She can't," Doro replied before explaining how the widow had hidden when the bootleggers arrived. "She only saw their vehicle."

Taylor looked skeptical. "She's sure no one saw her?"

Doro nodded. "She seemed sure, although she didn't give many details. She was in a hurry to get away, and we wanted to learn about the bootleggers that her husband dealt with." Other questions had, unfortunately, gone unasked.

"From what you've said, Mrs. Fulton indicated not being as involved as her husband," Taylor observed.

"That's her story," Ev agreed before going on. "But she went to the speakeasies with him on at least one occasion."

"Have you been to one of those places?" Mrs. Taylor asked.

"Yes, ma'am, as part of my job," Ev replied.

The older woman's eyes went wide. "How exciting. What was the speakeasy like?"

"Ma," her husband said, "I'm surprised at you." His eyebrows rose as he spoke.

Mrs. Taylor pursed her lips. "I'm not going to one, but I'm curious about them. Aren't you?"

A rueful expression crossed his lined face. "A little. However, we won't be visiting any."

She clucked her tongue. "Of course not. But I'd like to know what one is like."

Doro repressed a chuckle as she listened. A glance at Ev revealed he was also amused.

"I've been in several," Ev said, "but a couple of times, I was part of a raid, so we didn't linger to observe the surroundings. I have general impressions. There's a band, a dance floor, and an extensive bar at many. There's food, often fancy, at the nicer ones."

"And the Zee-Yarrow speakeasy is nice?" the older woman asked.

Several moments preceded Ev's reply. "I've heard, it's classy," Ev said.

He had more than heard about the place, but Doro did not point that out. "Mrs. Fulton mentioned Patrick Sweebe being a charmer, but also dangerous."

"Could his family have been involved in the murder?" Ev asked Taylor. Possibly Zee and Yarrow

The retired sheriff finished his soup and leaned back in his chair. "That would keep them an extra step away. I've never known Patrick's grandfather or father to get violent. As for his brothers, I can see both of them getting involved in a murder. They've used their fists a few times, and neither one is as polished as Patrick. Of course, his pleasantry is all surface and little substance."

"How old are the other two?" Ev asked.

"Jake and Jamie are close to twenty, I think. About a year apart," Taylor replied. "They quit school a few years back. They've been running booze ever since."

A glance at the wall clock evoked Doro's next comment. "We'll have to keep moving in order to be back in Michaw by four o'clock." She did not want to miss Lowery Canton's call, and Ev would not want to, either.

Ev studied his wristwatch. "Before we go, Wade mentioned you not recognizing his description of the Cadillac roadster he saw the night of the murder, Sheriff Taylor."

"I've racked my brain, and I asked Ma. Neither of us recall seeing that kind of vehicle. Sorry," the older man said.

"So am I," his wife added. "I don't like knowing there's gangsters coming around, and I hate thinking locals are involved with them. My folks kept spirits in the house, and we did, too. Of course, not since Ohio went dry." Mrs. Taylor shook her head. "Not sure how I feel about banning alcohol, but it's the law."

"It is, ma'am," Ev agreed.

"Too bad it's one that's spawned more crime than compliance," the retired sheriff said. "I don't envy you, son, but I sure hope you find the killer or killers. Fulton working with more than one gang was foolish—not that he deserved to die for being a fool."

"I feel the same way," Ev said. "There's a possibility that young Alf Waggoner is involved with two gangs, as well. If so, he needs to know to lay low for a while."

Mrs. Taylor put both hands to her face. "He surely does, and he needs to stay away from his mother and sisters."

"If we find him, we'll say as much," Doro promised.

"Their cottage is only a few miles up the road. Turn right out of our drive. Small ramshackle place with a chicken coop and old shed way in back," Taylor said. "They need help but are proud. We take food over from time-to-time, and we hire the girls to help in the garden, when there's need. Anyhow, you can't miss the place."

"We'll find it," Ev said.

Silence fell over the group before the sheriff's wife got up and started to clear the table. Doro immediately joined her.

"I'll slice the pie," Mrs. Taylor said. "Then, the two of you can be on your way."

For the next few minutes, the group savored the dessert and more coffee. When Ev finished first, he was offered a second piece, which he readily accepted.

Briefly, worries about bootlegging and murder disappeared.

Chapter Seven

After they were outside, Doro glanced at Ev. "I hope Alf is somewhere safe. I agree with Mrs. Taylor about him staying away from his family."

"While I'd like to talk with the boy, I have to concur. If Alf knows too much, gangsters won't hesitate to go after his mother and sisters. With luck, we'll learn something from them."

"I hope he isn't involved in the murder," Doro said.

"Me, too. Odds favor the murderer being in the Zee-Yarrow or Kesler gang. It could've been done on the spur of the moment or planned ahead of time."

"Which we need to find out," Doro added.

"We do. That and a lot more."

The hurdles ahead seemed nearly insurmountable, but that had been true during previous cases. After considering what they already knew, Doro voiced an idea. "What if someone else killed Mr. Fulton? We can't be sure Alf wasn't involved or Mrs.

Fulton. And why was Jug Barnes coming back from Sylvania that night? Did he ever say?"

Ev sat up straight and swiveled to face her. "Did those ideas pop into your head, or have you been considering them?"

A long sigh escaped Doro. "They've been in the back of my mind. Saturday night, I didn't think Mrs. Fulton was a good suspect. But she didn't seem forthright in the diner. Also, Alf disappearing could be a clue." When Ev rolled his eyes, she went on. "Jug Barnes was dismissive when I spoke with him in town."

"Do the two of you chat much?"

"Of course not. I ran into him and asked a couple of questions."

Ev's dark brows rose. "A couple."

"He was in a hurry, but I wonder about him. And Mrs. Fulton, too."

"We can't completely rule Mrs. Fulton out, although I'd put her down the list. As for Jug Barnes, he was coming back from Sylvania after dinner at one of the restaurants. Wade says that's not unusual."

"He'd know Jug's habits better than I do," Doro admitted.

For a long moment, Ev searched her face. "Why didn't you mention any of this at the constable's station earlier?"

Her gaze went to a point beyond him. "Because I don't have any solid reason to wonder about any of them, and your old boss wouldn't have appreciated me wasting his time on flights of fancy."

Laughter rumbled out of Ev. "You don't have flights of fancy. You have good insights."

Doro met Ev's gaze. "I sense a *but* coming."

He lightly clasped her hand. "Wade and Lowery both talked to Barnes. Neither is suspicious of him, which doesn't mean you're wrong. I hardly know the man, so I can't be sure of his guilt or innocence."

"But you'd put him down the suspect list, too."

"I would," he replied. "Same with Alf. I don't see motive for either of them or for Mrs. Fulton. But there's a lot we don't know. The motive appears to be Fulton working with rival gangs and stealing booze from one or both. Although that could be wrong, it is our working theory."

"And a sound one."

"But a sound theory isn't always right," he said. "Maybe Barnes wanted booze, and Mr. Fulton caught him in the barn. I'd label it possible, not probable, though. Let's get going. We might get a crucial piece of the puzzle today." Ev held the driver's door for Doro before going around the car and climbing in.

When they were on the road, she spoke again. "What will you do if the case isn't solved before classes start?"

"I'm trying to be optimistic, because that would be tough. My first duty is to the college. My second is to the town. Professional, not personal duty."

The undercurrent in his words and tone confused her. "I don't think of anything in my personal life as a duty."

"You don't? You've stayed here because of your grand-mother, haven't you?"

"Mostly because of her," Doro replied. "Having lived all her life in Sylvania, she doesn't want to move at her age. Of course, I don't want to leave Michaw, and I'm much younger. We're people who put down tap roots, not just roots. My parents would've stayed, but my mother's health forced them to move."

"Your dad didn't go to Colorado right away, though."

"No, he didn't. We all hoped Mother could come home. Now, it seems unlikely. Anyhow, for the first couple of years, my uncle was there and my grandmother went to stay for a long while. Dad and I visited every summer and at Christmas. Now, my uncle has moved on." She chuckled. "Gramma Rose says he's got shallow roots."

"Some folks do."

"You've lived in a few places," she observed.

"Only three. Detroit, Toledo, and Michaw." He paused. "I meant what I told the Taylors. I'm not planning to leave. I might be later than some in putting down a taproot, but I have."

Her heart swelled with the implications of his statement. "Better late than never."

Several moments of silence passed before Ev replied. "You're right."

Since he did not continue, Doro chuckled. "Nice to hear." She released his hand to downshift, and he sat back again. "The Waggoner homestead should be coming up."

Ev sat up straight. "There's a small place up a ways."

She glanced to her side of the road. "That's probably it." When they reached the building, Doro turned in. The front yard, such as it was, had more weeds than grass, and an area of bare dirt passed for what could be a driveway. "I don't see Alf's jalopy."

"That's good. I'd like to quiz the sisters and mother without him around."

Before Doro could reply, a girl of about fourteen appeared on the front porch. Her long blonde hair was pulled into two braids. Small and slender, she wore a housedress so faded that determining the color was impossible. A study of the house revealed it was also worn and washed-out. The last coat of paint was long-gone, leaving the wood bare. The home looked even worse than she had imagined after listening to Sheriff Taylor.

"Who are you?" the girl asked. "What do you want? My mama isn't home."

Before answering, Doro slipped out of the vehicle. Ev was immediately at her side. "This is Deputy Constable Mallow, and I'm Doro Banyon. We're from Michaw."

The girl's gaze went from Doro to Ev. "We got a lawman around here."

"We've heard the town is temporarily without a constable," Doro observed.

Red rose in the girl's round cheeks. "We still don't need interference."

"We don't plan to interfere," Ev said. "We only want information, miss...what's your name?"

The girl shoved her hands into her pockets. "We aren't supposed to talk with strangers. Especially none with a fancy automobile."

Doro and Ev exchanged a knowing glance. When he gave a slight nod, she faced the girl again. "We aren't bootleggers, and we aren't after your brother."

Tears flooded the youngster's blue eyes as her bravado deflated like a bad tire. "He's got to make money, or we won't have much food on the table this winter. He isn't doing anything so wrong. Really he isn't." Her plaintive tone revealed a host of fears.

"We don't think he is, either," Doro said, although that was not quite accurate. But if Alf was only an errand boy for rum-runners, and not involved in the murder, he was in little trouble. Maybe none at all. She hoped that was the case, because his mother and sisters clearly needed him.

"No, we don't," Ev added. "But I'm afraid he may be putting himself, and possibly your whole family, in danger by being a messenger for more than one bootlegging operation. By answering a few questions, you could help him and your mother and sisters."

She shifted from one foot to the other. "I've only passed through Michaw, so how do I know you're the deputy?"

Ev smiled as he reached into his jacket pocket and pulled out his badge. He handed it to the girl. "Here you go."

She turned it over and studied it. "I've never seen a constable's badge up close. How do I know it's real, and you're who you say you are?"

After taking the shiny metal pin back, Ev went on. "I don't suppose you have a telephone to call and find out."

She shook her head.

"My full name is Everett Mallow, and I'm only the part time deputy. My full-time job is being the Michaw College campus security officer. I don't have a badge for that."

Wonder lit the girl's gaze as all suspicion ebbed from her expression. "We went by the campus a couple of times. So pretty with lots of building. I love learning things, and I want to go to college, but Mama says I gotta quit school and get work after this year." Her lips trembled as she spoke. "I get all As, but it doesn't matter, I guess."

Doro's heart constricted. College was out of reach for many youngsters, especially girls. She and Aggie often discussed what they could do about that issue. Now that women professors had won the right to marry without losing their jobs, they could push harder for more scholarships. It might take time, but this girl was a few years away from finishing high school. She needed assistance. Her family needed it. Somehow, Doro would help her. Surely, the youngster could work after school to help out. For now, Doro focused on the most pressing problem. If Alf was working for more than one bootlegger, he was endangering his family. "Something may happen to change her mind before next summer. I work at the college, and we're planning to offer more scholarships."

"My teacher told me about them, but she said I'd have to go as far as Toledo or maybe farther. She didn't say anything about Michaw College," the girl said.

"She wouldn't know about our initiatives. They're still being discussed on campus, which is where I work," Doro put in.

Her blue eyes went wide. "You work there. What do you do?"

"I'm a librarian."

"Oh, I'd like to do that. We have a little bitty library in town. I love to go there," the girl said.

"We'll have to see that you visit our library soon," Doro said. Maybe the girl's whole class could come, but working out the details would have to wait. "Now, would you answer some questions for us?"

After a moment, she nodded. "My name's Charlotte."

"It's lovely to meet you. I'm Doro Banyon."

"Come around to the back door," Charlotte said. "These steps aren't safe."

A glance at the porch revealed the truth of the statement. More than one plank was bowed and rotted. "That's fine. We'll meet you there."

As Doro and Ev made their way around the house, he pointed out more signs of decay. "The place looks ready to tumble down. Look at the windows. More than one is boarded up."

"I doubt they can afford to replace glass," Doro murmured. She gestured toward the shed sitting off to one side. "They have a few chickens, but the coop could use repairs, too."

"It could. I'm a little handy," Ev said. "After we solve this case, I'll come over and see if I can fix the porch stairs and the henhouse. Not sure Mrs. Waggoner will let me put in new windows, but I'll talk to Wade about it."

Doro slid her hand into the crook of his elbow. "You're a good man, Everett Mallow."

A boyish grin lit his handsome face. "I'm glad you think so, Dorothea Banyon."

Warmth spread through her before she murmured. "I do."

When Ev faced her, he looked both solemn and hopeful. "Someday, I hope we both say those two words in another place."

Heat suffused her cheeks as she met his steady gaze, and emotion formed a lump in her throat. "I—uh—I..." Her voice trailed off.

Ev glanced away. "Too soon. Let's go and talk with Charlotte."

When he started forward, Doro held him back although he did not face her. "It isn't too soon to think of such things. Just too soon to plan."

Relief filled Ev's gaze as he looked down at Doro. "Wise words." Then, they walked on.

They had not gone more than a dozen steps when Doro gestured to the woods two-hundred yards from the house. "There's the shed."

Ev narrowed his gaze. "It looks decrepit."

"True, but I wonder if it's used."

"The roof looks half torn off, so probably not." Doro released her hold on his arm when they got to the corner of the house, where Charlotte—along with two younger girls who were clearly twins—was waiting for them.

"These are my little sisters—Harriet and Janice," Charlotte said.

The twins were around twelve, so hardly little. While they looked exactly alike, they looked nothing like Charlotte. Although younger, they were as tall as she was. Both had auburn hair, freckles, and green eyes. The pair stared at Doro and Ev without saying a word. Again, Doro smiled. "It's nice to meet you, girls. My name is Doro Banyon, and this is Deputy Constable Everett Mallow, who is also the campus security officer at Michaw College."

"Charlotte says you didn't come after Alf," the one twin said in an accusatory tone that smacked of disbelief.

"That's right. We only want some information that might help your brother stay out of trouble," Ev replied.

The other twin scowled. "Why should we believe you?"

A barely audible sigh escaped Ev. "You all know how your brother is earning money."

The three Waggoner girls blanched. Only Charlotte spoke. "We do, and we know he could get into trouble." She faced her sisters. "We might be able to help him, if we answer some questions."

The twins appeared to be skeptical, so Doro sent a silent appeal to Ev. He nodded his understanding.

"Before I came to Michaw, I worked for the Prohibition Bureau as a federal agent. I can assure you that we never arrested delivery boys and messengers like your brother. If Alf is only doing those things, he's not in big trouble." Ev looked at each of the sisters in turn. "Bootlegging is a profitable but risky business. The men who do it often get violent. You've probably heard about the murder over by Michaw."

He never discussed his time with the Bureau, and very few townsfolk in Michaw knew about his previous job. Neither did most people on campus, so Doro was surprised by the admissions. Clearly, Ev wanted to reassure the sisters.

All three girls, the color draining from their faces, nodded. Only Charlotte spoke. "I heard in town." She swallowed convulsively. "Alf does chores for those folks, and I went with him a few times because Mrs. Fulton needed help canning. A couple of men came while I was there. They had an automobile as fancy as yours, and they were dressed real nice. She told me to stay away from the windows and not go outside until after they left. Alf and Mr. Fulton spent a lot of time in the barn with the pair."

Doro started in surprise. "How long did they stay?"

"Maybe an hour," Charlotte replied. "Even though Mrs. Fulton warned me not to look out, I took a peek. The four of them were carrying crates to the big automobile."

"Do you know what kind of car?" Ev asked.

Charlotte shook her head. "No, sir. I don't know much about them. But it was blue."

The description was little help, since many vehicles were that color. "Can you describe the men?"

Charlotte's brow furrowed and her eyes narrowed. "One was handsome. Blonde and blue-eyed. Taller than Alf. More muscular, too. He was only twenty feet away when I saw him. The other man was farther. Maybe forty feet. I couldn't tell his age, but he was about the same height as Mr. Fulton, who was standing beside him. Sort of medium build. He had a hat pulled down sort of low, so his hair didn't show much. It was probably brown."

"Could you tell if one or the other was in charge?" Ev inquired.

"The man in the hat seemed to be. He didn't carry much at all. Alf and the blonde did most of that. Mr. Fulton helped a little," Charlotte said.

Ev ran a hand over his face. "Did you see what direction they went when they left?"

"I couldn't look out too long, for fear of Mrs. Fulton catching me. I'm sorry." Charlotte looked distraught. "On the way home, I pled with my brother to stop working with Mr. Fulton. But he said it was good money, money we need. I couldn't deny that."

Again, Doro felt a stab of sympathy. The family was struggling through no fault of its own.

"If Pa hadn't gone to France, everything would be fine," one of the twins said.

Charlotte slipped an arm around her younger sister's shoulders before facing Doro and Ev. "We weren't rich, but we had plenty of food and the house wasn't tumbling down. Pa worked real hard on the farm. He rented a lot of the land, but Mama couldn't so we're down to a garden. So far, Mama has been able to pay the mortgage on the house, so we can stay here."

As Doro looked toward the back of the lot, she noted a variety of vegetable plants. At least the family had food to put on the table, but growing children needed more filling items. Although there were a few chickens, they might not lay enough eggs to make a full meal for the entire family, especially in fall and winter. Again, Doro wondered how she might help. But that would have to wait until the murder case was closed. Ensuring the Waggoners stayed safe was the current concern.

Charlotte faced Ev. "You say you won't arrest my brother, but how do we know you're telling the truth?"

"If your brother wasn't involved in the murder, he's in no serious trouble. And I'll find another job for him," Ev promised the girls. "With classes starting at the college soon, there may be something. If not, there are other places in the area that might need help."

As Doro studied the three young faces, she saw hope warring with disbelief. "I'm sure there's something else for Alf. But do any of you know more about his comings-and-goings?"

The twins looked at Charlotte, who shrugged. "Alf doesn't tell us much at all, and he lies to Mama."

"How do you know he lies if he doesn't tell you things?" Doro asked

Pink rose in Charlotte's cheeks. "He's said a little."

"Even a little might help," Doro suggested in an encouraging tone.

"We won't tell your brother anything that the three of you share," Ev assured the girls. "I'll only pass the information along to other lawmen, and only if absolutely necessary."

"Why should we believe you?" one of the twins asked. "You're a copper."

Charlotte was quick to chastise her sister. "Harry, that's a rude term."

Harriet pursed her lips. "That's what Alf calls his kind." She jerked a thumb at Ev. "Coppers and Prohis."

Doro grimaced at the derogatory term for Prohibition agents. She would have joined in chastising Harriet, but Ev spoke first.

Amusement glittered in Ev's silver gaze. "I've been both."

Harry put her fisted hands on her hips. "So, there's no reason for us to believe you. All you want is to put Alf in jail."

The humor ebbed from Ev. "No, Harry. I don't want that at all. I'd like to help your brother and your entire family. We need your cooperation, though."

The sisters looked at one another. Then, Charlotte turned back to Doro and Ev. "All right. What do you want to know?"

Since getting out pencil and paper might spook the girls, Doro focused on listening intently. But she let Ev ask the first question.

"How long has Alf been a runner for bootleggers?" he inquired.

Charlotte swallowed convulsively. "About five years ago. He started helping some wealthy couple in Michaw. Doing chores and such. At least that's what Alf told Mama."

"The Parsons," Doro murmured.

"Yep, that's the name," Harry put in. "I remember cuz I thought the man was a preacher."

Her twin jabbed Harry in the ribs. "I didn't."

"Shush," Charlotte told both girls. "If you can't contribute something important, be quiet."

The twins scowled, but neither spoke again. Doro had trouble withholding her amusement. As an only child, she had not had a bossy older sibling. Harriet and Janice clearly did. Perhaps, the younger girls knew something of import, so she turned to them. "Do either of you have details about your brother's activities?"

Harry shrugged. "He don't tell us much."

"Sometimes, we can't help but overhear people talking. We don't mean to," Doro suggested.

Harry and Janice looked at one another before the latter spoke. "You tell 'em."

"Like you say, sometimes we happen to hear something without meaning to," Harry said.

"That's true for all of us," Ev put in.

Although she still seemed hesitant, Harry finally continued. "Jan and I was in the shed." She jerked her thumb at the tumble-down building twenty yards away. "We was getting tools to weed the garden when we heard an automobile come in. It wasn't long before we heard Alf talking to some other man."

"When was this?" Doro asked.

Harry shoved her hands into her skirt pockets and rocked back on her heels. "Monday."

Doro's pulse rate sped up. "Did you recognize the person?"

"We didn't ever see him," Jan put in. "We was too scared to come out until he left."

Disappointment filled Doro, but she smiled at the girls. "Understandable."

"It is," Ev agreed, "but what did they talk about?"

Harry wrapped her arms around her waist. "The man said Alf better hide out cuz folks thought he was involved in the killing. Alf swore he wasn't, but we was worried cuz he was gone all Saturday and Sunday. He showed up right before the man came."

Disappointment filled Doro. "Did your mother see this man?" Mrs. Waggoner had expressed concern about Alf's absence, but he had come home on Monday.

"No. She was already gone to work at a house in town," Charlotte replied.

"I see," Doro murmured. "Does she know he was home?"

"No, miss," Charlotte said. "He told us not to let her know he'd been here. Then, he took off right after the man left." Worry lined her youthful face. "We haven't seen him since then."

"Do any of you know more about your brother's associates?" Ev asked.

"Associates?" Harry's brow furrowed. "What's them?"

"People he worked for," Doro supplied.

"Nope," the twins said in unison.

Several moments of silence followed the assertion before Charlotte addressed her younger sisters. "Did you see the automobile?"

Harry gnawed on her lower lip. "Got a peek. It was a black truck, but I only saw the back end."

"Will that help Alf?" Charlotte asked.

"Maybe," Ev said, his voice somber. "I thank you girls for talking with us. If Alf comes home, please don't tell him. All right?"

After a moment, Charlotte and her sisters followed suit. "Is it okay to tell Mama?" the older girl asked.

"Sure," Ev replied. "And tell her not to worry about Alf. Right now, it seems like he wasn't involved in the murder. As for the rest, if he cuts ties to all bootleggers, I'll help him out as much as I can."

Doro noted Ev not making a solid promise, which was wise. The boy might be too involved to escape all punishment.

"When he comes home, tell him to stay here. We've got more work to do in arresting Fulton's killer, but I'll be back after that," Ev said.

"It would be good if all of you kept close to home for a few days," Doro suggested.

Ev nodded. "It would."

"All right," Charlotte agreed. "I'll tell Mama."

Because the girls looked morose, Doro addressed them. "When Officer Mallow visits again, I'll come along and bring a treat for everyone." A chorus of *thank yous* followed.

After saying their farewells, Doro and Ev were back in the car and on the road again in short order.

"The truck could belong to Jug Barnes," Doro said. "His is black."

"Yep, it sure could. I doubt if any of the gangsters drive a truck." He smiled. "You could be on to something by suspecting Jug. I'll tell Lowery when I talk to him."

"What would be his motive to kill Mr. Fulton? I haven't worked that out."

"If Fulton kept booze to sell himself, he could've had local customers. Jug is apt to be one of them. He came of age well before Prohibition. Many folks kept spirits on hand, and plenty of them still like a nip."

Doro considered his observations. "Mrs. Taylor mentioned that. My parents didn't keep much liquor on hand, and none after Ohio went dry. Gramma Rose and Grampa Ben had a brandy decanter for medicinal purposes or so my grandfather claimed."

"That's possible. Others like a tipple every night. Jug could be one. If so, there could've been an argument over payment when he stopped to make a purchase."

"In which case, the killing was probably accidental."

Ev nodded. "But hitting someone in the head isn't."

"True." Doro thought back to Ev's words. "From what you told the sisters, you feel confident Alf wasn't involved in the murder."

"It's more of a gut feeling than confidence. Knowing the kid a little and his jalopy being out on the road to Sylvania that night lend credence to my supposition. Timing is part of it, but

I don't think the kid would be laying low if he'd been there. He'd be more apt to be with the Keslers or Zee and Yarrow."

"That's a good point."

Laughter rumbled out of him. "I'd like to think I make a few."

After a sidelong glance at Ev, Doro chuckled, too. "You make many excellent points. You're a fine lawman, and I'm sure you were an extraordinary federal agent."

"Really?"

The odd note in his voice made Doro wonder if Ev sought reassurance. Surely not. But she offered it. "Your old boss wouldn't have sought you as a consultant, if you hadn't been great at the job. Not only that, Wade thinks the world of you as a deputy and everyone at the college respects you, too. Especially President Adams. He's your biggest supporter." As soon as the words were out, Doro knew they only told part of the story. "Maybe not your biggest."

"And who would that be?"

Doro swallowed over the lump in her throat, but she did not look at him. "That would be me."

Only a moment passed before he responded. "And I'm yours. I know you want to be the library director, and I want that for you, Doro. No matter what happens between us, I always will. And I'll always do whatever I can to help you get the job and be successful in it."

His sincerity and assurances touched Doro deeply. Ev was not only a good man, he was an unusual one. And she was lucky to have him in her life.

Chapter Eight

Twenty minutes later, when Doro pulled into Michaw, Ev stirred. With the heels of his hands, he rubbed his eyes. "Sorry," he mumbled in a sleep-thickened voice. "I'm not much company today."

"You're worn out." Doro pulled to a stop in front of the constable's station.

Ev sat up straighter as his expression grew solemn. "Lowery is here."

Doro glanced at her wristwatch. "It's only three-thirty, and he was calling at four. I wonder why he came back."

"Let's find out."

Ev's serious tone sent ripples of uneasiness through Doro, but she preceded him into the station. Agent Canton was seated with Wade at the desk in the corner, while two other men, their backs to the door, sat facing them.

Canton rose and nodded. "Professor Banyon, Ev. We didn't expect you back so soon, but I'm glad you are."

After Doro sat down, Ev took the chair next to her. "Why? What did you find out?"

The federal agent ran his hand over his clipped hair. "The agent who goes to the Kesler brothers' fancy place has an informant who overheard talk about Fulton stealing booze."

"We were just talking about how that meshes with what you and I suspected, Ev," Wade said.

"Very little was left in the barn on Saturday when we were there," Ev agreed. "Now, it looks like it was gone when the gangsters arrived."

"Exactly," Canton said. "Unfortunately, my agent didn't find out if Fulton robbed stock from the Keslers, the Zee-Yarrow gang, or both. He only knows that some of the Kesler boys went that night and found very little booze left."

"Just like Ev and I did," Wade added.

Doro considered the revelations. "So, the Zee-Yarrow men must've been there first, which means one of them killed Mr. Fulton."

"It seems that way," Ev said, "although we need more solid evidence to be sure."

"And we need to know who was there," Doro put in.

"Exactly," Ev murmured.

Canton released a long, low sigh. "What we can say for certain is, whoever was there first probably took all the booze, although we can't be sure. They could've killed Fulton or the next visitors might have. I'm not willing to rule out the Keslers yet."

The other lawmen concurred and, after consideration, Doro did, as well. As much as she wanted the case solved quickly, coming to the right conclusion was critical. For a moment,

Doro mulled over the widow's revelations. "Mrs. Fulton hid for a time. I don't know where or for how long, because we were interrupted. Shortly after that, she hurried off." Was that significant? Doro still was not sure, and she hated to voice possibilities in front of Lowery Canton.

"I wish we knew everything she does," the federal agent observed. "Even if Mr. Fulton didn't inform his wife about his stealing, the bootleggers are probably suspicious. They want to know where the missing liquor is being stored."

"Don't they suspect Zee and Yarrow of having their men grab the stuff?" Doro asked.

"They do, and so do I, but the Keslers think the liquor is being hidden for now. At least that's the talk," Canton replied.

Logic dictated Doro's next words. "If they think Mrs. Fulton knows, they wouldn't kill her, but they'd want to find her."

"Exactly right." Canton crossed his arms over his chest. "We've got a lot of missing puzzle pieces. The informant who works for the Keslers thinks they could've been involved. Due to that, my agent who's been going as a customer is making a point of being there early tonight and staying late. They're more closed off to new blood than Zee, so he probably won't worm his way in as part of the Kesler gang."

"Are you sending an agent there, too?" Wade asked.

"In the past, a couple have gone as customers," Canton replied. "Ev is one of them."

Doro wanted to shout that Ev was not an agent anymore, but something in his expression put a lump in her throat. "I thought you just went in a few weeks ago to check the place out."

Ev shifted in his chair and avoided her gaze. "That's right, but I was in the place several times last year."

While those facts seemed innocuous on the surface, Doro could not shake her uneasiness. Why had he gone last year? "Your previous visits were as a customer."

After clearing his throat, Ev replied. "Ostensibly, yes."

When he still did not look at her, Doro felt her anxiety surge. Annoyance joined it. "Exactly what does that mean?"

An uncomfortable silence filled the room before Canton broke it. "Last year, we wanted to put someone undercover with the Zee-Yarrow gang. Ev was my first choice, but he left us before that happened."

Some of Doro's tension drained away. "So, you had another agent do that?"

"No, we got word about the Purple Gang planning to move into Toledo, so we had to focus on them. Zee and Yarrow fell down the list. It didn't happen, maybe because we worked with the Detroit field office to keep them from spreading their influence."

The admission failed to reassure Doro, who figured she knew why Canton had driven back to Michaw instead of merely calling. While eavesdropping operators were a concern when discussing the murder, talking about going undercover with bootleggers was far riskier. What if an operator along the line had a friend or relative working for rumrunners? The activity was common enough to make it a concern.

"And I left the Bureau not long after that," Ev added.

Since neither he nor Canton had been forthright, Doro asked a pointed question. "Do you want Ev to go undercover now?"

The agent leveled his gaze at her. "*Yes,* is the short answer, but we'll have to discuss it further before he decides."

One glance at Ev sent a chill through Doro. He wouldn't say no. "Exactly what do you want him to learn?" While the question was bold, knowing the parameters seemed crucial. Was Ev being sucked back into his old job? He'd told the Taylors that he had roots in Michaw and planned to nurture them. Would old duties and loyalties cut those roots? When no response came, she clarified her query. "Is he only investigating the murder, or is he also digging into other transactions?" The previous summer, he wouldn't have been investigating a murder, so looking into other dealings must have been the goal.

Ev gave her a half-hearted grin. "I'm not doing anything yet."

"No, but you will be," Doro said.

Before Ev could respond, Canton replied. "Both, although the murder is first and foremost. Zee and Yarrow may not be behind it, but Sweebe's connections out here have me leaning toward them. If we find out that gang is responsible, we'll want to know who actually did the deed. Who hauled out that booze, where is it, and who killed Fulton? Those are all important questions. Having someone inside is key. And remember, I have another agent trying to get inside the Kesler gang, if he can manage it."

Uneasiness plagued Doro. No matter who killed Mr. Fulton, Ev was going into the lions' den. "What we learned from Sheriff Taylor and the Waggoner girls may prove useful." Although she sounded calm, Doro was swamped with anxiety, along with a need to know what would happen next and how soon Ev would leave. "Are you sending Ev today? Or doing more planning?"

Canton frowned. "You've been helpful, Professor Banyon, and I appreciate that. Further planning and discussion will have to stay among us lawmen."

For a long moment, Doro stared at him in disbelief. "I wouldn't reveal any details. Or even tell anyone."

The federal agent cleared his throat. "Perhaps not, but you still won't be involved in this part of the investigation."

His steady tone and set expression provided little hope of changing his mind. Despite that fact, Doro felt frozen in place. When Ev spoke, she turned toward him.

"I won't be leaving right now, so I'll stop by Wheaton Hall later," Ev said.

"Ev, the professor doesn't need to know what our plans are," Canton put in.

Ev lifted his chin and stared at the other man. "But I'm still talking with her before I leave, Lowery. Or I'm not going."

A resigned sigh left Canton. "All right."

Knowing she could talk with Ev before he undertook his new role, Doro rose. After bidding the men farewell, without looking at Agent Canton, she headed to her vehicle. For the moment, cracking the case left her mind only to be replaced by anxiety for Ev.

Ninety minutes later, Doro got the word that Ev was in the foyer. Since she wanted to talk with him before he left, she put Tee on her lead and hurried downstairs. The pup yipped with delight when she saw Ev, who went down on one knee to scratch

Tee's ears. Despite the pep talk she had given herself on the way to see him, Doro felt ill-at-ease. She did not want him to go undercover, but she had no right to say so. When he rose to face her, she forced a smile. "You probably have very little time."

"Not a lot, but enough to take a walk with my two favorite girls." His grin did not quite reach his eyes.

"Tee would love that," she murmured. "So would I."

He nodded. "Let's go."

Although drawing a deep breath proved impossible, Doro kept pace with Tee, who darted as far ahead as she could. For several moments, silence reigned. Finally, she expressed a platitude. "She loves her jaunts around campus."

"In a few weeks, she'll be making rounds with me again."

"I hope so."

Ev clasped her forearm, so Doro stopped walking but said nothing.

"Please look at me." Entreaty was in his deep voice.

After a long inhalation, she did. "I didn't mean it in a bad way." More like an anxious, fearful way which only made her feel foolish and needy, when she was neither. At least, she never had been.

One corner of his mouth twitched into a faint smile. "I know, but you were worried about me getting deeply involved with the Bureau again, and I said I wouldn't. Now, it seems like I am, but this assignment won't last long, and I'll be finished forever afterward. I promise you that."

Doro searched his expression and saw sincerity and more. He would not lie to her, but Ev was loyal and honorable. "What if you're needed in the future?"

"I told Lowery that I'd only take this assignment with the understanding that this case is the end of the line for me. No consulting and no returning."

"And he agreed?"

"He did, but he's caught in a bind. You heard him say I was the one being set up to go undercover with the Zee-Yarrow gang last year. Mr. Zee wanted me to join, and he was happy to hear I'd been in the place earlier in the month. Or so an informant told another agent."

"What about Yarrow?"

Ev shrugged. "He wasn't around the last time I was there, and he may not be now. Lowery's informant hasn't seen Yarrow for over a week, but the man will let Mr. Zee know I'm available now. Zee liked me, so it should work out. He's arranging a meeting for tonight. If it goes well, I'll stay in Toledo and probably for a couple more nights. Maybe a little longer."

After absorbing his statement, Doro felt doubt bubble up but fought it back. Putting Ev on the defensive was not her desire. "What's the excuse for you showing up again after a year?"

"Of course, you'd ask a logical question," he murmured.

"Will I get a logical answer?"

Ev chuckled. "Last summer, I told them I had to go to Cincinnati for other business. Then, Lowery floated the idea that I got caught and went to jail."

"Meanwhile, you were in Michaw."

"Yep. It's why I've mostly stayed here for the past ten months. Going into Toledo could've been risky."

Briefly, Doro mulled everything over. "But you went into the speakeasy earlier this month. Didn't Zee ask if you wanted to work for him?"

"He and Yarrow were both at the lakeshore place. No one else asked any questions, but I wasn't there for long."

That relieved some of her concern. "I got the gist of what Agent Canton wants you to do, but can you tell me more? I won't tell anyone—except Aggie." Would he reveal details?

Regret turned his silver gaze to stormy gray. "I know you won't, and I'm sure you've got a good handle on it already. For one, I'll try to find out about Mrs. Fulton. The agent going to the Keslers' place is doing the same, and neither of us is apt to find that an easy task. Her safety is paramount, but finding her husband's killer is next."

"She acted so strangely," Doro murmured. "I have to wonder why she seemed hesitant to reveal more. Was she afraid or involved?"

His brow furrowed. "You said you were interrupted before she revealed where she hid."

"We were. By the waitress." Doro chewed on her lower lip. "Mrs. Fulton seems genuinely sad over her husband's death, so I'm just overly suspicious."

"Maybe. Maybe not. Besides, one of the gangs—Zee and Yarrow or the Keslers—must be behind the killing. Either the other undercover agent or I should find out for sure. With some luck, we'll also discover who actually killed Mr. Fulton and the motive."

The revelations lifted some of Doro's trepidation. "When you identify his murderer, or murderers, you'll be done with the undercover assignment."

He released her arm, only to take her hand and intertwine their fingers. "I should be able to leave when I know about the murder and Mrs. Fulton. Locating the booze can fall on other agents."

The feel of his rough palm against hers sent warmth through Doro, and she yearned to never let go. But let him go, at least for a few days, she must. "You're a fine lawman, so you'll get the information and be back here soon." When Ev grinned, Doro knew he appreciated the vote of confidence.

"I'll do my best."

"I know you will. You always do." As they finished their walk and returned to Wheaton Hall, Doro focused on the present. Although holding hands was still considered rather forward for a couple not yet courting, neither of them let go until they stopped at the door of the women's faculty residence. She reluctantly released his hand. "I'm glad you took time to walk with us."

"Me, too." Ev reached to ruffle Tee's floppy ears, and the little dog pranced around. "You be a good girl and take care of Doro. We'll go to Sylvania for ice cream when I get back." He stood and faced Doro. "If you want."

"It sounds lovely."

"I can't call you while I'm undercover, but I will as soon as it's over. Lowery will stay in touch with Wade. I've asked him to let you know I'm fine."

Relief filled her. "Good."

His gaze bored into hers. "Monday, the place is closed, so I'll only be able to meet with Lowery then—probably in the morning. Don't worry if you don't hear something until after that."

She nodded, although not worrying seemed impossible. "All right." Other troubling thoughts came to mind. "What if Alf is more involved than we know? If so, he could be at the speakeasy. He'd recognize you right off."

"I told Lowery and Wade what you said about the kid, Barnes, and Mrs. Fulton. They both agree that all three could be involved but, like me, they think those folks belong down the suspect list. Wade thinks Jug was a small-time customer of Fulton. He could've been at the Waggoner place warning the kid."

"Interesting," Doro said. But were the facts significant? "All of you have more experience in investigations than I do, but it worries me that Alf or even Jug might be there and reveal you're a lawman. The same with Mrs. Fulton."

He squeezed her hand. "Lowery already described all three to the informant. He only saw Mrs. Fulton in Zee and Yarrow's place with her husband a week or more ago."

"Which fits her story."

"It does, so will you stop worrying?" he asked in a cajoling tone.

"Probably not," she admitted, "but I'll try."

"Distraction can alleviate worry." Ev's gaze rested on her lips for a long moment. "Too bad it's broad daylight."

Heat scorched her cheeks. "I agree," she said with enthusiasm.

A chuckle escaped him. "We'll go for ice cream late in the day, and get back after sunset. Fewer prying eyes."

"Great idea."

Chapter Nine

F riday morning, Wade dutifully reported that Ev was undercover with the gang. Doro felt mixed emotions. She wanted to locate Mrs. Fulton and find her husband's killer, but she hated knowing Ev was in grave danger. At least he would check in with the Bureau, sometimes via the informant, on a daily basis, and word would be passed along. Wade shared that news with her.

That happened on Saturday and Sunday. Ev was supposed to meet with Canton on Monday, since the place was closed, so Doro did not expect to hear anything until the next day. Maintaining a calm demeanor proved challenging, but she kept busy preparing for the coming school year.

When no word came on Tuesday, Doro asked Aggie to walk to the constable's office with her. She half-expected Wade to be out, maybe with agents and deputies to arrest accomplices in Fulton's murder. But he was in the office alone, since Colleen's work hours ended at four, and the clock read five-thirty. Doro's uneasiness escalated when she noted the grim expression on Wade's face. "What's wrong?" The answer was not reassuring.

"Not necessarily anything," the constable replied.

As the two friends approached the counter where Wade stood, Aggie linked her arm with Doro's. The support was welcome.

"You haven't called, so I wondered what happened," Doro said. Only the greatest effort kept her tone even.

Wade glanced at Aggie and back at Doro. "I talked to Lowery Canton a half-hour ago. Ev didn't make their meeting yesterday, and the informant hasn't seen him today, either."

Doro's pulse pounded in her ears. "Is he going to the place to check on Ev?"

"He's basically an errand boy, so he goes when they need him. Just showing up might be suspicious, but he'll stop in the kitchen after-hours. He won't ask about Ev, but he'll look around." Wade picked up a pencil and rolled it between his hands.

"And hope to see him." Which Doro thought was a poor plan. "Can't Canton send another agent, someone they wouldn't recognize? Just as a customer?"

Wade shifted forward and put the heel of one hand to his forehead, as if warding off a headache. "Tonight, they've got a raid planned at another speakeasy across town from the Zee-Yarrow place. Every agent is tied up."

Aggie squeezed Doro's arm. "Not even one could check on Ev?" her friend asked.

Wade did not respond directly to the comment. "Lowery thinks Ev is fine, or they'd hear something. He says it's not unusual for an undercover agent to miss a meeting."

Resentment toward the federal agent rose from Doro's core. The man ought to be more concerned. "Ev told you about my suspicions regarding Mrs. Fulton, Alf, and Jug. What if one of them was at the speakeasy, recognized Ev, and told the bootleggers?"

Wade nodded. "That's possible, but not likely. As for their guilt, I don't discount them, but we haven't found a motive for any of those three. Alf is probably an errand boy, not that he couldn't have been involved. Maybe forced to hit Fulton over the head. The kid might not have figured the man would die. After all, it was hitting his head on the wagon that killed Fulton."

"The same could be true of Mrs. Fulton or even Jug," Doro suggested.

"Yep. Either of them might've hit Fulton out of anger and never considered him cracking his head so hard on the wagon edge." Wade released a long breath. "But Jug is stronger than the widow, so he'd be a better suspect that she is."

"I know more about Mrs. Fulton than Jug Barnes, although he got snippy with me the other day," Doro said.

"Jug isn't easy to know," Wade admitted. "My longest conversation with him was the night of the murder. Typically, he stays on his farm although he goes into Sylvania every Saturday night for dinner."

Briefly, Doro considered the various points. "Ev and I had something to eat before the movie, and we didn't see him. Of course, there are several restaurants in Sylvania, so Jug could've eaten elsewhere."

"He likely didn't get there until later," Wade pointed out.

"Because of farm work," Aggie put in.

"Yep," Wade agreed.

"So, he should be off the list," Doro said with dismay.

"No, just toward the bottom. You may not remember because you were still a kid, but Jug frequented the bar in town before Ohio went dry. I imagine he was a customer of Fulton, if nothing else." Wade's comments revealed more about the farmer.

Doro put one hand to her mouth. "Do you think it's important?"

"No way to be sure," Wade admitted. "I've known Jug since he came to town more than two decades ago. Never known him to get into an argument, let alone a fight, so hitting a man over the head, even if Jug didn't mean to kill him...it doesn't seem likely."

"I suppose not," Doro admitted, but uneasiness filled her. Being undercover, Ev was vulnerable. Shaking her apprehension was impossible. So was going on as if nothing was wrong. "You know the password for the speakeasy since you were there recently."

Alarm blanketed Wade's face. "You're not thinking of going."

"Of course, she isn't," Aggie put in, but her voice lacked certainty.

The idea of not knowing Ev's fate was intolerable. "Why not? Plenty of people go to speakeasies. It's nothing unusual," Doro said, as her mind kept churning. "Besides, Agent Canton may be fine with Ev's safety in question, but I'm not and I don't think you are, either." She looked directly into Wade's eyes as she spoke.

He stared down at the battered countertop for long moments. "I'll admit not knowing bothers me, but Lowery wouldn't leave Ev in the lurch."

The hesitance in Wade's tone was more than matched inside Doro. "He may not think of it the way we do. He sends agents into danger all the time. If he's lost any, Canton has to go on without sorrow and sentiment." While the man might feel bad temporarily, Doro knew she would never completely recover if Ev died. Just the thought froze her insides with icy terror.

"Which none of us, especially you, can do," Aggie observed, her expression soft with sympathy.

Wade's nostrils flared with a sharp intake of breath. "I can't argue with any of that, but going to the speakeasy is risky."

Although Doro realized Wade was right, she felt an overwhelming urge to find Ev. Or at least to find out what happened to him. "I'm going whether or not either of you comes along. I'll get in somehow."

"That wouldn't be easy," Wade pointed out.

Doro clasped her hands together. "I can't just wait and see. I need to know if he's all right. I need to go to the city."

"Doro, you can't do that. It's too dangerous for a young woman to visit such a place alone, especially when you don't know the password," Wade insisted.

"I agree with him," Aggie put in. "What if you disappear and Ev is fine? I don't want to face him with that kind of news."

Doro exhaled and inhaled several times before replying. "You aren't worried, Wade?"

His nostrils flared with a deep inhalation. "I am, but I don't like you taking chances. Ev wouldn't, either, because you could disappear, too. Not that I think he's actually gone. Just busy. Or something."

Wade's weak excuses only solidified Doro's resolve. "All kinds of people frequent speakeasies regularly. They don't disappear. They drink, eat, dance, and maybe gamble." A wedge of silence followed her observation.

Aggie slid her hand out of Doro's elbow and laid it on Wade's arm, which rested on the counter. "If you were in Ev's place, I'd feel the same as Doro. I don't like her going but..." Her voice trailed off.

For long moments, the pair gazed at one another. As Doro watched, she felt the silent communication, the same sort she had witnessed between her parents. When Wade clasped Aggie's fingers, Doro held hope.

"I understand," he said. "And you'll go with her."

A soft smile touched Aggie's lips. "I will because best friends stand with one another."

The lopsided grin on Wade's face telegraphed his next words. "In less than a year, Ev and I have become close friends so, even though the lawman in me thinks it's not the best idea, I'll go with you. But the password may have changed since I was there."

Relief and hope lifted Doro's spirits. "We'll have to hope it will still get us in."

Hoping was at the top of Doro's list. She had to get into the speakeasy and find out about Ev. Exactly what she'd do or say if he wasn't in sight, she was not sure. But she would learn something tonight. She had to. "What time do such places open?"

"Around eight o'clock," Wade replied. "What about clothes? You aren't going in your current attire, are you?"

"Heavens no," Doro replied. Her dress was barely fashionable, and certainly not right for a saloon. "I wore a flapper outfit to last October's costume party, so that will be perfect. Aggie has a similar ensemble, which she hasn't worn."

Wade turned his attention to his sweetheart. "Why not?"

"I didn't feel comfortable wearing it to the party, and I haven't had the occasion since," Aggie replied.

"But you do now," Doro said.

"I'll be interested in seeing you in it," Wade said, his grin back in place.

Color crept into Aggie's cheeks. "What will you wear?"

Wade reddened. "I have a zoot suit. It was for a Halloween party that one of my railroad buddies had some years ago. It should still fit, but it'll need pressing."

Happiness and hope buoyed Doro. "When should we leave? We won't make it by the opening time, if we don't hurry."

"There's no need to be there as soon as the doors open. It might make us conspicuous, which I want to avoid," Wade said. "I'm still not sold on the idea, but I know the two of you will go, with or without me."

"I will," Doro confirmed.

Aggie took Wade's hand. "I will, too."

He gently squeezed her fingers. "Then, I'll pick you both up around eight-thirty. How will you explain your clothing if any of your neighbors see you heading out?" he asked.

She and Aggie exchanged a glance, before Doro spoke. "We can wear coats. Even though it's warm, they'll cause less interest than flapper get-ups."

"I agree," Aggie added. "Maybe luck will be with us, and we won't see anyone."

"Some luck would be wonderful," Doro murmured, but the only luck she wanted was for Ev.

*

Wade did not appear until shortly after nine o'clock. Aggie tried calling him at the office and at home before contacting his mother, who relayed that he should be back any time. She had few details about his absence but it was official work. When Aggie reported the news, she looked as anxious as Doro felt.

"I'm sure Wade is fine," Doro said.

"Of course, he is," Aggie agreed, but she did not relax until he appeared at the door of Wheaton Hall. Then, she darted toward him. "What happened? Where have you been? Is something wrong?"

He put both hands up. "Whoa. One question at a time."

A sheepish smile touched Aggie's lips. "All right. Let's start with the whole story."

Wade chortled. "Since we're already late, why don't I tell you in the car?"

Both young women agreed and, as soon as Wade pulled on to the road out of Michaw, Doro spoke. "Go ahead."

"I got a call from Mr. Bailey. He'd been in town for dinner and was on his way home and saw a vehicle behind the Fulton place."

"Really? Who was it?" Doro leaned forward to put her head over the edge of the front seat.

"He wasn't sure. It was already dusk, and he didn't recognize the vehicle. Said it looked black, but the descending darkness could be the reason for that," Wade replied.

"Besides, many are black. What did you see when you went out?" Doro asked. There was no doubt in her mind that he had gone.

"Not much. Bailey had a flat about a mile from his place. By the time, he walked home and telephoned, at least fifteen minutes had passed. I went right out, but no one was around. I checked the house and the barn. Even though nothing looked to be disturbed, I can't shake the idea that someone was looking for, and maybe found, booze. The night of the killing, Ev and I checked for a secret hiding place and didn't find anything. Neither did Lowery or his agents. It's a puzzle," Wade said. "But Bailey saw two figures. One was a man, medium height and build. The other was shorter. Maybe a woman or a boy."

Realization struck Doro. "It could've been Jug with Alf or Mrs. Fulton. She didn't tell us everything. Since Jug was most likely a customer of her husband, he might've gone back. With Alf, since she's probably in the city."

"Or gone," Aggie suggested.

"All are possibilities. Same with another bootlegger checking to see if any booze was left," Wade pointed out. "Bailey didn't know if it was a truck or a car, so Jug might've been there."

Doro sat back in the seat. "I suppose."

"Tomorrow morning, I'll make more calls. Maybe someone else got a look at a vehicle around that same time," Wade said. "It's unlikely to be related to the killing, but it pays to check."

"Which is why I want to go to the speakeasy," Doro said. "It might pay to check on Ev."

"We'll see," Wade replied.

The two words did nothing to ease Doro's mind. Nothing at all.

༄

Less than an hour later, the oppressive heat and humidity bore down on Doro like a stack of wet wool blankets. She and Aggie had shed their coats in Wade's vehicle, but the slight breeze through the open windows did not alleviate her discomfort.

Once they arrived in the city, Wade parked around the corner from the saloon and went into the bar first, while Aggie and Doro went to the end of a narrow alley that led to the entrance. After watching Wade enter the establishment, the two friends waited for several moments before approaching the bulky figure by the front door. Clad all in black, the man stood well over six-foot-four. His dark hair was swept back from a raw-boned face set in hard lines and, when Doro and Aggie stopped a few feet from him, his eyes narrowed. "Never seen you two before," he muttered in a guttural voice.

"No, it's our first visit," Doro said, proud that her voice did not waver. The doorman, or bouncer, or whatever he was, made her wonder about her plan. But she wanted to find Ev, and this place was their first step. "My cousin's sweetheart is already here, and we're joining him. He told us this place is the bee's knees." The last two words were key to getting inside, according to Wade. But had the secret passage phrase changed recently? Surely not, since Wade had entered with only a short delay. Nevertheless, despite her flapper attire, abbreviated as it was, sweat dampened her back. Cloying mugginess and rampaging nerves combined to send Doro's pulse rate soaring. Beside her, Aggie was pale and wide-eyed.

The man's bushy black brows rose a fraction. For a long moment, he stared directly at Doro. Then, he grinned. "It is. Enjoy yourselves, girls."

"Thank you," Doro replied as she stepped inside when the door opened. "Wade is already here, so there's nothing to fret about." The comment was as much to reassure herself as Aggie. Now that they were in the bar, butterflies were doing the Lindy Hop in Doro's stomach. Added to her heart rate and perspiration level, she felt completely off-balance.

"I know, and I hope he sees us right off."

"He will." Their plan was for Wade to intercept the young women as they entered the speakeasy. Doro mentally corrected herself. The strategy was hers, and she'd had to be mighty persuasive to garner the lawman's agreement.

"This place is a madhouse," Aggie observed.

As Doro scanned the saloon, she had to agree. Dancers, gyrating to jazz, crowded the floor in front of the bandstand while patrons stood three-and-four deep at the bar lining one wall. On the other side of the expansive room, tables and chairs provided a place to rest...and drink. Bottles of all shapes and sizes dotted the tables and filled the shelves above the bar. An array of sparkling glasses was also on the ledges. Prohibition was not in evidence here.

After her survey, Doro took a longer perusal, not to find Wade, but to see if Ev was on the scene. A shuddering breath left her. What if he wasn't here? What if something had happened to him? That seemed far too likely. Fresh sweat broke out across her back, but from fear instead of heat.

As Doro perused the interior again, she saw Ev—tall and lean—striding toward her. A host of emotions assailed her before a smile began to form. Then, she noted his set expression, and her relief faded.

Silver fire flashed in Ev's gaze as he stopped two feet from her. "Let's dance," he muttered from between clenched teeth.

Since the band had struck up a slow tune, Doro was amenable. They had danced several times in the past, and each occasion had been memorable. But this time, Ev looked resigned—or maybe furious—instead of pleased. Because she was not sure what to say, Doro stepped into his arms as an answer. At first, he was stiff and restrained but, after a few moments, Ev relaxed. So did Doro. As packed as the floor was, they could not swirl around as they had on previous occasions. But the crowded conditions led to him pulling her close to avoid being jostled by other couples. She could not object, because being close to him was a tonic. The anxiety that had stalked her for the last few days ebbed. He was safe, at least for now, a fact that overshadowed his annoyance at her arrival. She took a reassuring breath and inhaled the clean scent of his aftershave. The urge to touch his smooth cheek, which must be freshly shaven hit Doro, along with a wave of embarrassment. A couple of previous dances, several chaste kisses, and one social outing did not make them sweethearts. While she was dressed like a flapper, Doro was not among that fast set of girls. Not at all. She was a college librarian and had to maintain some sense of decorum, even in an illegal bar.

"What are you doing here?" he whispered in her ear.

"Looking for you."

Ev stumbled before righting himself. "What? Why?" Confusion and dismay laced his tone.

Doro left her head fall back, so she could see his face. When she had last seen him, Ev had been exhausted. The purple smudges beneath his eyes were now black. Had he slept at all? "You thought you'd only be gone a couple of days, but it's going on five, and Canton said you didn't make your meeting with him yesterday."

His dark brows rose. "You talked to Lowery?"

She shook her head. "No, Wade telephoned him."

For a moment, his thick lashes fluttered down before he looked directly into her gaze. "I hoped I'd be back sooner, and I didn't have a way to tell Lowery I couldn't meet him."

"Why couldn't you?"

Ev's gaze traveled around the interior. "I don't want to talk about it here." Again, his voice was hushed. "But you can tell me what brought you. If Lowery was really worried, he could've sent another agent."

"As you've said, they're under-manned, and they're all tied up tonight."

A long sigh escaped him. "True, but you didn't need to take a risk by coming here. I'm surprised Wade agreed to your scheme. I saw him as soon as he came in." Ev pulled back far enough to study Doro's expression. "And I still don't understand how you connived it."

In high heels, Doro stood only a half-head shorter than Ev, which meant she could peer over his shoulder instead of holding his steady gaze, so she did. He was far too skilled at reading her state of mind, especially when their eyes met. "Connive is a strong word. I've been anxious and upset. I haven't slept well for several nights even before you disappeared, Ev." She scanned his face.

Briefly, he averted his gaze. When he looked at her again, Ev did not repress his emotions. "I'm glad to know that, even though I don't want you to fuss and fret." Before she could answer, he hurried on. "And I don't want you here, either."

The two statements seemed contradictory, which evoked a gasp from Doro. "What?" She felt, more than saw, his long exhalation.

"I'm undercover," Ev murmured.

A snort-laugh escaped Doro. "I realize that. Even if I hadn't already known, I could tell. The pin-striped, three-piece suit in black-and-gray. The round collar shirt and black tie. The expensive tie pin and matching cufflinks." She laid a hand on the gem-studded bar holding his tie. "That's not like anything I've ever seen you wear. But you've gone undercover in the past. Is this get-up from those days?"

When he chuckled, Ev looked like himself—not a boot-legger. "Yep. I kept the suit, tie, shirt, and shoes. The jewelry is borrowed from Lowery."

"He goes undercover?" she asked with surprise.

"Occasionally," Ev replied. "Back to my point. I don't want the crooks tying the two of us together, so it's this one dance. Then, you'll be on your way. You, Aggie, and Wade. I plan to talk to him when I get home, because he shouldn't have brought you girls here."

Several heartbeats of silence passed before she spoke again. "What if I said he followed us?"

A guffaw left Ev. "I wouldn't believe you, because he came in ten minutes before you and Aggie. Somehow, you convinced him to come."

Seconds elapsed before Doro admitted the truth. "By saying I'd come on my own."

"Oh, Doro. That would've been hazardous."

When Ev's hand tightened on hers, Doro peeked at him from beneath her eyelashes. His expression was set in hard lines, while his gaze constantly scanned the room. "In the Chicago train station, you assured me you were only consulting with the Bureau, which wasn't dangerous at all. Your words. Last week, you were only working to solve Mr. Fulton's murder. Again, no hazards in that. Again, your words." Beneath her hand, his shoulder stiffened. "Now, you're undercover, which is perilous, isn't it?" She did not keep the annoyance from her voice. While happy to see Ev was well, Doro wanted some concession before leaving.

"There's no sense in lying," he muttered.

"But you would if you could." Doro did not try to keep the exasperation from her voice. Not raising it was a challenge, because she wanted to shout at him. But letting others overhear them would be reckless.

The tension left him. "Only because I don't want you getting hurt, which is why you, Aggie, and Wade need to leave here right away." His fingers splayed out across her back. "If Lowery Canton didn't need help on the case so badly, I wouldn't have taken this job. I'd much rather be in Michaw tonight. Or at a movie in Sylvania. With you."

The sincerity in his voice pulled on her heartstrings. "I wish we were there, too. But we will be as soon as we solve the case."

Instantly, he went rigid. "There's no *we* involved. Not at this point. Wade needs to escort you and Aggie out of here, and I plan to tell him as much when this tune ends."

Doro was about to reply, when a middle-aged man of short stature and bulky build approached them. A feral smile curved his thick lips, and the scents of liquor and tobacco wafted around him. She fought to keep her disgust from surfacing.

When the music ended, he looked from Ev to Doro. "Who is your charming friend, Edward?" As the newcomer tugged on his shirtsleeves, impressive diamond cufflinks glittered in the lamplight.

Doro could not help but notice his attire was even slicker than Ev's outfit. Clad in a three-piece navy pinstripe suit with a round collar white shirt and silver-blue tie held in place by a diamond stickpin, the man exuded wealth and power. Since the double-breasted suit jacket hung open, the heavy gold pocket watch and chain tucked in one vest pocket were visible. He had to be a bootlegger, and a successful one. After a moment, Doro turned her attention to Ev, whose jaw had tightened.

Tension rolled off him in waves, but he schooled his features into a bland mask. "Miss Mary Smith. She's in town visiting a cousin. At least that's what she just told me. We're newly acquainted." He cleared his throat. "Miss Smith, this is Cal Zee, the owner of this fine establishment."

Doro blinked her eyes, hoping the gesture made her seem awestruck, but she noted her new fake moniker. "You have a lovely place, Mr. Zee," she said in an even tone that masked her inner turmoil. Helping Ev maintain his cover was of paramount importance, so she followed his lead. "I'm glad my cousin and her beau talked me into coming tonight." When Ev scowled, Doro stopped speaking. Evidently, he did not want her saying too much. Since his safety ranked far higher than her curiosity, Doro simply smiled at the bar owner.

"My business is one of the best in Toledo. Fine liquor, wonderful music, excellent food, and some backroom games." When Zee winked, his thin mustache—as black as his slicked back hair—wobbled. As the band began another number, he focused on Doro. "Would you do me the honor of a dance?"

The question momentarily held her mute, while she contemplated refusing the invitation. Finally, unsure how the man would react to being turned down, she agreed. "Of course," she replied, not looking at Ev, since such a gesture might be construed as asking for advice or permission. If the two of them were strangers, Doro would not seek his counsel. A quick glance at him revealed Ev was maintaining a stoic stance. Only the slightest hint of apprehension clouded his gaze. When Doro turned back to the saloonkeeper, he led her on to the floor. As they walked away from Ev, she felt his gaze bore into her. Or did she imagine that?

Luckily, the music was a fast number, so Doro and the speakeasy owner were not in each other's arms, a bonus since she disliked the odors of smoke and booze clinging to him. But she hated how he eyed her up-and- down. At least, they weren't touching. Nor were they able to converse due to the band's volume. When the song ended, she thanked her partner and hoped she didn't sound as insincere as she felt.

"My pleasure." A smirk blanketed his heavy features.

Although Doro had been eager to visit the speakeasy, she felt increasingly anxious about saying something wrong, ruining Ev's persona, and putting him in danger. Conversing more with Zee could be a trap. "I should find my cousin."

When Doro turned away, Zee grabbed her hand and tucked it into the crook of his elbow. "How disappointing. I hoped we might get better acquainted."

Despite being shorter than she was, the bootlegger had a potent grip. He could easily overpower her, which increased her uneasiness. She scanned the room and saw Aggie standing beside Wade. Both were facing the bar. Would they notice if Zee pulled her out of the room? Ev was not in sight, which sent a sense of abandonment through Doro. While her mind said his departure made sense, her heart hurt. Was his withdrawal related to his anger about her appearance? Or to his undercover role? Not knowing, she repeated her plan. "I'm worn out from dancing, so I should join my cousin." And get away from the bootlegger.

"The pretty young lady who came in with you?" Zee asked.

The man was observant, another reason for Ev not to return to Doro's side. He might put up a solid front, but she was not sure about her acting ability. "Yes."

"She has an escort, but you don't."

Since Doro was unsure how to respond, she hedged. "No. I came with them."

"Do you come out often? I haven't seen you here before, and I'd remember such a lovely lady."

"This is my first time at your place." And at any speakeasy, but he need not know. "My cousin hasn't been here before, either. She'll expect me to rejoin them."

"I'll escort you over to her."

Although Doro wanted to turn down the suggestion, she agreed with a forced smile. "Thank you."

As they approached Aggie and Wade, Doro noted both looked uneasy. Wade's tension grew when she introduced Cal Zee to them. Since Ev had used fake names, and common ones at that, she did, too. "Mr. Zee, this is my cousin, Anita Johnson, and her beau, William Moore."

"You must call me, Cal, Miss Smith," Zee said.

"Then, please use Mary for me." Doro kept her attention on the bootlegger, but she felt sure Aggie and Wade got the message: be careful and use assumed names.

The saloon owner extended a broad hand to the constable. "Good to meet you."

After shaking hands, Wade replied, "Same here."

"Mr. Zee. That is, Cal," Doro began, "owns this establishment."

"How nice," Aggie murmured.

Wade nodded. "It's a great place." He injected enthusiasm into his tone and countenance.

Zee's brow furrowed. "You haven't been here in the past? I thought I'd seen you before, William."

Out of the corner of her eye, Doro noted Wade slipping his arm around Aggie. The protective gesture made her wish Ev hadn't disappeared. How she longed for the reassurance of his arm encircling her. More than once, he had offered warnings about how dangerous bootleggers were. But hearing caveats was not the same as actually meeting a gangster. Cal Zee's manner sent darts of apprehension shooting through Doro. And not only for herself.

"I've been in," Wade replied.

Zee nodded, but his intense gaze remained on Wade. "That's probably why you seem familiar."

"I'm sure it is," the constable agreed with a grin. "This is the first I've gotten my sweetheart to come along."

The bar owner turned to Aggie. "You don't drink or you don't dance? Or you don't approve of speakeasies?" A smirk curved his thick lips.

A long moment passed before Aggie responded. "None of those, really. I have an ailing mother. Someone stays with her while I work, but getting out in the evening is hard. Tonight, a neighbor offered to keep her company, so we could show my cousin a good time."

Since her friend's story flowed in a remarkable, believable manner, Doro had difficulty hiding her surprise. Who knew

Aggie could spin such tales? Or look so giddy and excited when she had to be as nervous as Doro.

"I hope you're having a good time, Mary," Zee said to Doro. "I'd like to make it better by inviting the three of you to our private room."

The suggestion put Doro on edge, and she was about to politely turn him down when Ev joined the group.

"Excuse me, sir, but you're needed in the office," Ev said to Zee. He did not take even a sidelong glance at Doro, Aggie, or Wade.

Zee scowled. "Is it important?"

"Mr. Yarrow thinks so, sir." Ev kept his gaze fixed on the bootlegger.

The suspicious partner was on the premises, which created additional anxiety inside Doro. Clearly, Ev needed to watch his step. And so did she, since a slipup might lead to disaster for all of them.

Resignation lined the other man's face as he turned back to Doro. "I'm sorry, doll. I'd love for you to stay while I sort out the issue. Ed can show the three of you to the private dining room. I'll be down when I can."

Tension rolled off Ev in waves making Doro realize he wanted to refuse, but how could he?

"All right," Ev murmured.

"Food and drink are on me." Zee lifted Doro's fingers to his thick lips. "Enjoy yourself and don't hurry off."

When his damp, meaty lips touched her skin, revulsion spread through Doro, and she nearly snatched her hand away. Since such a gesture might create suspicion, she resisted. All the same, relief filled her when Zee went on his way. But no such emotion appeared on Ev's face. His handsome features were carefully schooled, while his silver-gray eyes looked like pond ice on a wintry morning. Doro forced herself to smile at the bootlegger. "We can't stay too late because of my aunt."

"I won't be gone for long." Zee turned to Ev. "Make sure the pretty lady and her friends are treated right, and don't leave them to fend for themselves."

"Of course not," Ev agreed.

Doro detected a note of reluctance in his voice, but the speakeasy owner didn't seem to notice. Instead, the man bowed to her and hurried away. When Aggie slipped her hand into the crook of Wade's arm, Doro did not follow suit with Ev. After all, they had supposedly just met. If a third party observed them, like one of Zee's goons, she did not wish to create speculation.

"Lead on, Mister..." Aggie let her voice trail off as she addressed Ev. "I don't believe we've heard your surname."

His expression softened but only slightly. "Barrington. Edward Barrington."

Wade stuck out his hand before introducing himself and Aggie, although he was careful to use their newly assumed names. Then, he nodded at Doro. "You've already met Mary."

Ev's gaze flickered to Doro. "I have."

His tone indicated their meeting had not been a great experience. Perhaps, he was covering up, so no one got wise to them, but Doro felt bereft. She had wanted to know Ev was safe. Clearly, he didn't appreciate her effort.

When Wade spoke again, he sounded tense, too. "Why don't you show us to that private room? We can't stay a lot longer, due to Anita's mother. The friend sitting with her needs to leave by midnight."

After a curt nod, Ev turned away. "Mr. Zee wants me to keep you here until he comes back."

When he stalked off, Doro scowled at his back. Before she could launch a snotty remark, Wade took her by the elbow. "Let's go, ladies."

Chapter Ten

Within a few moments, the quartet entered a softly lit room tucked into a back corner of the building. A massive crystal chandelier sent shards of light throughout the space, while cut-glass sconces were placed strategically at each booth lining the walls. Unlike the main area, no tables were in use. Because booths offered more privacy? Probably so. A combo played soft jazz in the far corner, but the small dance floor was empty. As Doro glanced around, she saw a handful of couples eating, drinking, and conversing. The overall atmosphere was low-key.

Ev stopped inside the door before gesturing at an isolated booth across the room. "Let's take that one."

As they crossed the space, several men lifted their hands in greeting, while Ev responded in kind. After they reached the booth, Aggie slid into one side, and Wade sat next to her. Doro scooted to the back on the opposite bench and, after a moment, Ev took his place on the seat beside her. With only a foot between them, she once again caught the scent of his shaving soap. Hints of citrus with undercurrents of allspice filled her nostrils. Why was she noticing that again? Doro hadn't noted the smells until they had crossed paths in Chicago. But she'd been aware of the aroma on Saturday night. Close perusal revealed he had shaved right before picking her up, so he must have done the same tonight. But not for her benefit, since her appearance was a surprise. Now that she thought about it, Mr. Zee had appeared to be freshly shaven, although his odor was not as pleasant. Was it a habit for bootleggers to spruce up before they came to a speakeasy? Their clothing was certainly immaculate and stylish. A waiter approached while she was trying to regroup. Tall and muscular, he exuded power and strength and sophistication.

"May I bring drinks and food, Eddie?" the young man asked as he set a bowl of peanuts in the middle of the table. "I could also provide an assortment of canapes."

"Good evening, Patrick. I saw shrimp and crab cocktails in the kitchen earlier, so maybe four of each, as well," Ev said before glancing around the table. "How does that sound?"

As soon as she heard the waiter's name, Doro went rigid. Only the greatest effort had her feigning a calm demeanor. Although she wondered what Aggie and Wade thought, she kept her attention on the young man.

"Great," Wade replied, although his voice held little enthusiasm.

Aggie murmured her agreement with a similar lack of zest.

"What about you, Miss Smith?" Ev asked. "Anything appeal to you?"

During their date the previous weekend, Doro had mentioned shrimp cocktails being served on the train during her trip home from Colorado. And she'd expressed her enjoyment of them. Did Ev want to please her? Or was he putting up a façade for the waiter? "I'd love a shrimp cocktail," she replied. "I had one on a train trip, and it was wonderful."

Some emotion flickered in Ev's silver gaze before dying away. "Then, bring an extra one for Miss Smith," Ev told the young man.

"Very good. And for beverages?" When Patrick grinned, his pale blue gaze glittered.

"I've had a long day, so coffee for me," Ev replied.

"Same here," Wade added.

Since the room was cooler than outside, or even the main area, Doro asked for the same drink. Aggie followed suit.

A grin kicked up the corners of the waiter's mouth. "If you want something cool later, let me know," Patrick said before moving away.

When he was out of earshot, Doro turned to Ev. "Is he who I think he is?"

"He is, which is enough said," Ev replied before focusing on Wade. "Mary mentioned how she learned about this place, and how to gain entrance."

How he kept his voice and expression well-modulated, Doro did not know. He acted like they were all virtual strangers, when nothing was further from the truth. And he had deftly cut off further conversation about Patrick Sweebe. Doro yearned to know more, but the waiter could come back at any moment.

Wade's jaw briefly tightened. "So, she and Anita told me."

As Ev slanted a glance at her, Doro folded her hands on the table and stared at them. "Mr. Zee has seen you here," she said to Wade.

"Yep. A friend told me about the place a while back," Wade said, his own voice holding an amused note.

"I see. Have you come often?" Aggie asked.

Wade faced her. "Only twice. The last time was about three weeks ago. I was looking for another friend. Someone who was late getting home, so I searched for him. It worried me. Since he'd mentioned this spot before leaving, I thought it was worth a try, but we just missed each other."

"How nice of you to check on your friend. He must be important to you." Beside Doro, Ev shifted to look at her, but she kept her attention on Wade.

"He's a good friend and a fine man, but he takes some risks that worry me," Wade replied.

A long exhalation escaped Ev. "I'm sure they're calculated risks."

"So, he says," Wade murmured.

For a long moment, Doro studied Ev's expression, which gave little away. "In any case, he's lucky to have people who fret over him."

Something akin to a chuckle left Ev, but when he spoke, his tone was dead serious. "He is. Very lucky."

Relief filled Doro, but anxiety remained. She had not liked Ev being overprotective, her term, in past cases. Perhaps, her concern for him was equally unwelcome now. "Sometimes being fretted over can feel stifling."

Ev turned to face her. In the dim light, his expression was hard to gauge. "Having people who care about your welfare is a gift, and it should be appreciated." He paused for a heartbeat. "Their concerns should be taken to heart, but acting on concerns might put them in danger."

The implicit warning was not lost on Doro. "Some things merit taking a risk." Some emotion flashed in Ev's gaze, but Patrick's return interrupted the conversation. While the young man served the ladies, Ev shifted farther away from Doro.

Patrick grinned at Doro. "Two shrimp cocktails for you, miss." After providing food to the others, he took cups of coffee off his tray before putting a pitcher of cream and a bowl of sugar on the table. "Holler if you need anything. I'll check back later." He glanced at Ev before scanning the others and winking at Doro. "I hope we can dance later. I get off work shortly."

She forced a smile. Although he wore a waiter's apron, the young man was dressed much like Ev—stylishly and expensively. His cornstalk blonde hair was neatly trimmed, and confidence emanated from him. Mrs. Fulton's assessment of him was correct.

"Mr. Zee wants us to wait for him here," Ev told Patrick. "Unless the young lady dances with him again, I don't think she'll be on the floor."

Patrick's blonde brows rose a fraction. "I know better than to get in the boss's way," he said in a cryptic tone before nodding to the others and slipping away.

Ev slumped back in the booth. "When I go to the office, I'd like the three of you to leave. Mr. Zee may be down here before then. If so, mention the ailing mother again and insist you have to go."

"Sure thing," Wade readily agreed.

Aggie nodded. "I'll be ready to leave."

When Doro said nothing, Ev turned to her. "What about you? Will you be ready?"

"How late will you be here?" she asked.

A genuine grin lit his face. "Answering a question with a question is a dodge. Or so I've heard."

Because he had heard it from her. And more than once, Doro smiled in return. "True enough. But when do you plan to leave?" His immediate response was to scan the room. Doro did the same. So far, Ev had kept the conversation impersonal. Was he considering a deeper discussion? She hoped so, because further explanation could provide reassurance. And Doro wanted reassurance. Leaving him here among gangsters, men who would not hesitate to kill a federal agent, deeply disturbed her.

As Ev sat up straight, his body radiated tension—much as it had earlier. "Patrick won't be back for a few minutes, at least." He exhaled sharply, but his jaw was as taut as his shoulders. "If there's some news, you might as well tell me."

Uncertain, she glanced at Wade, who was playing with his crab cocktail. Abruptly, Doro realized none of them were eating much, which also might draw unwanted attention, so she stabbed a shrimp with her fork, bathed it in cocktail sauce, and popped it into her mouth. As much as she loved the shellfish, Doro barely tasted it, and swallowing seemed like a Herculean task. Once the little delicacy was down her throat, she smiled.

"Delicious." After Aggie and Wade dug into their appetizers, she addressed Ev in a low murmur. "There's a little."

Light flashed in Ev's gaze. "What?"

"Not much. A vehicle was seen at the Fulton place just after dusk tonight. I got the call as I was getting ready to come here," Wade said.

Interest sparked in Ev's eyes. "Who called you?"

"Mr. Bailey. He'd been in town and was headed home," Wade replied. "Have you learned anything that would illuminate who was there?"

"A man and a boy could describe plenty of the guys in this crowd. Most of the runners are youngsters," Ev said.

"Like Alf," Doro suggested.

Ev nodded. "Much like him. In need of money and/or excited about getting involved with gangsters." He looked back at Wade. "Has Mrs. Fulton been found? I figured on getting an update from Lowery yesterday."

Although right beside Ev, Doro could barely hear him. Wade seemed to understand, though.

"No word yet," the constable replied.

Once again, Ev looked around the room. "No one is in the adjacent booth, so we can talk more freely, but Patrick will be back soon, and others could stop."

Because Doro considered herself to be an adequate sleuth, she felt foolish for not noting that. "I didn't notice we're somewhat isolated."

Ev winked at her. "As an employee of Mr. Zee, I need to be alert about who comes back here."

"Being vigilant about all comings-and-goings in this place is wise," Wade added. "And you're a sharp guy."

A half-smile kicked up one corner of Ev's mouth. "I have to stay on my toes."

Despite the grin, his muscles remained taut. Did he ever relax while undercover? Doro doubted it. Once again, she scanned the room. About half of the booths were filled with elegantly dressed couples, while the rest—except for the empty one next to them—held only men. Were they gangsters or customers?

"Our waiter is interesting," Aggie observed.

One corner of Ev's mouth lifted. "He is. Patrick and I have chatted quite a lot. I haven't learned anything, but neither has he."

The comment indicated Patrick might test Ev. Was Yarrow doing the same? But being suspicious of a newcomer didn't mean they were involved in Fulton's killing. Not that either of them would hesitate to murder an undercover agent like Ev. Doro wrapped her arms around her waist to quell a shudder.

"Are you cold? I could give you my jacket, since your dress is..." Ev's voice trailed off. "It doesn't look like it'd keep you warm."

A chuckle rumbled out of Wade as he glanced from Doro to Aggie to Ev. "The girls told me these outfits were originally worn to a costume party last fall."

"Doro's was," Aggie said.

Ev's focus did not leave Doro. "I remember, although the feather headband is a recent addition."

Heat scorched her cheeks at the memory. The previous October, shortly after she and Ev had solved a murder, Doro had gotten locked out of Wheaton Hall while using the back stairs to go to Aggie's apartment. Her intention had been to avoid being seen while in the scanty dress. No such luck, although Ev was the only one who had been passing by. While suitable for a costume party or a speakeasy, the gown was hardly appropriate daytime attire for a college librarian.

After studying Ev and Doro, Wade made an observation. "There's more to the story."

A chuckle escaped Aggie. "Quite a bit more. Doro was coming to show me her costume. Since she didn't want everyone to see it, she went outside to those steps. While out there, she saw little Tee and tried to get the puppy. We'd been feeding her for a while but couldn't get close enough to bring her inside."

Wade's forehead furrowed. "I heard about Ev catching the dog, and the two of them deciding to share care of her. Never heard about Doro wearing that dress when it happened."

"The dress has nothing to do with us rescuing Tee," Doro rushed to say.

"It must've grabbed Ev's attention," Wade suggested with barely repressed laughter.

Aggie gently elbowed her sweetheart. "Wade, don't tease them."

Ev's glare was tempered by the color rising in his tan cheeks. Despite the dim light, his flush was easy to see. "She was on the steps by the third-story door. I didn't know if she was locked out or what."

A guffaw left Wade, but he hurriedly shoved more crab cocktail into his mouth. Aggie stifled a giggle and ate more of her appetizer, too.

Since she did not appreciate the amusement coming from across the table, Doro spoke in the tone she used with errant students. "I wore this outfit so I'd fit in tonight, and I do."

Ev's gaze met hers. "We're both fitted out in clothing suitable for the setting, which is wise." Although the observation was valid, his lips twitched and his eyes glinted.

The humor in the situation was not lost on Doro, but she fought to keep from grinning. Ev looked good in the gangster suit. He looked good in everything.

"You make an attractive couple," Aggie observed.

"Now, who's teasing them?" Wade asked.

A slight smile played across Doro's lips. The bantering was friendly, and Ev seemed to cope with it well. She should, too. "These are suitable outfits for the next costume party on campus. Even though I've worn mine, I may use it again."

"It's not too soon to plan on going," Ev observed.

Warmth spread through Doro. The annual event was two months away. Despite her fear for him, she grinned. "No, it isn't." With determination, Doro brought her attention back to the present. "We have other matters to go over now, though."

Several moments of silence followed before Ev swallowed hard and turned his attention to Wade. "Doro is right. We've got items to discuss before I head to Zee's office, and the three of you go home."

Abruptly, a chill replaced the warmth encompassing Doro because the gangster made her skin crawl. "How long will you stay here?"

"I'm not sure," Ev replied. Once again, he scanned the room. When he continued, his voice was barely audible. "Lowery wants to nail Zee and Yarrow. "Even if they weren't behind Mr. Fulton's death." Doro made the statement with certainty.

"Yep," Ev agreed. "He told me how close the Bureau is to nabbing them when I got to town last week, so that changed things."

Doro wanted to point out his reassurances that he'd be home as soon as the murder case was solved, but how could she object to catching violent gangsters? "And you'll stay here until Canton gets what he wants," Doro murmured.

A long moment elapsed before Ev responded. "I've got a conundrum. I'm inside where I might get important details to bring a big operation down, even if no one here was involved in the killing. But I'm not convinced that's the case. More information is needed."

Doro's insides knotted. Gathering information took time, and she wanted him out of this place soon. "What about Mr. Zee's partner? You thought he might not be around, but he is, isn't he?"

With one hand, Ev rubbed his neck. "Yep. Cutter Yarrow came in tonight."

Anxiety skyrocketed through Doro, keeping her from forming a coherent reply. A year ago, the man had not wanted Ev in the gang. That had probably not changed.

"Cutter," Aggie echoed. "That's a strange name."

Ev lifted his head and met Aggie's gaze. "It's a nickname."

"I'm afraid to ask how he got it," Doro admitted.

A wry smile touched Ev's mouth. "All I'll say is that he carries a switchblade."

Although Doro's pulse pounded in her ears, she schooled her features. "Is he in here now?"

"He may be talking to Mr. Zee, and he'll be at the meeting later." Ev glanced at his wristwatch. "But that's not what's important. I saw him drive into the back lot earlier. He was behind the wheel of a two-tone blue LaSalle phaeton."

Doro gripped her fork. "That's interesting." It was far more than interesting.

"I'll say. What about the Cadillac that I saw at the Fulton place?" Wade inquired. "Have you seen one similar to it"

"Nope," Ev replied. "Just the LaSalle."

"I'll pass the news on to Lowery?" Wade asked. "Anything else you want me to tell him?"

"Share your observations from this evening. As far as more details, tonight's meeting may offer them. There's a guy who may have inside information on Fulton's death.

"Do you think this guy was involved?" Wade asked.

Ev shook his head. "Maybe. Maybe not, but he knows details. I feel sure of that."

Doro studied the people, customers and employees, on the other side of the room. "Is he in here now?"

"No, he's not," Ev said. "He runs errands, but he often comes in at night. At close of business, many of us meet in the kitchen. That's usually when he shows up. With some luck, I can speak with him privately for a moment. If the meeting in Zee's office doesn't run late."

"What's the usual conversation at the end of the day?" Wade inquired.

"Pretty general stuff. Saturday night, this guy—Ollie Carlisle is his name—mentioned the Fulton murder, and he got shushed up right away. I've tried to get that guy alone, but to no avail." Frustration lined Ev's face.

Wade laid his fork down. "What about the Keslers? Have they come up in conversation?"

"Only in terms of a simmering feud, which could bubble up and boil over any time. They're definitely the biggest rivals of this group," Ev said.

"That sounds ominous," Aggie observed.

"It's not unusual," Ev told Aggie. "Rumrunning is a profitable business, and no one wants to cede ground and lose money."

Maybe not, but it troubled Doro. She had no chance to comment since Patrick's return interrupted.

"You haven't made much of a dent in the food. I hope nothing's wrong with it." The waiter glanced at the nearly full dishes.

"Not at all," Doro said, before dousing another shrimp with cocktail sauce and shoving it in her mouth. Thank heavens, the waiter had not returned a few moments earlier. But Ev was facing the room with an unobstructed view, so he would have seen anyone who approached their booth, and all of them had spoken in hushed tones.

Wade ate more of his crab cocktail, while Aggie smiled. "I'm not as hungry as I thought."

The waiter looked at Ev. "Guess you're not, either."

Since Ev had not taken a bite, the observation rang true. Doro understood why his appetite lagged, because her own stomach was in knots. Chewing and swallowing were challenging. She hoped her anxiety did not show. As Doro glanced at Ev, she was impressed at how calm he seemed. Only moments ago, a host of emotions had been in his silver eyes. Now, they looked like ice chips.

"I'll eat more later," Ev replied. "I need to get to Mr. Zee's office shortly."

Patrick's eyebrows rose. "Best to go lean and hungry."

What in the world did that mean? Doro had no idea, and Ev's response did not offer any insight.

"It always is," he said.

"Yeah," Patrick agreed before looking around the table. "Can I bring anything else?"

The consensus was that they were set, so the waiter—or whatever he really was—departed. When he was out of earshot, Doro addressed Ev. "What did he mean about going to the meeting *lean and hungry*?"

"It's just a phrase they use around here," he replied before lifting his coffee cup and taking a long swallow. The brew had to be cold, but Ev continued to drink, and the cup partially obscured his eyes.

"Why do I not believe you?" Doro asked with asperity. "It seems like I've heard it used in the context of hunting." Ev could all too easily be the hunted.

Ev made no reply, and a lingering silence fell before Wade entered the fray. "We should be on our way, so Ev can get to his boss' office."

Doro did not miss Ev sending his friend a look of gratitude, which escalated her annoyance. Of course, the two lawmen would support one another. But why not explain the expression? Surely, Ev wasn't being sent out to intimidate other boot-leggers or some such thing? He was a temporary Prohibition agent, which ought to preclude him taking part in illegal activities. But did it? Doro did not actually know.

"That's a good idea. I need to be on time or early, and I'd like to know all of you are safely out of here," Ev added.

"Don't most customers get out safely?" Doro asked. "If there's no raid."

Ev ground his teeth. "There's never been a raid, as I told you already. That doesn't mean you should hang around."

Annoyance ballooned into exasperation. "I'm not planning to hang around or snoop around, as you like to say." Doro fought down her frustration before continuing in a softer tone. "I don't want you worrying about what I'm doing, so I'll heed your warnings. Please remember, I'm concerned about you. I don't want last Saturday's night out to be our last one." After the statement was out, Doro cringed at her boldness. While she was hardly the typical young miss, she was not usually outspoken in social situations.

"I promise it won't be," he said with certainty.

While Ev's response comforted her, Doro knew following through on such a pledge was not in his control.

Chapter Eleven

As the group made its way to the exit, a lean man of medium height approached them. Clad in what Doro thought of as typical gangster attire—charcoal gray pinstripe suit, a white dress shirt with a round collar, a black tie with a matching kerchief in his jacket pocket, and a black vest–he must be Cutter Yarrow. Like his partner, Cal Zee, this man sported a diamond-studded collar pin. A glance at his hands revealed a heavy gold ring, also with diamonds. Most telling of all, a three-inch scar curved from the outer edge of his left eyebrow to his ear. Doro fought back revulsion. Not because of the imperfection, but because of how he must have gotten it.

"Good evening, Mr. Yarrow," Ev said.

Before replying, the gangster scanned the group, which had paused when Ev spoke. "Cal expects to see you in twenty minutes," Yarrow bit out.

The man's terse tone and forbidding expression escalated Doro's anxiety, as did knowing he had been at the Fulton place the night of the murder. At least his vehicle had. While Zee hid his ruthlessness behind a charming façade, Yarrow did not. When his slitted gaze focused on her, she struggled to remain calm.

"I'll be there," Ev replied in an equally flat voice.

Yarrow turned back to Ev. "What are you doing with these people? I just spoke with Cal, and he mentioned you entertaining them in the private room."

Ev's chin lifted a fraction. "That was at Mr. Zee's request."

"But you danced with her." The man jerked a thumb at Doro. "Did Cal suggest that?"

Something in Yarrow's manner revealed he knew his partner had not proposed Ev escort her on to the dance floor. But why did it matter?

"No. I asked her on my own," Ev said.

A sneer curved Yarrow's thin lips and made his scar more prominent. "You've been working for us almost a week, and you haven't slow danced with any other ladies. I thought maybe you only liked the fast numbers."

The words were more accusation than statement, but Doro's heart soared. Ev had not been squiring other women around the speakeasy. Had his action tonight undermined his role? She hoped not.

"Am I not allowed to do that?" Ev inquired. "Other employees do."

For several moments, Yarrow stared at Ev. During that time, the phrase *if looks could kill* kept running through Doro's mind. She glanced at Wade, who had the same composed countenance as Ev but, when Doro focused on her best friend, she noted Aggie appeared to be as uneasy as she felt.

"They do, but we assumed you had a sweetheart somewhere." Yarrow snickered. "When I saw the two of you together, I figured she finally came to see you."

Almost too quickly, Ev rushed to refute the idea. "There's no sweetheart, and I never laid eyes on Miss Smith until tonight."

Again, Yarrow let a period of silence develop. "You may be telling the truth, or you may be a skilled liar like most undercover Prohis." The derogatory term for federal liquor agents fell like drops of acid from the bootlegger's lips.

Doro felt the blood drain from her face, and she could only be glad for the dim light that should hide her pallor. When the gangster again studied her, she fought for control. She couldn't, wouldn't react. Not when Ev's safety was on the line.

A snort left Ev. "That's ridiculous, and you know it."

Yarrow spun back to face him. "I don't know everything about you, but I'm working on it. Cal may trust you, but I don't. Never did. You were supposed to join us last year. Then, you disappeared."

Although the statements were implicit and explicit threats, Ev's demeanor did not change, nor did he directly address the challenge. "I'll have to earn your trust."

Yarrow's eyes became narrow slits. "I'll be at the meeting, so don't be late." As he spoke, Yarrow pushed back his jacket to reveal a holster and gun alongside a sheath and knife.

The latter reminded Doro of Ev's earlier revelation about a switchblade. Her stomach roiled. Yarrow suspected Ev was a federal agent, which meant the meeting could end in an execution. Surely, Ev realized the danger. Could she convince him to leave with them?

"I won't be," Ev assured the other man. "Now, I'd like to see these nice folks outside."

"Be quick about it," Yarrow said before spinning on his heel and stalking away.

As she grabbed at Ev's sleeve, Doro released a pent-up breath. "You've got to get out of here," she whispered.

His response was to lay his hand over hers. "Let's all get going."

"Good idea," Wade said.

Although she wanted to say much more, Doro let herself be led along. She needed privacy to repeat her request. No, request was too tame a word. Demand fit better. She'd demand Ev come with them. Somehow, they would find Mr. Fulton's killer and locate Mrs. Fulton without Ev continuing to risk his life. And Canton could take down the gang with some other strategy.

Ev nodded. "Where did you park?"

"The car is down a couple of blocks and around the corner," Doro replied.

"I should have time to see you to your vehicle," Ev said.

Wade tucked Aggie's hand into the crook of his arm. When Ev followed suit, Doro jolted in surprise.

"It'd cause more attention if I didn't properly escort my pretty dance partner out," he murmured.

"I see," she replied and let him lead the way.

When they reached the kitchen, Wade addressed Ev in a muted voice. "Is there anything you need me to do right now? Other than call Lowery Canton first thing tomorrow."

"Nope. But thanks," Ev replied before pointing to the right. "This way is shorter." As he led them through the kitchen, they ran into Patrick. Ev stopped. "I'm going to escort Miss Smith and her friends to their vehicle. I'll be back momentarily."

The waiter grinned as his gaze swept over Doro. "You're a smart guy, Ed. Smart and maybe lucky, huh?"

Ev did not comment. Instead, he grasped Doro's elbow and took her outside. This time, Wade and Aggie trailed them. When they reached the alley behind the speakeasy, Ev paused. "Be careful. This road is paved with bricks, so the surface is uneven." He released Doro's elbow and slid his arm around her. "Leaning on me might help you keep your balance. Those heels look dangerously high."

The suggestion touched Doro, and she readily agreed. "Good idea." As they made their way toward the main street, she let her worries drift away. For a few moments, she could pretend the two of them were enjoying a night out with Aggie and Wade. One of many, she hoped.

The only sound was their footfalls on the hard surface until they reached the end of the alley. Then, she stopped and faced Ev. "I didn't want to say anything until we were out of earshot of your—uh—of the gangsters, but since Yarrow suspects you're a lawman, you can't go to that meeting."

His jaw tightened, but he did not meet her gaze. "I have to go. They'll probably talk about a weekend shipment. Besides, I still need to find out where Mrs. Fulton is and pinpoint who murdered her husband. All those answers may be inside the gang."

"Not necessarily, since the Keslers might be responsible for Mr. Fulton's death. We can't be sure Jug Barnes isn't involved. Or even Mrs. Fulton. We could find other ways to investigate," Doro shot back. Some of the ideas were weak, but she used every excuse to get Ev to leave. "Yarrow has a gun and a knife and, from what he said, you aren't likely to walk out of Zee's office."

Ev ran a hand over his face. "He's trying to intimidate me because I'm new. It's his way with every new guy. Besides, I can't simply walk off the job."

Anger combined with fear to provoke Doro's next words. "Would you rather be carried off? Because that's likely to happen if you go back in there."

"Doro..." Ev barely got her name out when Wade interrupted.

"I've got to side with Doro on this. Yarrow made a barely veiled threat, Ev. He evidently hasn't obtained solid proof about your role, but he's skeptical. You won't learn much, even if Mr. Zee likes you and doesn't let him..." Wade's voice trailed off, but his meaning was clear.

Doro pressed her point. "See. Wade agrees with me, and I bet your boss would, too."

"Wade can talk to Lowery in the morning," Ev replied.

"It may be too late by then," Doro protested. Why was he being so stubborn? Surely, he recognized the inherent risk. She looked at Aggie, who gave a slight nod.

"Doro and Wade are right, Ev," Aggie said. "You're taking a terrible chance by going back into the speakeasy. Even if that awful man doesn't shoot you tonight, he'll be scrutinizing your every move. So will the rest of them. How will you find out important details?"

Ev shifted from one foot to the other. "Yarrow hasn't liked me from the start. I'm sure he's filled Zee's ear with his suspicions all along, since he's hinted before that he's watching me." He turned to Wade. "If I thought my neck was in a noose, I wouldn't go back."

Dismay filled Doro. Why didn't Ev address her? She was a reasonable person. A glance at Wade revealed his discomfort. "Why not call your boss tonight?" she asked.

"From where?" Ev asked. "It's after midnight, so no stores are open and there aren't any telephone booths in this area. I sure can't call from in there." He jerked his thumb at the building.

"Do you know where Mr. Canton lives?" Aggie asked. "We could drive to his place, and you could talk with him? It wouldn't take long if his home isn't far."

Ev's expression softened. "I don't want to involve the two of you any further." Clearly, he meant Doro and Aggie.

Exasperation caught hold of Doro. "Because there is danger."

"Driving off with you wouldn't look right. Not after I've said we all met tonight," Ev asserted.

"No one in the gang ever leaves with a flapper?" Doro asked. When Ev stared at her, heat scorched her face, and she glanced away.

"I don't have much time before I need to be in Zee's office." Ev reached out for Doro's hand. "I'm taking a calculated risk, but I'll be careful. Very careful, and I'm competent at my job."

At first, she let her fingers lay limply in his. After several moments, Doro intertwined them. "I don't doubt your competence," she murmured.

"Then, let's not argue," Ev replied in a weary voice.

The urge to keep pushing for him to leave now was intense, but Doro did not want to part on bad terms. Not like they had in May. Not when this might be the last time that she saw him. Bile rose in her throat, and she swallowed it down. "All right."

His winning smile surfaced. "Thank you."

A period of silence fell before Wade ended it. "Why don't I get my Packard? That would save you girls walking farther in those fancy shoes. I'm sure Ev would wait with you."

"Of course," Ev readily agreed.

"My heels aren't as high as Doro's," Aggie put in. "so, I'll go with you. Doro and Ev can chat for a few minutes."

Her friend's suggestion, while not subtle, was welcome. Doro yearned for more time with Ev. A lot more, but a little was better than none. What if his reassurances were for naught? Her usual enthusiasm for sleuthing was muted by the dangerous situation at hand. "That sounds good, since my feet are hurting."

Ev looked down at her. "Then, you need a rest." He jerked his thumb toward a bench on the main sidewalk. "We can sit there."

"All right." Getting off her feet truly was a wonderful idea, because Doro had not lied about her aches and pains. Each toe felt like it was on fire.

Wade nodded. "We'll be back quickly."

As soon as the other pair turned away, Ev ushered Doro to the bench, where she gratefully took a seat. An inaudible sigh left her.

After sitting down, Ev bent to study her feet. "Do they hurt terribly?"

Not wanting to admit how awful she felt, Doro shrugged. "I won't be wearing shoes like these every day, and it's only a minor discomfort."

"If you say so." Ev's tone indicated disbelief.

Doro could not help but chuckle. "If you must know, my toes are burning and my ankles ache. I have no idea how flappers dance all night in such shoes."

Ev laughed along with her. "I've wondered the same thing."

His comment gave her pause. "Mr. Yarrow indicated you don't dance with a lot of flappers." The revelation had eased her mind, but the gangster might not know every detail about Ev's actions. As she thought back to earlier in the evening, Doro recalled Mr. Zee, who hadn't been surprised to see Ev on the floor.

"He isn't around all the time, but I haven't danced with many. Maybe a handful."

"I see." The idea of other women in Ev's arms bothered Doro far more than it should have. Yarrow had mentioned Ev only engaging in fast dances. Was that the case? Should she ask? They were stepping out, not courting, so she had no claim on him. In retrospect, she realized she had no right to make him give up his undercover role, either. She folded her hands in her lap and stared down at them. When his fingers wrapped around hers,

Doro kept her downward focus. He didn't need to view her reaction, which was wholly out of line.

"Doro, I have to play a role. It doesn't go beyond one dance with several women each night. I'm pretty good at the Charleston and the Lindy Hop. If you recall, Yarrow mentioned me not slow dancing with ladies until tonight."

"And you haven't, even when he wasn't around?" she asked pivoting toward him.

He winked. "There's only one girl I want to hold in my arms when slow music is playing."

She shifted one hand so she could entwine their fingers. "Is that so?"

"Absolutely," he murmured. In the lamplight, his gray eyes shone silver.

"That's good because there's only one guy I want to dance with."

Ev gently squeezed her hand. "Good to know. As long as it's me."

Another chuckle left him. "Of course it is."

While she enjoyed the lighthearted moments, Doro could not shake her sense of impending doom. She needed reassurance. "You said Yarrow has acted suspicious about you all along."

"He has. Yarrow likes to keep new guys on their toes. None of them want a federal agent in their midst, which is understandable, so they're wary. Yarrow's spiel was to prod me, or one of you, to slip up and reveal something. And you stood up to the challenge."

The praise chipped away at Doro's anxiety. "I didn't want to say or do anything that might ruin your cover."

"And you didn't. I was proud of you. Very proud. You're not only a fine sleuth, you're shrewd."

"Fine amateur sleuth, you mean."

His hand cupped her face. "You'd be a good professional one, not that I think you should quit your job as a librarian."

"I don't plan to, but it's nice to know I have options." The lilt of laughter lightened her response.

A serious expression blanketed his handsome features. "I can think of at least one more."

Before she could reply, an automobile flew down the street and careened toward the alley. Because the vehicle passed so close, the occupants and their weapons were clear. Doro gasped. "The men in the backseat had Tommy guns. Are they agents?"

"No, I would've been alerted to a raid. Besides, there's one at another place tonight. At least there was one planned."

His words jogged Doro's memory. "That's right."

Ev grabbed her arm as he spoke and rushed to the nearest storefront door. "Stay back here until Wade and Aggie come for you. No one will see you if you're in this recessed area. Just don't move until they pull up. Then, hurry into Wade's car and go."

When he turned away, Doro grabbed his jacket sleeve. "Your boss hasn't been able to get in touch with you. How would he get word to you about a raid? Maybe they changed locations."

Although he kept looking toward the alley, Ev froze in place. "A good point."

"Do all the agents in the local office know you're undercover?"

He shifted to look at Doro. "No."

"So, they might shoot you if you rush in," she pointed out.

His shoulders slumped. "Possibly, and I shouldn't ruin my cover in any case."

Before Doro got another word out, Wade pulled up to the curb and stopped. As Ev darted out to open the back-seat door for her, another vehicle—a large black roadster—roared toward them and shots rang out.

"Get out of here, Wade," Ev shouted as he shoved Doro to the ground and twisted to take most of the impact before covering her with his body. "I'll take care of Doro. Come back around in a few minutes."

As Ev got her out of harm's way, Doro saw Wade drive away. Then, she saw nothing. Despite the muggy air, she shivered. With Ev shielding her, her view was blocked. Her anxiety grew by leaps and bounds when the second car slowed down before stopping near them. As the vehicle came to a halt, Ev rose to his knees and withdrew a revolver from his inside jacket pocket.

"Looks like one of Zee's and Yarrow's men," a male voice called out. "And his gun is in his hand."

"Sure does," another said. "Let's take care of him. That'll be one less to enter the fight. Get his moll, too."

As more shots cut through the night air, Ev gasped and fell against Doro. He was no longer a shield. He was a dead weight. Terror ripped through her, but she could not move and did not try. What if doing so hurt him more? After the gangster car careened away. Doro's muscles went slack, but her mind roiled with fear. "Ev. Ev. Can you hear me?"

After a moment, he rolled off her with a groan. "I'm...all right. What...about...you?"

His ragged tone and irregular cadence sent fresh fear coursing through her. Doro struggled into a sitting position and stared at him in disbelief. The streetlight revealed a wet splotch forming on his shoulder. "I'm fine, but you've been shot."

Ev glanced at his upper arm as if he needed to get confirmation. "It's only a flesh wound," he corrected, struggling to his feet. "We need to get you out of here. Wade will surely be back soon." Ev glanced toward the alley. "I'll wait with you to make sure." He wobbled before righting himself and reaching down to help her up. As he did, he groaned again.

"You're really hurt." Doro followed the statement by stepping around him. Even in the dim streetlight, the spreading dampness was evident.

Briefly, he stared at her as if in disbelief. Finally, his fingers went to the area. "It's not bad." The tremor in his voice belied the assertion, so did him sinking to his knees.

She dropped next to Ev and wrapped one arm around his lean waist. When a shudder ripped through him, Doro fought for control. Panicking would not help Ev, but he was too heavy for her to lift. As she looked up and down the street, she prayed to see Wade's Packard appear.

Doro's shaking hand went to Ev's sleeve, which was now soaked with blood. His blood. A lump of terror rose in her throat. Their budding relationship could not, should not, end this way. Cracking the case was not as important as his safety. Not nearly as important. She'd give up amateur sleuthing forever before seeing him wounded and...Doro did not let the worst outcome form. Ev would be all right. He had to be.

"Ev. Can you hear me?" Her voice wavered, but she continued. "Aggie and Wade will be back any minute." How she wished Ev had not told them to take off. What if they had encountered another carload of gangsters? What if they'd been shot? But no shots had come from any place else. With determination, Doro reined in her apprehension. "Ev..." This time, he cut her off.

"I hear you," he mumbled, but his voice trembled more than hers did.

She clasped his ice-cold hand and willed her strength and warmth into him. "Hang on."

His eyes did not open, but a weak smile curved his lips and his fingers tightened slightly on hers. "I will."

She wanted to ask how bad the wound was, but he wouldn't admit to a serious injury. He'd try to reassure her when he needed to conserve his energy. With her thumb, Doro stroked the back of his hand, waited, and prayed.

After what was likely a few minutes but felt like hours, Wade's familiar vehicle came down the block. When he stopped, the constable called out. "We heard gunshots. What happened?"

"Ev got hit." Doro grasped his arm and tugged him toward the vehicle. Her pulling became more urgent when more and more gunfire, emanating from the alley behind the speakeasy, filled the air. "Come on."

"You go. I need to get back inside. Otherwise, Zee and Yarrow will wonder where I am," Ev insisted.

"You got shot. If you ever go back, you can tell them that." Doro kept yanking on his good arm. His weakened condition became obvious when she was able to tug him along with no resistance.

"Doro is right," Wade, who had stepped out of the Packard and come toward them, said. "Come on, Ev. We all need to get out of here before more gangsters arrive."

Despite the heavy shadows, the play of emotions on Ev's face was clear. At the same time, his gaze grew cloudy with confusion. "Let's go," Doro urged him again. Leaving Ev in the midst of a battle between gangsters was her worst nightmare. And what if cops came? He couldn't, wouldn't shoot at them, which would throw him under additional suspicion. A policeman could shoot him. One bullet wound was one too many. Another could be fatal. She clutched his good arm more tightly. "You can come back later, after we find out what's going on." The statement was meant to mollify him. If Doro had her way, Ev would not return to the Zee-Yarrow gang.

When Ev failed to respond, Wade did. "The girls need to be in a safe place."

That observation seemed to break Ev's will. "Let's go." Only a moment's hesitation preceded Wade helping Doro before nearly lifting Ev into the automobile.

As soon as the back seat door closed, Wade jumped into the driver's seat, pulled back into the right lane, and drove on. For several minutes, no one spoke. Then, Aggie turned to look at Doro. "What's going on? Wasn't that gunfire? Who shot Ev? And what about the speeding car? I didn't have a good view."

A low laugh left Wade. "That's a lot of questions, but I'd like answers myself."

"Ev understands what's happening," Doro said, "but he got shot, so let's discuss details after we get help for him."

"Shot," Aggie echoed as she swiveled to peer into the backseat. "How bad is it?"

"Probably a graze. Some antiseptic and a bandage will take care of it," Ev insisted, although his voice still wobbled.

"Shouldn't we go to a hospital?" Aggie asked.

"Not necessary," Ev murmured.

"Since we don't have supplies with us, you should at least see a doctor," Doro said. She felt more than heard a sigh leave him.

"It's the middle of the night. No doctor's office is open," Ev replied.

"Since you can't go back to the speakeasy tonight, we either need to go home or head to Lowery Canton's place. Your choice," Wade put in.

Doro held her breath waiting for Ev's response. Her choice would be to head to Michaw. What would Ev want? When a period of silence developed, she decided to press for the expeditious course of action. "Even if your wound isn't serious, it needs to be treated. It'll take nearly an hour to get home. If you keep bleeding, you may pass out. And please don't say that's impossible."

A resigned sigh escaped him. "Lowery lives about ten blocks away on Glenwood Court. It's a small apartment building. You can drop me off there," Ev replied.

His curt cadence made Doro think the wound hurt more than he was admitting, but she held her tongue. After getting the injury clean and bandaged, they could discuss Ev going home—at least for a short time.

Within ten minutes, Wade stopped in front of a two-story Spanish revival apartment house. A few carriage lights illuminated the stucco walls with their dark brick trim. "I hope he's back from the raid, but it is late."

"It is," Doro agreed as she scanned the building. "Nice place."

"I remember when this place was built," Aggie said. "My family lived a few blocks away, and my brother and I sometimes passed by here going to and from school. It was different from any building I'd seen before then."

"It's definitely not like any homes in Michaw," Wade added. "Pretty small, too."

"Less than a dozen apartments, I think," Ev put in. "I visited Lowery a few times when I lived in the city."

Since Ev's voice sounded odd, Doro shifted toward him. "How do you feel?"

"I'm fine," was his reply.

"I'm sure." Doro failed to keep a cryptic note from her tone. When he made no response, she scanned the area. "It looks like there are exterior entrances to many of the apartments. Where is Agent Canton's door?"

"His place lies on the end of the right wing. We can get there through the archway," Ev replied.

Since that apartment was close to the curb, Doro breathed a sigh of relief. Ev might say he felt fine, but how far could he walk? Not far was her guess.

"Let's get you inside and check your injury, Ev." Wade spoke as he stepped out of the car.

Ev did not again suggest being dropped off, which was wise since Doro noticed he had trouble with the door handle. After he extricated himself, she joined him on the sidewalk while Wade assisted Aggie out of the vehicle. "I hope he's home and awake," Doro said. From their vantage point, no lights were visible from the end apartment. What would they do if Canton was still away from home?

"The dining room does double-duty as an office, and that's in back. He's probably there, since he sleeps very little during big cases. And if he was on a raid tonight, he may not rest at all," Ev said before pointing to a brick walkway leading to an arch where two doors were visible.

When Wade moved alongside Ev and took his arm, the two slowly led the way. As they moved along, Doro thought Ev leaned on his friend more and more. They had done the right thing by coming here for help.

After they passed through the arch, Ev and Wade went to the door on the right. Wade knocked without releasing his hold on Ev, who swayed on his feet.

Doro's heart pounded against her ribs while they waited. How long could Ev remain upright? Not knowing had her fretting more and more.

A few moments passed before footsteps approached from inside the apartment. When they stopped, a male voice echoed with surprise. Evidently, the senior agent availed himself of the peephole, which was sensible. Checking who was at his door in the middle of the night was a safety measure.

"Ev. What in the world brings you here?" The door swung open before the last word was out. Canton scanned the group. "Come in. I'm sure there's a story behind all of you coming."

Wade and Ev let the two women precede them into the apartment's narrow foyer, which was dimly lit with light from the adjacent parlor's lamps. The group followed their host into the room. When the man turned back to them, his gaze fixed on Ev's shoulder.

"How bad is it?" the agent asked.

"It's a flesh wound, and a minor one at that," Ev replied.

For several seconds, Canton stared at his agent. "All the same, let's get into the kitchen and look." He turned to the other three. "See that he sits down, and I'll be back with my first aid kit. There's a basin under the sink. Filling it with hot water would be a good idea."

"We'll tend to all that," Doro assured him.

Canton nodded. "He knows where the kitchen is," he said before leaving them.

"Let's go," Wade said.

Ev's response was to return to the front hall and turn toward the back of the apartment, but he let his friend provide more support. Light poured out of the kitchen, where a large oak table and several chairs sat against one wall.

"Sit down," Doro told Ev. When he did not object, she wondered again how he really felt. In the bright light, the wet area on his sleeve was much more obvious, and the splotch was larger. Anxiety warred with logic. If he had lost a lot of blood, Ev would not still be on his feet. So not a lot but a good amount.

After Ev took a seat at the table, Doro retrieved the basin. "Aggie, would you see if there's a big pot to heat water?"

"Of course," her friend said, before looking through the cupboard next to the stove. "Found one."

"Let me fill it," Wade said.

By the time the water was hot, Canton was back. "We need to get your jacket off."

"Right." Ev yanked at the material, but it did not give.

Doro watched with concern. Being too weak to pull off his outerwear was not a good sign.

"Stick your arm out," Canton said.

Ev followed the order but slumped against the back of the chair as he did. At the same time, his eyelids closed. Doro, fearful he might faint and fall to the floor, stepped forward. Wade must have had the same fear, because he put a hand on Ev's good shoulder.

Within moments, the jacket was off and a red-streaked shirt sleeve with a ragged hole was revealed. Doro shifted her focus from there to Ev's face. Although the injury was troubling, his color remained fair, so he could not be badly hurt. Could he? When his gaze met hers, Ev grinned. She smiled in return. "Let's get your wound cleaned and bandaged."

His lips flattened. "Lowery and Wade can do it. You and Aggie wait in the parlor. We'll be out shortly."

Doro stiffened at what sounded like rejection. She opened her mouth to object, but Wade spoke first.

"That's best," the constable said. "It's not seemly for two young unmarried women to see a man..." He cleared his throat.

Heat scorched Doro's cheeks. She had not given a moment's thought to propriety. Only helping Ev seemed important. "Going to a speakeasy isn't seemly, either."

Ev's mouth quirked up at the corner. "No, but let's not compound the issues."

"No, let's not," Aggie agreed as she took Doro by the arm.

Canton turned to Doro. "I've dealt with gunshot wounds before. From what I can see, this one isn't bad. If I'm wrong, I have a doctor friend down the block, and I'll call him. All right?"

The federal agent trying to placate her made Doro realize her feelings for Ev were evident. Not that she was trying to hide them, but they had only been out together once. "Of course." Hurriedly, she turned on her heel and went to the parlor. Aggie followed.

After the pair took seats on the divan, Aggie squeezed Doro's hand. "You heard Agent Canton. He knows what he's doing, and Wade will help."

Her friend's reassurances did not ease Doro's anxiety. "Ev's shirt is all bloody, and the material is clinging to his skin. I hope they're careful getting it off. He has to be hurting terribly already. Ripping the cloth loose could make it worse." A soft sigh escaped Doro. "I sound too...I don't know...concerned." Actually, *concerned* was too mild a word for her feelings.

A sympathetic smile softened Aggie's countenance. "It's natural to worry. After all, getting shot is serious, but there wasn't as much blood as I would've expected." Her expression became serious. "I understand you wanting to help, but it wouldn't be appropriate."

"Appropriate." Doro echoed the word with disdain. "We saw Wade and Ev when they were sick in May."

"Which bordered on inappropriate," Aggie pointed out. "But they were fully clad, albeit in pajamas, and Dr. Silven was down the hall. Now, we're in the apartment of a Prohibition agent after being at a speakeasy."

Resignation replaced resentment. "I know, and you're right. Besides, Ev didn't want me in there." Her gaze drifted toward the kitchen. His rejection stung.

"I'm not sure that's the case. It's more him knowing you and I shouldn't see him half-undressed," Aggie pointed out. "And he may not want you witnessing the wound. Even if it's not serious, it can't be pretty."

"I suppose not," Doro murmured. While she had found murder victims, Doro had never seen their raw wounds. She didn't really want to witness Ev's torn flesh. She only wanted to help him.

Chapter Twelve

Fifteen minutes later, the three men joined them. Doro's attention immediately went to Ev, who was ambling between Wade and Canton. Was he weaker? Was he paler? Were they at his side because he might pass out? Muted light from two stained glass lamps offered scant visibility, but both possibilities bothered her. Knowing Ev would not want to be smothered, she bit her lower lip to keep from suggesting he lie down. Instead, she scrutinized his attire. Canton must have given him a clean shirt, which pulled tightly across Ev's broad shoulders, one of which sported a bulky bandage. Blood was not coming through. A good sign. Wasn't it? Her disquiet at a high ebb, Doro swallowed convulsively.

"That didn't take long," Aggie said in a bright tone.

"Nope, it didn't," Wade put in as he took a chair next to the divan. "Lowery is skilled at tending wounds."

"He is," Ev agreed, "but I knew that already."

Doro's gaze narrowed on him. "Was he around last October when you got shot?"

Ev's expression resembled that of a boy getting caught with his hand in the cookie jar. For several moments, he was silent. Finally, he shrugged. Then, he winced. "He was."

"I see." And she did. She saw Ev was accustomed to being shot. Had it happened more than twice? Would it happen again? If he stayed with the Prohibition Bureau, even temporarily, the likelihood was strong. Surely, they could crack the case another way.

Canton took a chair across from the two women and gestured to Ev to sit on the sofa with Doro. "Let's go over what happened. Wade and Ev didn't tell me much. We were otherwise occupied, but we want to talk now."

"We're happy to help," Doro replied.

"We are," Aggie agreed.

Ev turned to Doro. "Since I wasn't at my best after shots rang out, you can provide better descriptions." A rueful grin touched his lips.

Briefly, Doro considered the moments before, during, and after the vehicles—guns blazing—had sped by. "Ev and I were sitting on a bench, waiting for Aggie and Wade to pick us up." Warmth spread through her as she recalled their exchange. When Ev shifted to look at her, Doro cleared her throat. Now was not the time to think about personal matters. "One car sped past us and into the alley. It looked like the men in the backseat had Tommy guns. I wondered if they were agents conducting a raid, but Ev didn't think so." She focused on Canton. "He was sure you would've gotten word to him."

"Absolutely, but I had no inkling of this development," the agent agreed. "Then, what happened?"

Doro continued. "Ev didn't want to ruin his cover, but he wanted me out of harm's way, so we stood in a nearby doorway. As soon as Wade's vehicle appeared down the street, we started to the curb. Ev was helping me when another car careened toward us and gunshots rang out. It was black with running boards." Reliving that event sent a shudder through Doro, but she focused on revealing every detail. "The men yelled to each other about Ev being one of Zee's men. Then, they fired at Ev. A flurry of bullets. I'm not sure how many." As Doro spoke, she recalled her terror. Ev was lucky he had only been hit once. So very lucky.

"And they went on?" Canton asked.

She gathered her troubled thoughts in order to answer. "They did. Wade drove up within a couple of minutes, and we rushed into the car."

Canton turned to Aggie and Wade. "Could either of you identify the vehicles?"

Aggie shook her head. "After the gunshots, I worried about Doro and Ev, so my attention was on them. I heard squealing tires and gunshots, but I couldn't identify the cars."

"I didn't get a good look at the first one, but the second bore a strong resemblance to the Cadillac I saw leaving the Fulton place the night of the murder," Wade said. "Except that one was burgundy with black trim."

Silence echoed in the room as the others stared at Wade. Ev was the first to find his voice. "As dark as it was, a burgundy car could've looked all black. If it's the same vehicle, we've identified the owners of both cars seen at the murder scene. The gangsters tonight had to be from the Kesler gang, probably shooting up the speakeasy to get even for Zee and Yarrow attacking one of their places recently." His assessment rang true and reinforced how rival gangsters operated.

"You're on the right track," Agent Canton said. "Not that it narrows our list of suspects down much, but it solidifies that the killer is probably with one of the two operations. In the kitchen, you mentioned Yarrow owning a blue LaSalle roadster. He's done dirty work in the past, so he might've gone to the Fulton place himself." Canton turned toward Ev. "What do you think?"

"That seems quite likely. But was Mr. Fulton dead when Yarrow left? Or did a Kesler kill him?" Ev posed the questions.

As she listened, Doro thought about other bits and pieces. "Mrs. Fulton told us about Phil Kesler going to their place, but he drives a sporty vehicle, not a Cadillac roadster."

"That's right," Aggie added. "She didn't know the make, but said it was one that young men like."

Canton rubbed his forehead. "Maybe someone else from the Kesler gang went to see Fulton."

"Or Phil might've borrowed a car from one of his brothers," Ev suggested.

"That seems plausible," Wade put in.

Fresh frustration built inside Doro. "Which still doesn't narrow our list down."

"You're right about that," Ev said. "I'll find out more when I go back later tonight. I should get going. Zee and Yarrow will wonder where I am."

"If they're not shot up," Wade said in a strained tone. "I don't want to tell you what to do, but maybe wait until morning, at least."

A long sigh escaped Ev. "I don't know. I'm not thinking clearly."

The idea of Ev heading back to the speakeasy took Doro's breath away. Was he serious about returning? What a horrible idea. Instead of being blunt, she spoke an obvious—albeit, less incendiary—fact. "Because you're exhausted and hurting. Please don't say you aren't."

Ev bowed his head. "I can't argue about either one."

Canton held up one hand. "I don't want you going back tonight. We need to find out what happened at the speakeasy. Although the Keslers were likely in those cars, I need hard facts, not supposition. The police are surely there by now, so I'll get a call soon. Even if Zee and Yarrow are all right, they'll head out of town for a while. The two of them go to a lakeshore house at times, and Sweebe might head home. Hard to say for sure."

Doro sat up straighter as she focused on the federal agent. "What about Mrs. Fulton? Wade must've told you what a neighbor saw at her home this evening."

"He did," Canton agreed.

"We've got more work to do," Ev said. "Maybe a lot."

"Maybe not," his old boss observed. "We're a lot further in the investigation than a few days ago. One big break could lead us to the killer and, with luck, to Mrs. Fulton, who may be a victim or a suspect."

The statement rang true, but Doro wished the big break would come quickly. As always, solving a crime involved gathering puzzle pieces and, as always, some bits had to be discarded. "She acted oddly when we met, but I chalked it up to fear."

"So did I," Aggie agreed.

"Which could be the reason," Wade put in.

"It could." Lowery looked from Wade to Ev. "We need to find out what caused tonight's shoot-out and how much damage was done. Why don't you head home to recuperate? If and when you take up your undercover position, you'll have the excuse of being wounded to not report immediately. Besides, have they told you exactly where their lake hideout is?"

"All right," Ev agreed. "And no. They didn't share that, so I can't turn up there."

"Another good reason to lie low for a few days," Canton said. "Although I'd like you to learn more about Sweebe, if you can do it covertly. Unfortunately, he'd recognize all four of you now."

"We'll be cautious," Ev said.

"Sure will," Wade agreed. "Sheriff Taylor might ask some questions for us, even though he's retired. I'll check with him. For now, we ought to get on the road home."

"I agree," Ev said, "but I hate to leave my vehicle in the city, and I'm not sure about driving yet."

"Where is it?" Canton asked.

"In back of the hotel where I'm staying," Ev replied.

The agent nodded. "I'll see it gets moved to where Zee-Yarrow and the gang won't see it. We'll let them think you took off, too."

"Probably wise," Ev observed. "Everyone knows to scatter if the feds or rival gangsters come. It'll probably be a few days, maybe more, before they open the saloon again. If it wasn't completely shot up."

A shiver rippled through Doro and, when she met Aggie's gaze, she saw her friend's reaction was similar. Wade must have noted it, too, because he patted Aggie's arm. In the tense silence that followed, Ev shifted toward Doro, but it was Canton who spoke.

"The bunch of you barely missed being in a possibly deadly situation," the agent said as he looked from Wade to Aggie to Doro. "Ev and Wade know how to handle themselves, of course."

The implicit warning was not lost on Doro, but she did not respond. Although going to the speakeasy had been risky, she would do it again. If she, Aggie, and Wade had not been there, Ev would've gone to the meeting in Zee's office and probably not walked out. The possibility solidified Doro's certainty: she had done the right thing.

"Entering a speakeasy is inherently dangerous," Ev added.

Doro turned to face Ev. Although his voice had an edge, his gaze glittered with some softer emotion. "You made sure I was safe after the bullets started flying. I was fine, but you weren't." His quick action had ensured her safety, something she would never forget. Nor would she forget he'd taken a bullet himself. Not ever.

Ev's nostrils flared with a sharp intake of breath. "I'm not seriously injured."

Repeating the assertion did not make it true. Minor wounds often got infected, which was a real concern, but she did not say so. All of them knew that was a common complication with any type of injury. "I'm glad."

Canton clearing his throat broke the spell. "We all are."

Color seeped into Ev's pale face, as he glanced at his boss. "I understand taking a couple of days away. At least until you find out what went on after we took off."

"We'll see what happens," Canton said. "You may not be going back at all. It's not worth risking your life to get a few details that you might find in your own backyard. I definitely want to find out more about Patrick and his family, and about Alf Waggoner. I doubt if Sweebe is also working for the Keslers, since he's tightly woven into the fabric of the Zee-Yarrow gang. That kid Alf might've done jobs for the brothers, though, and he could've been at the Fultons' home tonight."

"But who was the bigger man at the Fulton place last evening?" Doro asked. "The description is vague, but it sounds like Jug Barnes."

"It does," Canton readily agreed. He ran one hand over his face. "I talked to the man and, although I feel sure he's bought bootlegged liquor, I'm not convinced he killed Fulton."

"We've said it could've been an accident," Doro pointed out, "since it wasn't the blow from the bottle that killed him. It was Mr. Fulton hitting his head on the metal corner of the wagon when he fell."

"True, and we have to keep that in mind, along with everything else," the federal agent said.

Ev slumped back into the corner of the divan. "There's still a lot to consider," he said in a weary voice.

"Unless there's more to discuss right now, we should get on the road. Ev needs to rest, and I'll be up early to make sure all is well in Michaw," Wade said.

Canton nodded. "All of us could use some sleep, although I'll be up for a while. I'll be in touch tomorrow. The agent patronizing the Kesler place was on tonight's raid at another establishment, but he'll go there tomorrow afternoon. Actually, this afternoon. They open earlier than most speakeasies." The telephone ringing interrupted the conversation.

Canton jumped up. "That could be about tonight's shootout or about our raid. I'll be right back."

Fresh anxiety weighed heavily on Doro's heart and mind. Although she could not pinpoint why, she thought the call related to their case, not the other events.

Chapter Thirteen

When Canton came back ten minutes later, his expression was impossible to read. He stood by his chair instead of sitting down, which brought Doro to the edge of her seat. Ev was the first to speak.

"You look like you got important news."

Canton's lips twitched. "You know me well. I did, and not about the shootout or our raid." His gaze moved to Doro. "Mrs. Fulton has been trying to call you since just before midnight."

Surprise made Doro's jaw drop. "How do you know that?" And why was the woman telephoning her again? Canton's admonition that the widow could be a suspect or a victim rang in her ears.

"Her friend convinced her to call the Bureau office. Several of my agents were still there, and one spoke with her," Canton replied. "Both women say they're terrified, so they're willing to let us protect them."

"Did the agent think she was telling the truth?" Ev asked. "It could be a set-up."

A harsh breath left Canton. "It could, so we need to proceed with caution."

"What's your plan?" Ev asked.

"My agent told the woman that Professor Banyon would call her back as soon as possible, but Mrs. Fulton prefers to telephone again herself," Canton replied. "We need to go to my office, if the professor agrees."

"Of course," Doro said. "Where has Mrs. Fulton been since last week?"

"She supposedly rented a room at a cheap hotel downtown. Today, her nerves got the better of her, and she went back to her friend's home. They waited until late to place a call to Michaw," the senior agent explained. "At least that's the story."

"Our town operator goes off duty at midnight, although she'll rouse to take emergency calls," Aggie put in.

"It's different in the city. More than one operator is on duty overnight," Canton said.

Ev leaned forward and focused on the federal agent. "If the woman is really worried about her safety, why is she still in town?" Ev asked. "It makes little sense, since she told Doro and Aggie she was leaving. How do we know she isn't working with bootleggers?" Tension was in his voice and his expression. "She could've been with one at her house earlier tonight. That would explain the figures."

Canton grimaced. "We can't be sure."

The brief exchange had Doro's mind churning. "Do you think she's been held by one of the gangs since last week, and they're using her to set a trap?" She agreed about the situation being odd.

Ev's jaw clenched. "It seems possible to me."

"To me, too," Wade agreed.

With a sigh, the federal agent sat down. "I can't rule it out, either."

For several moments, silence filled the room. During that period, Doro shifted to study Ev. Tension radiated from him in waves, which did nothing to lessen her anxiety. "Maybe I can learn more when I talk to her."

Ev faced Doro. "Talking is fine."

"That's all I'm planning to do," she replied with a smile.

"Good, because you and Aggie don't need to be in harm's way," Ev said.

"I agree," Wade added in a firm tone.

Canton cleared his throat. "After the call, we'll discuss how to proceed. It's fifty-fifty that Mrs. Fulton is being used by gangsters. If the woman is out on her own, I'd like to get her under our protection. She trusts the professors, not the rest of us." He glanced at his wristwatch. "I told my agents I'd be at the office in fifteen minutes. Mrs. Fulton is calling back in a half-hour."

Ev got to his feet. "Then, let's go."

Fifteen minutes later, the entire group was in the Prohibition Bureau office, where a half-dozen agents waited. One of the group, a tall blonde in his early thirties, stood up immediately.

"Mrs. Fulton called back already," he said. "I tried to reach you at your apartment, Lowery, but you'd already left."

The man's stern expression and flat tone put Doro on edge. Was the woman backing out?

"What did she want? The professor is here to take the call," Canton said.

The other agent glanced at Doro and back at his boss. "She decided she wasn't staying near the telephone booth. She and her friend are in a restaurant on the outskirts of town."

"On Chicago Pike?" Doro asked.

The blonde nodded. "Yep."

"That's where we met her last week," Aggie put in. "How did she get in at this hour?"

"Her friend owns the place," the blonde agent replied.

Surprise filled Doro. "She didn't act like she knew anyone when we were there."

Aggie nodded. "Not at all."

"She may be a good actress," Canton observed.

Doro thought back to the meeting at the diner. "Now, the waitress's actions make more sense. Maybe she's the friend and owner."

"You could be on to something," Ev observed.

The others agreed. Although they had all taken seats, no one looked at ease. While conversation ensued, Doro waited anxiously for the telephone to ring again. When it did, she jumped to her feet.

"That's got to be here," the blonde agent said. "There's a telephone diner, and she planned to call from there."

"Let one of us answer," Canton said before snatching the receiver. He only spoke a few words before gesturing to Doro.

She moved forward to take the base and earpiece. "Hello, Mrs. Fulton. Are you all right?"

The widow spoke quickly and quietly. "Please come. We need to get out of here."

The plea tugged on Doro's heartstrings. Despite her doubts, she found herself agreeing. "We'll do what we can. Just stay inside. If there's an outside light, turn it on."

"There isn't," Mrs. Fulton replied before giving additional details about when the place opened and such. "Come to the back door. We'll wait there."

For a moment, Doro tried to picture the building. "Can we drive around back?"

"Yes. There's a narrow drive and a little parking area behind the diner. Don't bring a bunch of lawmen. Just your friend and the constable. Maybe a couple of Prohis. Not a lot of them. I'm too afraid."

A knot of dread formed in Doro's stomach. Something did not ring true, but she agreed. Working out details would be done with the lawmen. "Of course. It'll take us a half-hour, maybe a little longer to get there."

"We'll be here." Then, the woman hung up.

Doro followed suit before turning to face the others. "She doesn't want a bunch of agents coming along, but she mentioned Wade. How would she know he was with us?"

"A darn good question," Ev muttered.

"It could be an assumption," Wade pointed out.

"It could," Canton agreed. "Or she heard from someone who was in the speakeasy."

"Someone who might be holding her hostage," Doro said.

For long moments, deadly silence echoed in the room. "That's a major concern," Ev said.

"It is, so we'll take every precaution, but we can't ignore the woman. She's a civilian who is in danger, no matter if she's being forced to call us or not." Canton focused on Doro. "What else did she say?"

"She wants us to pick her and the friend up at the place. It doesn't open until six o'clock, but the cook comes around five, so we need to be there before four-thirty," Doro replied with what the widow had shared. "One agent can come to the door with me. Wade and Aggie can be in a vehicle parked in back."

"She knows I'm along, too?" Aggie asked.

"Yes, and an agent can escort me to the back door," Doro replied.

"I'll be going with you," Ev said.

"Good," Doro murmured.

His expression did not lighten. "She has a lot of details, which make me suspicious and uneasy."

"Me, too," Wade added.

Canton gestured for the other agents to join the group by the door. "We'll need all of you along to provide security. Discreetly, of course. I wish I'd seen the place, but Professors Banyon and Darwine can fill us in."

"Hold on, Lowery." Ev held up a hand. "Doro and Aggie can ride along, but they stay in a vehicle until we see the situation."

Doro turned to Ev, who looked as tense as she felt. "The diner is in the open, except for some bushes and trees behind the parking area. Not much else is out there. A service station and a church across the street, and a few houses scattered around the area. The closest is at least three-hundred yards away."

"That's not good." Wade reached for Aggie's hand as he spoke.

Canton ran a hand over his face. "The service station won't be open, and no one will be in the church. We can go in as few vehicles as possible. I'm going to assume the area isn't well-lit at night, since most places on the outskirts aren't."

"Assuming can be dangerous," Ev pointed out.

A rueful smile touched Canton's mouth. "Sometimes, it's necessary. None of us likes how this is playing out, but Mrs. Fulton may be in grave danger, and the same with her friend."

"Let's not forget that this friend is probably the one whose husband runs booze," Wade put in.

"I haven't forgotten," Canton assured him.

"I still don't like it," Ev said. "I can go up to the diner by myself."

The blonde agent turned to Ev. "The women won't answer the door, and I'm not sure breaking in is a good idea."

"Neither am I," Ev replied. "I planned on knocking. If they want protection, they'll come out. If they're held by gangsters, we'll avoid a trap."

Doro laid a hand on his forearm. "You'll be walking into it."

He bowed his head but said nothing.

"You'll be right there with me, so everything will be fine." Despite her own misgivings, the last was said with certainty, because Ev would let nothing happen to her. "What about you? Are you well enough to go?"

"Sure," he said. "It's my left shoulder, and I'm right-handed. No problem for me."

A host of potential pitfalls filled Doro's mind, but she withheld them. Ev would go, no matter what. And so would she.

"I'll have several city cops, too," his old boss said. "You and Professor Banyon will have plenty of us around to watch what happens. We don't have much time, but I'll make a call. The chief of police will help, and he might have ideas on where to hide our vehicles."

"And I'll be there," Wade assured them.

"So will I," Aggie put in.

Although Ev did not answer, he looked tense and hard and unyielding. "I'm outvoted."

Doro laid a hand on his arm. "She's truly frightened. She's been upset and angry, too. She wants her husband's killer brought to justice. That's understandable."

Ev lightly clasped Doro's fingers where they rested on his forearm, but he kept his focus on Canton. "Make the calls."

Canton headed toward a door toward the back of the main office, while his agents went to various desks.

"It'll be fine," Doro told Ev. "She may have additional information that she was too afraid to share last week."

"That's true," Aggie put in. "She probably really wants protection now."

While Doro agreed, uncertainty dogged her. But she would not let Ev see. "I think so, too."

"We'll find out shortly," he murmured.

Before Doro could respond, Canton was back.

The senior agent signaled for his men to again join them. "Several Toledo police officers will be there, too, along with the chief. He knows the diner and gave me some ideas on where to park and hide."

"It'll still be dark," Ev shot back. "How are other agents and policemen going to see us and what's going on?"

"Wade can keep the headlights on. That'll help," Canton said. "It'll work out fine. I know we're taking a risk, but I don't have many options. We'll have plenty of men outside, so we'll get the women. One way or another."

Did the man believe what he said? Doro could not tell, but she agreed that they needed to proceed. Beneath Doro's hand, Ev's arm went stiff. As she watched him, she saw the tension spread through his body. Despite Canton's assurances, a lot could go wrong. Ev knew it, and so did she.

The next ten minutes were spent reviewing the plan. At the end of that time, the group headed outside. Before they got to Wade's Packard, Ev caught Doro's arm and stopped her. "You don't have to go. We can pick up Mrs. Fulton without you."

"Oh, Ev. You heard what Agent Canton said. She'll disappear if I'm not there. I don't think she was involved in her husband's death, and she should have protection." A host of emotions played across his handsome face. Doro felt, as much as saw, Ev's dismay and doubt. Despite Canton's reassurance, she felt both echo inside her. While the senior agent had seemingly taken all precautions, he was not infallible. No one was. When Ev did not respond, Doro continued. "The meeting place has a lot of areas for agents and policemen to hide. We only need to enter the parking lot and let Mrs. Fulton see me. She and her friend should hurry out. Then, we'll be on our way." At least she hoped that's how the scene would unfold.

Briefly, Ev bowed his head. After a moment, he again met her gaze. "Gangsters can hide, too."

"But the other lawmen will get there ahead and see them," she reasoned.

He released his hold on her. "All right. Let's get it over with."

Chapter Fourteen

When they got to the sidewalk in front of the office, three unmarked cars sat at the curb. "I see the police chief," Canton said. "I'll talk to him before we head out. Since the ladies know where we're going, give us ten minutes head start. We'll get set up before you arrive."

"Sure thing," Wade agreed.

Ev merely nodded.

Within moments, Ev and Doro climbed into Wade's vehicle, while he and Aggie sat in front. After chatting with the chief, Canton drove off with three agents inside his automobile. The others traveled separately, as did the Toledo police.

Wade did as he'd been directed and waited ten minutes before leaving. Since Ev looked tense and grim, Doro did her best to keep the conversation light. Wade cooperated with his usual affability, while Ev only added terse comments on a sporadic basis. Aggie made an occasional comment, but she sounded anxious herself. And who could blame her? Anyone with sense would have doubts.

When they got close to the diner, Doro sat up straighter. "It's not far now."

Aggie peered out her window. "Over there, Wade. There's a light coming out the back of the building."

"I see a couple of cars next to the church," Doro observed.

"There are also two next to the service station," Ev said.

"The rest must be on the other side of the woods behind the diner," Wade suggested as he downshifted. "I'll pull around to the back lot but stay where it's dark so we're not seen by Mrs. Fulton and her friend."

"Canton gave me a gun before we left the office," Ev said. "You've got yours handy?"

"Absolutely," Wade replied.

Doro's heart hammered in her ears, and she breathed deeply and slowly to gain composure. If Ev sensed the depth of her anxiety, he would end the meeting before it began. Dim light from a nearby streetlamp provided the only illumination inside the car. Wanting reassurance, Doro turned to Ev. A glance at him revealed he had donned what she now considered his federal agent persona—steely gaze, tight jaw, squared shoulders.

After a fleeting moment, he faced her. "You sure about this?"

His voice was as stoic as his demeanor. "Very sure." Doro, forcing a smile, injected confidence into her tone.

Ev clasped her hand. "Just remember. Take no chances, no matter what."

The reminder resulted from genuine concern, so she nodded. "Of course."

"Let me remind you that Mrs. Fulton and her friend will be just inside the kitchen. There looks to be decent lighting inside there, but don't get too close to her. Let them come to us."

The discussion in the Prohibition office had centered on the plans and included the caveat that to avoid a trap, Doro and Ev were not to go far into the parking lot without staying alert. Canton had emphasized this was an unnecessary step, but he wanted to address Ev's worry. Unfortunately, the admonition escalated Doro's anxiety. Was Mrs. Fulton, willingly or unwillingly, involved in a ruse? The question plagued Doro. Once again, Doro took a deep breath. "I understand," she murmured.

"I'll be right next to you," Ev added.

"Be careful," Wade said. "If something happens, you've got plenty of back-up, and I'll be one of them."

Ev clapped his friend on the shoulder. "I know you will."

Aggie, who sat in front with Wade, swiveled around. "I know you'll both be fine."

"Thanks," Doro replied before letting Ev help her out of the vehicle. When he tucked her hand into the crook of his arm, she felt her tension ebb. Nothing bad would happen. Not to either of them. Mrs. Fulton had been truly grief-stricken over her husband's death, so she was not responsible. Doro clung to the belief like she would to a life raft in choppy water.

As they crept toward the diner, Ev whispered to her. "Let's be cautious. Even though help is here, and there's been no trouble, restraint is best. We'll stop at the side of the doorway, so we aren't silhouetted in light. When we see Mrs. Fulton, go ahead and call out to her, like we already discussed. Then, we wait."

"I remember."

"I know you do," he said. "The reminder is also for me."

Doro knew he didn't need a reminder, just the knowledge that he was doing everything in his power to keep her safe. Her reply was to squeeze his arm. "Let's get it behind us."

When they passed through the parking lot, only one vehicle was visible. It had to belong to Mrs. Fulton's friend. As they got closer to the building, Ev slowed his steps and Doro did, too. He laid his free hand over hers where it was safely tucked against his side and gently squeezed it. Then, he pulled out his weapon and cocked the trigger. While she knew his action was wise, Doro felt a surge of renewed fear. She fought it back and focused on her surroundings. Staying alert could be crucial.

The small window in the back door revealed lights on in the kitchen, but no figures were visible. Since the door was solid, someone could be behind it. Anyone could be.

"Call out to her," Ev murmured in Doro's ear.

"Mrs. Fulton, I'm here with just one lawman," Doro managed over the lump in her throat. "You and your friend can come outside now." Silence resonated in the night air. "Mrs. Fulton. Are you there?"

The door opened a crack before a female voice replied, "Yes. Just a moment."

The delay increased Doro's uneasiness. Why didn't the women come out? She was about to ask Ev what they should do when he spoke again.

"There's someone inside near the window. A man from the size of the figure," he whispered as he stepped in front of Doro in a gesture of protection.

If bullets flew, they would hit him first. The thought was not reassuring to her.

"Go ahead and call out again," Ev whispered.

Doro licked her dry lips. "Mrs. Fulton, I'm here with my sweetheart. He'll drive all of us, your friend included, to safety." The shape did not move, and no reply came. "Mrs. Fulton?" Abruptly, the form moved and one arm came up. Doro did not take time to think. Instead, she threw herself against Ev. A whoosh of breath left him as they both fell to the ground, but he immediately wrapped his arms around her and rolled away from the door. At the same time, gunfire sounded. Doro went rigid with fear, but Ev did not moan or move. Surely, he had not been hit. Before she could ask, shouts followed the shots. From the corner of her eye, Doro saw men—hunched low and zig-zagging—racing toward the diner. Since they came from several directions, the shooters had to be lawmen, since they had been positioned in various spots. Relief made her muscles go slack.

"Are you all right?" Ev asked.

"Fine. What about you?"

"Fine, too," he replied, but his low groan belied the statement.

When he moved to let her up, Doro studied his features, which were contorted with pain. "You are not fine. Were you hit?"

"No. I banged my arm when we dove to the ground," he muttered from between clenched teeth.

Doro put one hand against his shoulder. No moisture came through the bandage and shirt, which was a good sign. "We can check it when we get out of here."

"It'll be all right."

All around them, men shouted and more shots ensued. Doro listened to see if she could determine how many people inside the diner were shooting, but that proved impossible. Then, a high-pitched scream cut through the air. "Maybe that was Mrs. Fulton," Doro murmured. She started to get up, but Ev pulled her back down.

"Wait. Someone could be holding her hostage," Ev whispered. "Some of the agents and officers undoubtedly went in the front door. Let's not rush to stand."

"All right," Doro replied.

After a moment, Canton's voice reverberated through the air. "We've got the culprits."

Immediately, Ev heaved himself to his feet and held out a hand to pull Doro up.

Wade joined them within a moment. "How are you two?"

"Good," Ev replied. "I didn't see who started shooting. Do you know?"

"No. I stayed in the car with Aggie," Wade said.

When Lowery Canton emerged from the diner's back door, Ev addressed him. "What happened?"

The agent looked at Doro. "Your hunch that the widow was held against her will for the past few days turned out to be true. Patrick Sweebe and a couple of others picked her up. She's been at Cutter Yarrow's place since then."

"Yarrow?" Ev echoed. "Is he here?"

"No," Canton replied. "He's too cagey for that, but we'll pick him up today. Sweebe and two others were with her tonight. His accomplices gave up quickly."

"What about Mrs. Fulton's friend?" Wade inquired.

"Not here," Canton said. "We'll interview the widow at the hospital and see what she knows."

"Is Sweebe still inside?" Ev asked.

"He is, but my agents will bring him out shortly. He's got a flesh wound. Mrs. Fulton's shoulder or collarbone is injured, so we'll go to the hospital. We can question both of them there. The two other guys, as well."

As Doro glanced around the area, she noted lawmen escorting Sweebe out. Although unsteady on his feet, he grinned at her when he got close. "Too bad we didn't have that dance. It may be a while before I'm free to get another chance."

"If you were involved in Fulton's death, you won't be dancing at all," Ev told him.

Patrick sneered. "I only went along with Cutter, because the old guy was not only working with the Keslers, he was stealing booze. Cutter wanted to set him straight, not kill him, but Fulton came at him. He fell and hit his head. Like I said. I was a bystander."

"Maybe. Maybe not," Ev said.

Some of Patrick's bravado slipped. "I'll tell you whatever you want to know. I'm not taking the blame for murder."

But was it murder if Yarrow had only wanted to scare Fulton? Doro wasn't sure, but she planned to ask later.

"Come on, Sweebe," Canton said. "We'll get you to the hospital and talk after you're treated."

Mrs. Fulton, on the arm of another agent, stumbled out of the diner. "I need a doctor." She jerked a thumb at Sweebe. "He needs to be in jail."

Doro searched the widow's pale face. "The police will escort you."

"I want you to be there, too," the widow insisted.

Doro glanced at Canton, who nodded. "All right."

After Mrs. Fulton was led away by two agents, Doro took Ev's arm. "You need a doctor, too."

"Maybe."

"Definitely," she murmured as they returned to Wade's vehicle.

Chapter Fifteen

Doro paced restlessly outside the treatment room while a doctor tended to Ev. Aggie and Wade had headed home after taking them to the hospital, and Canton went with Patrick Sweebe to another room. Two other agents stayed with Mrs. Fulton. Doro wasn't sure about Sweebe's accomplices, who had been led away at the diner. Maybe they were under arrest already.

An hour later, Ev emerged, looking tired and pale. Doro jumped to her feet. "How are you?"

"All right. The doc had to put in fresh stitches." He looked down the hall. "No word on the widow or Sweebe yet?"

"Just the basics," she replied. "Sweebe took a bullet to the shoulder. Mrs. Fulton broke her collarbone when she fell to get out of the line of fire. A doctor is taking care of her. Not much they can do for her except put her arm in a sling and give her medication."

Ev had just taken a seat when Canton signaled to them. "Looks like they're ready."

Doro took Ev's arm. In response, he reached for her hand. "I hope this doesn't take too long," Doro murmured. "Patrick seemed cooperative at the diner, but he might've changed his mind by now."

"If he's smart and innocent, he hasn't," Ev said.

"We'll see if he's either one," Canton put in. "First, I want to talk with Mrs. Fulton. The doctor let me know we can see her for a few minutes. Professor Banyon, I'd like you to come along."

"Of course," Doro agreed.

"You, too, Ev." Canton gestured to the half-open door.

Doro stepped into the small cubicle just ahead of Ev while the senior agent followed. The widow, her face pinched and pale, was propped against several pillows. "How are you feeling, Mrs. Fulton?"

"Tired and hurting," the woman replied.

"We won't keep you long, but we need details about your kidnapping, so the lawmen can arrest those involved," Doro told her. She paused for a heartbeat before continuing. "The same men are suspects in your husband's death."

Mrs. Fulton looked from Canton to Ev. "Did you arrest Patrick?"

"Not yet, ma'am," he replied.

Her gaze narrowed. "You better not let him go."

"We don't plan to," Canton said.

"And who are you?" the widow asked.

After explaining his role, the federal agent continued. "If you could tell us what happened, that would be useful." Canton pulled a notepad and pencil out of his jacket pocket before handing both to Doro. "If you don't mind."

"Not at all," she assured him.

The widow fingered the sling on her left arm. "After I left the diner last week, I was going into the city. My friend's husband didn't want me staying with them in the upstairs apartment at the diner. I didn't like leaving, cuz I felt safe there, but what choice did I have? He told me about a cheap hotel downtown. Some friend of his runs it. Abe and Beatrice figured I'd be safe there. Or so they said."

When the woman's voice trailed off, Doro filled in. "Was your friend's husband behind your abduction?"

Mrs. Fulton shook her head. "Nope. He works for the Kesler boys and didn't want to draw fire from the Zee-Yarrow gang. He didn't want me around cuz of that."

"What's his name?" Canton inquired.

"Abe Jacoby. My friend is Beatrice," the widow said. "She's not involved in the illegal doings. She's been after Abe to quit."

Although Mrs. Fulton sounded certain, Doro had doubts, but they were a small part of the case. "Mr. Jacoby knew who was responsible for your husband's death?" Doro wondered if the friend's husband had been involved in the shootout at the speakeasy.

Tears filled the widow's eyes. "He figured out somebody from the Zee-Yarrow gang had to have killed my husband, so he and Phil Kesler came to our place that night. They'd heard

John was in trouble with those gangsters. Plus, he had booze for them, too, so he knew they were coming."

"In Kesler's burgundy Cadillac," Canton observed.

Mrs. Fulton wiped the moisture from her cheeks. "Yes. Phil borrowed it from a brother. His vehicle is more easily identifiable."

Doro stopped writing. "Did you know men from the Zee-Yarrow would be at your place that night?"

The widow shook her. "John never said anything, so maybe he was surprised, too. He didn't take time to tell me anything other than to hide. Anyhow, I was scared silly by the time Abe and young Kesler arrived, so they drove me to the diner and I stayed there for a few days."

Sudden realization hit Doro. "When you left our meeting on Thursday morning, you went to the back of the diner and re-entered that way."

The widow briefly bowed her head before looking at Doro. "I did."

"And the waitress blocked me from following you on purpose," Doro suggested.

"Beatrice wanted to make sure you and your friend were occupied when I arrived and left," Mrs. Fulton replied.

Ev winked at Doro. "Like I've said before, you're intuitive and astute."

As always, his praise filled Doro with pleasure, but she addressed her next question to the widow. "What about your vehicle?"

"Abe drove it into the city and left it," she replied. "One of Kesler's men gave him a ride back to the diner."

Doro paused in her notetaking. "You didn't go into the city until after meeting with Aggie and me."

"That's right, but leaving the car there was to throw Yarrow off," the widow said. "When Abe returned to the restaurant, he confirmed that Yarrow and Sweebe were the ones who went into the barn with John. I honestly didn't know for sure until Abe told me what he'd learned from Phil Kesler."

"How did Kesler find out?" Ev asked.

The widow swallowed hard. "A man who does odd jobs and errands for the Keslers and the Zee-Yarrow gang was talking about John's death. He heard rumors when he was helping with a delivery at Zee and Yarrow's fancy place. When Phil Kesler got word, he talked to the man. Abe was there and heard everything the two of them discussed."

"I'm surprised word spreads so easily," Doro murmured.

"I'm not," Ev put in. "It isn't unusual for guys to do errands for more than one bootlegger, and gossip is common. Especially if it involves violence, since it's a way to warn others about being careful."

Doro tapped her pencil against the notepad. "I'd think men who work for two or more gangsters wouldn't want it known."

"As long as they're only doing odd jobs and not telling the cops anything, no one cares," Ev said. "And, like in this case, sometimes carrying tales is helpful to the gang. Phil Kesler would probably like word to get to the cops about who killed Mr. Fulton, since it'd take suspicion off him and his brothers."

"That makes sense," Doro observed before turning her thoughts back to the night of the killing. She shifted to study the widow. "Surely, they knew you were in the house. Why didn't they come looking for you?"

A stricken expression blanketed Mrs. Fulton's face. "As soon as John saw the headlights, he told me to get in the cellar. Just like I told you." She paused before continuing. "There's a trap door under the bed in our room. Not at all easy to see, unless you know it's there. It goes to a small corner that's walled off from the storm cellar."

As she listened, Doro pictured the Fultons' backyard. She had only been there once, but a clear image emerged. "I saw a big door at the back of your house, one that must be to the storm cellar. Wade and Ev looked down there."

"We did, and neither of us noted anything unusual," Ev added.

"John walled off the little room and put in the trap door to it. That way we could go down from the bedroom, instead of needing to go outside," Mrs. Fulton explained. "He was thorough and cautious, because it was our hiding place in case of trouble. Not just in case of a bad storm." Her voice trembled, and her eyes again overflowed.

Doro, who was an arm's length from the older woman, reached out to pat her hand. "I'm so sorry. You had to be terrified."

Mrs. Fulton swallowed convulsively. "I was, especially when John didn't come for me. I was worried, but there were no gunshots, so I hoped all was well."

Canton rocked back on his heels. "I wouldn't have figured Yarrow would haul booze himself."

"He never dirtied his hands on menial labor," the widow said. "I didn't hear any of the conversation, since I was in the cellar, but Yarrow probably watched the other two haul the liquor."

Disappointment deflated Doro's optimism. Relying on Sweebe for the truth was fraught with uncertainty, but he might squeal, if that kept his neck out of the noose. "How did you get out?"

Mrs. Fulton scratched her broken collarbone. "I waited and waited. Not sure what to do until Abe showed up. He was the only other one who knew about the secret room and access to it. Well, he and Beatrice, but she wasn't with him. Only young Kesler was."

While Doro did not doubt the woman, she wondered how Ev felt about the widow's assertions. A glance revealed he was weighing her words.

Lowery Canton folded his arms across his waist. "So, Abe Jacoby and Phil Kesler helped you get away, out of the goodness of their hearts." Sarcasm underscored his statement.

Mrs. Fulton's chin went up as she focused on the agent. "As far as I can tell, Phil Kesler doesn't have a heart, but he has a rumrunning operation and speakeasies to protect. He wanted to know exactly what John had been doing and with who."

Ev, who looked worn out, leaned against the wall. "What did you tell him?"

A long, low breath eased out of the widow. "Everything I knew. I thought the Keslers might settle the score with Zee and Yarrow."

The memory of squealing tires and gunfire echoed in Doro's head. Had the Kesler gang sought revenge for that night? But

Fulton had been working for both gangs. Hadn't he? "Why would they do that? Did the Keslers know your husband supplied booze to Zee and Yarrow?"

"They did, but John wasn't giving those two the best stuff. He saved that for the Keslers, because we knew their daddy from way back. He was Mr. Parson's partner in the speakeasy that replaced our saloon," Mrs. Fulton explained.

Several moments of silence followed the revelations. Why the woman had not shared that detail, Doro did not understand. She jotted notes, but her mind ran over the information again and again. The widow's words rang true since she had said the same that morning in the diner. "The Keslers didn't mind Mr. Fulton supplying inferior liquor to another gang."

"No. The brothers, like their father, only wanted top-notch alcohol for their customers, inside or outside of the speakeasies. The boys are a little rough around the edges, but they have a high-class clientele," the older woman observed.

Canton stroked his now-stubbled chin. "Did Yarrow and Zee know they were getting low-grade booze?"

Anxiety flashed in the widow's eyes. "Not until recently. The liquor they kept at our place was going from Detroit to Chicago, not to their speakeasies. If they needed some from a shipment, they took it out before it came to us. We stored alcohol in the barn, and Patrick Sweebe's brothers came for it within a few days, as a rule."

"What about the liquor you kept for the Keslers? What was its origin?" Canton asked.

"Usually, Canada. For a while, they got it from shipments coming across the lake, but the feds got on to that," she said.

A smile pulled up one corner of Canton's mouth. "We've been on to the route for years. I'd like to stop all traffic, but it's impossible. As for the Keslers, we had them under close scrutiny for quite a while."

Mrs. Fulton's expression softened. "Which is why they started having booze brought through Detroit instead of across Lake Erie. Their runs through Detroit started last year. John and I moving to the cottage outside Michaw made it easier to store liquor when the heat was on, and it would've been risky to take the liquor to the Toledo speakeasies."

"Was you husband also selling liquor to people in the Michaw area?" Ev asked.

The woman's gaze fell to her clasped hands. "When there were extra bottles."

"Bottles that should've gone to Zee and Yarrow," Canton suggested.

When Mrs. Fulton looked up, her expression was resolute. "Usually. Sometimes, he nabbed a few from the Keslers' stock, but not as often."

"Did Mr. Fulton deliver locally or did folks pick up bottles?" Ev asked.

"Alf Waggoner does chores for a few people. One is Jug Barnes. Jug likes a daily nip or two, so he bought booze from John now and again. Alf often took a couple bottles to him. Then, he and Jug took booze to others in the area."

The information evoked a question. "Would Alf and Jug have gone to your house that Saturday night?"

Mrs. Fulton put a hand to her head. "They were supposed to come for a case of liquor that John took out of a shipment going to Zee and Yarrow. I never saw either Jug or Alf that evening."

"They went back last night, and a neighbor saw them," Ev filled in.

Since that fact had not been established, Doro knew he was fishing.

"I don't know about that," the widow said.

"I don't suppose you know where Alf might be now, either," Canton put in. "He's only been seen once since that Saturday morning at your place."

For a moment, Mrs. Fulton seemed to weigh ideas. "If Alf isn't at home, he may be at Jug's farm. The boy enjoys helping with the animals, and Jug likes the company."

Although Alf's sisters had not mentioned the possibility, the explanations were compelling. "Now, what about Patrick Sweebe and Cutter Yarrow nabbing you?" Doro asked.

"After a day or so, Abe had my vehicle brought to a place not far from the diner. I drove his vehicle there, got mine back, and went into town."

Canton scowled. "I didn't like your vehicle being left there, since monitoring it all the time was impossible. The city police should've impounded it after no cab company had a record of picking you up."

Although she did not find the senior agent likeable, Doro admired his shrewdness. She addressed the widow with another facet of the story. "Did you leave for the city right after talking with Aggie and me?"

"Not too long after that."

The woman was cagey, Doro thought. "Were you followed into town?"

Mrs. Fulton shook her head. "I don't think so. I went to the little hotel and stayed there, except to go out once a day for food. Unfortunately, my luck ran out the fourth day. I tried to run, but Patrick caught me and dragged me into his vehicle. We went to Cutter Yarrow's apartment. He's the one who decided to use me to get coppers in their sights. Not that they expected so many. I didn't, either."

"Did Yarrow know Ev is a lawman?" Doro asked.

"Not for sure, but he was suspicious," the widow said. "Patrick was looking out a front upstairs window at the Zee-Yarrow speakeasy when your beau got shot. Patrick immediately told Cutter, which is why they wanted me to get ahold of you tonight. Well, this morning. They knew the Prohis raided another place and didn't figure on them getting involved at the diner."

"But Sweebe and Yarrow were wrong," Canton observed. "We wrapped it up faster than usual, but my men were still in the office."

"Luckily," Ev murmured. "But you called Doro in Michaw when Sweebe and Yarrow knew she'd been in the speakeasy."

"They wanted to make it look good. Then, calling the Prohibition Bureau didn't seem so odd," Mrs. Fulton said.

"If Yarrow knew about the raid, why call there at all?" Doro asked, puzzled by the turn of events.

The older woman looked at Lowery Canton before replying. "Someone inside your office is giving him information, so Cutter's aware one agent always stays behind when the others are on a raid."

Dismay, or maybe disgust, darkened Canton's gaze. "It's been how we operate for a while, and I've worried about our moves being revealed. Now, I've got another mystery to solve—finding the man taking money." His jaw tightened and released. "For right now, I need to know anything else that will lead us to Yarrow and help keep him and the others behind bars for a long time."

After plucking at the blanket covering her, Mrs. Fulton looked back at the agent. "I don't know who hit John. No one said, even though I asked."

Her statement led to another question from Doro. "How do you know your husband got hit?" She took care not to say where or with what.

Mrs. Fulton bit her trembling lower lip. "Abe and Phillip looked in the barn first, because there was a lantern glowing. When they rescued me from the cellar, Abe told me John was dead, but I had to see for myself..." Her voice grew hoarse before trailing off.

Doro gently squeezed the woman's arm. "I'm so sorry"

The older woman nodded but did not reply.

"We all are," Ev added.

A look of surprise crossed Mrs. Fulton's face. "What we were doing is illegal."

"But your husband didn't deserve to die for it," Ev told her.

"No, he didn't," Canton agreed.

As she glanced from Ev to Canton, Mrs. Fulton took a deep breath. "I suppose you'll arrest me along with the others."

The woman's fear was palpable, and Doro didn't blame her. "You didn't do anything so wrong by calling me. After all, you were being held prisoner, so you had little choice."

"Not tonight, but I agreed to the bootlegging," she said. "We needed the money, but still. It's illegal."

Ev pushed away from the wall. "It sounds like your husband made most of the connections and such. It's not my decision, but Agent Canton is a fair man."

Lowery's lips twitched. "You've been very helpful, ma'am. I see no reason to arrest you tonight, and I'll do my best to see that doesn't happen in the future."

"Thank you, thank you," the widow said in a tremulous voice.

Color crept into the agent's thin face. "Sure. Now, do you have a place to go? One of my men can drive you, when you're released."

"The doctor wants me to stay overnight," the widow replied.

"A good idea," Doro said, especially since returning to her home wasn't safe, but neither was going to the hotel or the diner. By morning, they could find a place for her. For now, she was safe and comfortable in the hospital.

A nurse entered the tiny room. "Our patient needs her rest."

"We were about to leave." Canton turned to the woman on the gurney. "Thanks for your help. I'll check on you in the morning."

After Doro and Ev bid farewell to the woman, they went into the corridor. "What next?" she asked.

"Talking to Sweebe, but I want to tell Ev what the other agents learned while he was getting stitched up," Canton replied.

The words sounded like a subtle dismissal, but Doro was not ready to walk away. She lifted the notepad. "I can jot everything down, so that it's in one place."

Canton looked ready to reject the suggestion, but Ev spoke first. "Doro has done a lot of work on this case. Tonight, she put herself in danger twice. She deserves to be further involved."

The federal agent's nostrils flared with a sharp intake of breath. After he exhaled, Canton nodded. "All right."

Doro couldn't repress a smile. "I'll jot down everything that your men learned."

"Good idea," Ev said with a wink.

"Indeed," Canton agreed. "The agents interviewed the two guys with Sweebe. All of them claim they're lackeys. You caught glimpses of them at the diner, Ev. Did you recognize anyone?"

"The one guy was familiar." Ev glanced at Doro. "Remember when I told you, Aggie, and Wade about the man who brought up the Fulton killing?"

Doro nodded. "Yes. Was he on the scene tonight?"

"Yep. He was," Ev replied. "I saw him get led away at the end."

Canton swiveled toward Ev. "You didn't mention someone talking about the murder to me."

Ev put one hand up. "Because he got shushed up right away. I tried to get him alone to ask what he knows, because he might've been willing to talk more."

"He definitely was," Canton agreed. "Turns out he was with Sweebe and Yarrow when Fulton died."

"Did he see what happened?" Ev asked.

"Nope. He was outside the barn," Canton replied.

"Do you think he's the man who told Philip Kesler about what happened that night?" Doro inquired.

"That's my guess," Canton replied.

"Ollie Carlisle," Ev said.

"That's right," Canton agreed.

Doro shifted toward Ev. "You told us about him earlier."

A frown darkened Canton's face. "Why don't I know about this discussion?"

Ev put one hand up. "I told Doro, Aggie, and Wade, so he could call you with information, since I wasn't expected to see you tonight." Briefly, Ev revealed what he had said to the others.

Doro looked at Canton. "It sounds like you already know about him."

The federal agent cast a glance her way. "Ollie does odd jobs around the speakeasies. Sometimes, he helps haul liquor. Anyhow, he'd admitted to going along because Yarrow planned to take whatever alcohol was in the Fulton barn. Carlisle and Sweebe carried most of it out before Fulton appeared. Carlisle was putting bottles in Yarrow's trunk when he heard Yarrow and Fulton arguing. Then, silence before Yarrow and Sweebe rushed out and got in the car. They sat in the front seat, while Carlisle got in back. He only got snippets of their conversation, but it sounded like Yarrow's the one who picked up a bottle and clobbered Fulton."

"Out of anger," Doro suggested.

Canton confirmed the supposition. "We already knew Yarrow is ill-tempered and highly suspicious. He's gotten into more than a few fracases."

"Hence, his nickname." Doro looked at Ev, whose jaw was set in a hard line. Was he thinking what she was: that he'd be dead now if he had gone to the meeting in Zee's office? Once again, her decision to go to the speakeasy seemed wise.

Ev ran one hand over his face. "Carlisle won't be a good witness, since he didn't actually see anything."

"True, which is why I plan to pressure Sweebe. If Yarrow is the one who hit Fulton, Sweebe may want to save himself by being honest," Canton said.

Doro wrestled with the possibilities. "How can you be sure that it was Yarrow who did the deed?"

"Carlisle has nothing to gain by targeting Yarrow," the federal agent said. "If anything, he took a chance by telling what he witnessed."

"I suppose," Doro murmured.

Ev laid a hand on her arm. "We'll find out more by talking to Sweebe. You're insightful, so just watching him will help."

His support buoyed Doro's spirits. They were close to solving the mystery, and the next interview might make all the difference.

Chapter Sixteen

Canton led the way down the narrow corridor to where two of his agents stood by a half-open door. "Stay here," he said. "I assume Sweebe is restrained." Both men nodded. The senior agent nodded to Ev. "Go ahead."

As Ev held the door for her, Doro slipped inside. Sweebe, who was manacled to the bed, looked up. "Hello again, little lady." He touched the thick bandage peeking out from under the hospital gown. "Some feminine attention will ease the pain from my gunshot wound."

Doro gave him a fleeting glance but said nothing.

Canton gestured toward the only chair. "Sit down, Professor."

Sweebe's eyes went wide as he scanned Doro from the top of her head to the tips of her toes. "Professor. Wow. I sure never imagined college faculty dressed in such an interesting manner. I miss your pretty feather."

Doro's hand went to her head. The band was gone, not that she cared. "You'll miss your freedom much more."

A snort of laughter left Sweebe. "Don't try and convict me before I have a chance to defend myself, pretty lady."

"Enough sweet talk," Ev said. "You said you're willing to give details about what happened at the Fulton house that Saturday night. If you're honest, it could help you. If not, you may cook your own goose."

The gangster's amusement dissipated as he stared at Ev. "So, Ed, you're a copper, just as Cutter suspected."

"I am a deputy constable in Michaw, and I'm helping the Bureau now," Ev confirmed. "Where are Zee and Yarrow?"

"Zee is probably at the lake house," Patrick replied. "Not sure where Yarrow went."

Canton stepped forward. "At the diner, you said a little, but we need more information now."

The amusement left Sweebe's expression. "Carlisle blabbed."

His supposition hung in the air, but neither Canton nor Ev confirmed it. "What would he know?" Ev asked.

With one hand, Sweebe massaged his neck. "If he said I hit the old man, he lied."

When both Ev and Canton nodded at her, Doro girded herself to ask the right questions. "Why don't you tell us what happened? Then, we can decide who's being honest."

Sweebe looked taken aback as he scanned her again. "Are you really a professor or are you an agent? I heard the Prohibition Bureau hired ladies, but you're the first one I've seen."

A slight smile formed on Doro's lips. "Maybe you've seen others and not recognized them." Her comment neither acknowledged nor denied his observation, which seemed best. Let the gangster think she was a fed.

He shook his head. "If so, I'm not as sharp as I used to be." His gaze moved to Ev. "But I didn't tag you as one, either. Cutter insisted you were, because he didn't believe the story about you going to Cincinnati and ending up in jail. He didn't realize you were right in Michaw, though. Of course, he only went to the Fulton place twice."

"One was the night of Mr. Fulton's death," Ev observed.

"Yep," Sweebe replied.

Several questions percolated in Doro's mind and, when the gangster did not continue, she asked one of them. "Why didn't you ever come into Michaw?"

The blonde shrugged. "Mr. Zee insisted we stay out of all small towns. Cutter agreed, because strangers stand out, and we don't need extra notice taken. In the city, we blend in better."

Recalling Patrick Sweebe's role as a waiter, Doro felt convinced he could maintain a cover himself. "I suppose that's important, especially when another gang targets yours."

His lips twitched. "That's right."

"How did Mr. Zee feel about you and Yarrow sparking the Kesler family's wrath?" Canton inquired.

A scowl blanketed Sweebe's face. "I didn't have anything to do with that. Cutter insisted on going to the Fulton place, grabbing whatever liquor was around, and scaring the heck out of Fulton, so he would stop filching booze and working with the Keslers. I thought Mr. Zee knew we were going, but he didn't."

Ev's gaze narrowed on the gangster. "How did he react?"

A guffaw left Sweebe. "Not well, and that's a big reason why he didn't listen to Cutter's suspicions about you. Of course, that might've changed at the meeting scheduled for last night."

The last sentence indicated *might* actually meant *would* which sent a chill through Doro, but Ev had no outward reaction.

"Does Mr. Zee know exactly what happened at the Fulton place?" Canton asked.

Sweebe bowed his head. "Mostly, he does. He didn't like it, especially after the Keslers shot up the speakeasy."

Ev braced his good shoulder against the wall. "Where are he and Yarrow?"

"It turns out Mr. Zee went to the lake alone," Sweebe replied. "Cutter is around town, although he may take off when he hears what happened at the diner."

"How will he hear what occurred? You and Carlisle are here," Doro said. "Your other henchman is, too, and he's talking."

"You're sharp, Professor. Or is it, Agent?" Sweebe asked.

Doro laid her notepad and pencil down. "It doesn't matter. What matters is you telling us the truth. So far, you haven't provided details, although we have many from Mr. Carlisle and Mrs. Fulton." While the statement was bold, it had the desired effect because Sweebe sat up in bed before looking from Ev to Canton.

"What all did they say?" the gangster asked.

A look of satisfaction covered Canton's face. "Tell us what you know, and we may share their other comments."

Long moments of silence passed. When Sweebe kept quiet, Ev chipped in. "You're in a tough place, Patrick. If you're blamed for Fulton's death, you'll face a murder rap."

All color fled Sweebe's handsome face. Was the man finally taking his situation seriously? Although what they knew did not place blame on him, getting Sweebe to corroborate stories from Carlisle and Mrs. Fulton was important. As was finding Yarrow. Doro searched her mind for a way to glean the necessary facts. Pushing the young gangster from worried to cooperative was key. "Just tell us what happened that night." Doro used her most cajoling tone and aimed for a concerned expression.

Sweebe bowed his head. When he looked up, he nodded. "All right, but I better not be turned out on the street for Cutter to come after me, and he will if he finds out I blabbed to feds."

"Even if you had nothing to do with Fulton's death, we're not sweeping your involvement in bootlegging under the rug," Canton said, "so, you won't be loose soon."

Resignation underscored Sweebe's response. "Better jailed than dead."

"Yep," Ev agreed. "Only one has a good ending."

"I guess." Sweebe cleared his throat and began telling a tale much like what Mrs. Fulton and Carlisle had shared, but with a first-hand description. "Fulton was yelling at Cutter while Carlisle and I hauled the last crates of booze out. We didn't bother with loose bottles. He kept saying the Keslers would be after him for not keeping their shipment safe. Cutter didn't care, because the old guy had filched more than a little liquor from us over the past six months. I walked back into the barn just as Fulton grabbed Cutter by the arm. Cutter had a big bottle in his hand and whacked Fulton, who fell against the wagon's corner. I knew right off he was dead, so we skedaddled. Carlisle and I did a quick search of the house in case Mrs. Fulton witnessed anything."

Doro paused in her notetaking. "She was in a hidden room beneath the house."

"So, she told us after we nabbed her," Sweebe murmured. "What kind of witness will she be if she was out of hearing and sight range?"

"Mrs. Fulton saw Yarrow's LaSalle pull in," Canton replied. "It's distinctive."

Sweebe nodded. "She didn't share that bit of information."

"Where did you put the booze?" Ev asked.

"Zee and Yarrow have several storage places in the city. This batch was good stuff, so it went to one close to the fancy speakeasy. Some of it is still there," Sweebe said. "Some is stored nearby."

"I need the address of the storage place," Canton put in.

After he provided the location, Sweebe continued. "If you catch Cutter, he'll try to push the blame on Carlisle or me."

"Not surprising," Ev commented, "but the evidence so far is heavily against him. Is there a chance he'll leave the area quickly?"

Sweebe shook his head. "He'll need to get money and belongings together first. He may already be doing that since it's after eight o'clock."

"Maybe so," Canton commented. "But getting into a bank will need to wait until nine."

The noncommittal statement made Doro think federal agents were already on Yarrow's trail. She hoped so.

Once they were back in the corridor, Doro handed the notepad and pencil to Canton. "You should be able to read my handwriting. If not, I'm happy to go over it with you."

After tucking the supplies into his jacket pocket, the agent addressed Doro. "As Ev said earlier, you've gone above and beyond an amateur sleuth's purview. I appreciate it, but I'm sure I can read your notes. Constable Lammers and Professor Darwine left after we knew Ev would be all right, so I had an agent bring his vehicle here. You should drive back to Michaw, though. Then, he ought to rest."

Pleasure spread through Doro. Despite Canton's initial attitude, the man now seemed to respect her efforts. "I agree on both counts."

Ev grimaced. "I'm fine. Besides, we need to find Alf Waggoner and Jug Barnes. Yarrow's apt to be in the city, but you never know."

Canton put one hand up. "I've got men hunting for Yarrow, and Lammers will check on Waggoner and Barnes. Talk to him when you get home. Your vehicle is in the hospital parking lot."

For a moment, Ev looked like he might object. Then, he nodded. "All right."

"I'll be in touch as soon as we find Yarrow," the agent said. "Until then, hold tight."

Although Doro knew Canton meant to wait patiently, she clasped Ev's arm. Hanging on tight to him was her first interest.

The trip home was punctuated with long silences, mostly because Doro felt exhaustion weigh down on her like an anchor. After a while, she figured Ev was asleep but he shifted to look out the window before speaking. "A new day has started."

"It has, but you should rest."

"My mind is whirling," he said. "Isn't yours?"

"It is," she admitted. "I'm relieved we found Mrs. Fulton and glad to know what happened to her husband."

"I am, too. There's some information to confirm and corroborate, but the killer is known. As for the bootlegging, Canton and his men will have their hands full. But that's nothing new."

Doro cast a sidelong glance at Ev. With the sun now climbing in the sky, his face was visible. The dark circles under his eyes seemed more pronounced. Exhaustion and pain might keep him down for a day, maybe two, but he wouldn't rest long. That certainty dictated her next words. "Will you go back and help them?"

"No," was his immediate reply.

"You're sure about that?"

"Absolutely sure. Identifying Fulton's killer was first and foremost. Once I got inside the Zee-Yarrow gang, getting information on their business was important. Now, Canton has plenty to move cases forward. I'm not sure he'll nab Zee, who's a lot more cautious than Yarrow, but he can grab some of the Kesler gang."

"Because Philip's vehicle was seen the night Mr. Fulton died and because they hit the speakeasy last night." Doro made both observations instead of questions.

"Yep. Wade will testify to what he saw. You might be called as a witness to what happened last night. At the very least, you'll have to give an official statement."

"Both are fine. I want to help put as many bootleggers behind bars as possible. They're a menace."

"They create a lot of violence," Ev murmured.

"But you think Alf is safe." Worry for the boy had not completely left her.

"I agree that he may be with Jug, and I'm sure Wade has checked by now. For that reason, I'd like to drive by the constable's office."

Dismay filled Doro. "I can do that after I drop you at your place."

"Talking with Wade won't take long."

"What if he's not at the office?"

An audible sigh left Ev. "Then, I'll go home."

Silently, Doro hoped Wade was out-and-about. However, as soon as she turned on to Main Street, Doro saw Wade's vehicle. "He's at work."

Ev chuckled. "You sound disappointed. Don't you want to know what he found out about Alf?"

"I do, but..." Her voice trailed off before she admitted how uneasy she still was. "Sure. Let's find out."

Although he gave her an odd look, Ev was at the driver's door to help Doro out before she killed the engine. She preceded him into the building, where Wade sat behind his desk and Aggie was across from him. Both looked at Doro and Ev as they entered.

"Come sit down," Aggie urged. "You two have to be exhausted."

After doing as her friend suggested, Doro waited until Ev also took a seat. "You haven't slept, either, have you?" she asked her friend.

Aggie shook her head. "No. I wanted to stay with Wade while he made calls."

The constable smiled. "Having moral support was nice. Our local operator was none too happy with me for getting her up early. Or keeping her on the line for a long while."

Doro could not help but chuckle. "I'm sure she wasn't, but what did you find out?"

"Alf was with Jug at his place. I talked to both of them." Wade glanced at Ev. "Jug admitted to going to Fulton's house the night of the killing. When they saw the LaSalle parked by the barn, they took off. When Jug came to tell me, Alf hid in his truck. After that, they went back to where the boy's jalopy was left."

"I'm guessing both of them were scared," Ev said.

"Very much so," Wade agreed. "But they still went back last night. The night of the murder, he and the kid were supposed to pick up some extra bottles of booze. They didn't find it, so it's probably in the area of the cellar where Mrs. Fulton hid."

"She could've told us," Doro murmured.

Ev sighed. "I'll tell Lowery, and he can find out. Maybe she was just too upset to think about it. She had a harrowing experience."

Since Doro did not disagree, she nodded. "Bootlegging has long tentacles."

"It sure does," Wade concurred. "Evidently, Jug has been the middle man for selling some of the filched liquor to folks in the area. He's a small player, so I called Lowery's office, but he was still out."

"They're looking to pick up Yarrow," Ev said before revealing what all had happened after Aggie and Wade left the hospital.

Wade released a low whistle. "It looks like the murder case, if it gets charged as a murder, is solved."

Ev slumped back in his chair. "It could end up as manslaughter, but there's plenty else to charge Yarrow with."

"It sounds like some of the Keslers are in trouble, too," Aggie observed.

"Running everything down will take time, but both gangs will be hampered, if not broken up, for a long while," Ev agreed.

"Where is Alf now?" Doro asked.

"Jug Barnes planned to take the boy home," her friend replied.

"Good," Doro said. "I'm sure his mother and sisters will be relieved."

"Since they don't have a telephone, I plan to drive out. I spoke at length with Jug, and he knows he may be arrested for rumrunning. I want to speak with Mrs. Waggoner about Alf. And with the kid, too," Wade said.

One glance at Ev revealed he planned to ride along, so Doro spoke up. "Why don't we all go? Having two ladies along would ease Mrs. Waggoner's mind, I'm sure."

A weary grin lit Ev's face. "I'm sure it would."

Chapter Seventeen

Aggie and Wade climbed into the front seat of his Packard, while Doro and Ev settled in the back. Humidity shimmered in the morning air. As they passed fields of ripening crops, Doro let the peace of the countryside fill her. Another case was almost at a close. For that, she was grateful.

When they reached the Waggoner place, Doro led the way to the back door and knocked. Alf's mother, clad in a threadbare robe with her gray-streaked hair in a single braid, answered. She did not ask why the two couples were at her house. Instead, she ushered them into a dank parlor and urged them to be seated. "I could make coffee."

"Please don't go to any bother," Aggie said.

"No, don't," Doro agreed.

The woman wrapped her arms around her narrow waist and shifted from one foot to the other. "Jug Barnes told me about some goings-on when he brought Alf home."

"He's still here?" Wade asked.

"Oh, yes," his mother, her voice now firmer, said. "And Alf won't be going any place in the near future."

The sound of footsteps intruded, and Doro nearly laughed when she saw three pairs of bare feet appear on the staircase. Alf's sisters wanted a front row view.

"Could you get him, ma'am?" Ev asked.

"He's gathering eggs, but I'll holler for him to get in here," Mrs. Waggoner said. She left the room and, within moments, she was shouting for Alf to come inside pronto.

Only a couple of minutes later, Alf, who looked tired and miserable, appeared in the parlor. After being reassured that the lawmen were not there to arrest him, the boy settled on a small wooden chair.

"You know I spoke with Jug Barnes, so I've got the story about the night Mr. Fulton died."

"I know," the boy murmured. "Jug says the killer and others will get arrested, but how you gonna get so many of them when you're out here instead of in the city?"

Ev leveled his gaze on Alf. "Constable Lammers and I can't make arrests in Toledo. The city police and federal agents do, and they'll work together to get the bootleggers, especially the man who killed Mr. Fulton."

Tears filled the boy's eyes. "He and his missus was always good to me. What about her? You told Jug about her being safe. Is that right?"

"It is," Wade assured him.

Doro nodded. "She's staying at the hospital today. When she's released, federal agents will make sure she's in a good place."

"Good, but what about my ma and sisters?" Alf wiped his eyes with a shirt sleeve. I'm afeared for them."

"What Jug told you is right. The men who kidnapped Mrs. Fulton are already under arrest. Her husband's killer should be caught soon. Neither him nor any of the others will be coming out here. They're too busy trying to elude the law," Wade said.

"Good," the boy replied.

Mrs. Waggoner did not look as relieved. "You're sure we're safe out here?"

"Like Constable Lammers said, the bootleggers won't be after your family. Alf didn't do anything against or to them. He was an errand boy, not the one who stole booze and sold it," Ev said.

The woman nodded. "If you say so, but is my boy in trouble for working with them gangsters?"

"If he cooperates with federal agents, Alf won't be arrested. Errand boys rarely are," Ev told her.

"You're sure of that?" Mrs. Waggoner asked.

"I am," Ev replied. "I used to work for the Prohibition Bureau, and its task is to stop the making and selling of booze. Kids who help them don't merit much attention."

The tension drained from Mrs. Waggoner's expression. "That's a relief."

Ev focused on Alf. "You may need to talk with federal agents, but I'll come along."

"And we'll both help you as much as we can," Wade added.

"What about Jug?" Alf asked.

"That remains to be seen. For now, stay here. We'll be in touch in the next couple of days," Ev said.

"He's not going any place at all," the boy's mother assured them.

The reminder had Alf frowning, but girlish giggles sounded from the upstairs landing. Doro fought to withhold her own amusement. Alf would have his hands full, if his sisters and mother had any say.

⁂

After having a day to rest, everyone met in the Michaw constable's office the following afternoon. Ev leaned back in his chair and folded his arms across his narrow waist. Weariness still lined his face, but relief shone in his eyes. Wade looked equally reassured. Doro felt her tension ebb as she studied the two lawmen and listened to their latest news.

Earlier, Lowery Canton had called to say Cutter Yarrow, and several other members of the Zee-Yarrow gang were under arrest, as were a few of the Keslers. The whereabouts of Cal Zee was still unknown, since his lakefront house was empty and there was no sign of him at either Toledo speakeasy.

"This case took more effort and more time to crack, but our part is finished." Wade, who was seated on the other side of his desk, braced his elbows on the edge. "I, for one, am glad."

"I'm sure all of us are," Ev added, "but two weeks isn't bad for an investigation with so many facets."

As Doro listened, she thought back to two Saturdays ago. At this same time, she had been getting ready for her evening out with Ev, and cracking another case had been far from her mind.

Aggie nodded. "I feel better knowing bootleggers won't be coming out here anymore. But what will happen to the Fulton place?"

"They were only renting it, so I suppose someone else will eventually," Wade replied. "At least she's safe."

"Lowery will make sure she stays that way until after the trials. Then, he'll help her get out of the area. She has a cousin in California, which would be a good place for her," Ev observed.

"As far as possible seems like a wise idea. What did Agent Canton say about Alf?" Doro asked, still concerned about him and his family. What if agents decided he was lying? Would the boy be arrested?

"Lowery knows the kid didn't do anything more than run messages and lug booze into and out of storage," Ev said. "He never met Yarrow or Zee, only Sweebe, who paid him. Jug Barnes didn't know any of them, since he was only taking liquor from the Fulton place to local folks. And getting some for himself."

Doro considered the information. "I wonder why he was in town that day getting a big envelope. Surely, they didn't send him cash."

Both Ev and Wade guffawed before the former replied. "Actually, one of Patrick's younger brothers did mail cash from Chicago from time-to-time. Not the brightest boy. Anyhow, it's not too likely charges against him will be pursued, unless he continues to be a go-between, which I doubt. He was only involved with Fulton, for the most part, and the Sweebes on occasion. If he keeps talking, Barnes should do himself good."

"Him telling me what he saw the night of Fulton's death also puts him in a better light," Wade added. "As for Alf, as long as the kid doesn't get involved with another gang, he'll be fine."

Ev nodded. "I plan to see that he has other opportunities."

A smile touched Doro's mouth. "Ev called his sister in Cleveland. Her husband's parents just lost the couple who worked for them. Mrs. Waggoner can take over as housekeeper, and Alf will be the handyman. All the younger girls need to do is help with chores and go to school."

"How wonderful." Aggie clapped her hands together. "It was so kind of you to do that, Ev. Does the family know?"

Ev colored slightly. "Not yet. Doro and I are going over this afternoon. Even though I think they'd be safe here, it's good to be sure."

"They'll feel better, especially Mrs. Waggoner," Doro put in. "And Alf won't be tempted to go back to working for bootleggers."

"Which is important," Wade added.

"It is," Ev said, "and my sister will tutor him, so he can finish his schooling that way."

Pride and admiration filled Doro. Ev was truly a good man, and she was lucky to have him in her life.

Chapter Eighteen

The next week passed in a flurry of activity as Doro and Aggie prepared for the coming semester, and Ev and Wade helped to wrap up the murder case. Although Doro saw Ev several evenings, they spent little time alone. On two occasions, he went into Toledo to talk with Lowery Canton, but Ev mostly worked on campus and in town.

Late on the afternoon of her birthday, he picked her up at Wheaton Hall, and they drove to Sylvania with no further discussion of the past few weeks. Although she still loved sleuthing, Doro was happy to have a break from the stress and strain.

"My grandmother's house is the rusticated cement block two-story with a porch on two sides," Doro said as she drove down Summit Street in Sylvania.

"The one with the maple trees in front?" he asked.

"That's it," she replied.

"A pretty place with lots of room around it."

She downshifted and pulled into the drive. Since she had visited the home hundreds of times over the past almost-two decades, Doro had long ago stopped scrutinizing the structure. Now, she studied it before turning back to Ev. Was there a trace of longing in his voice? "You lived in a house growing up, didn't you?"

"Yeah, but in the city where your neighbors are only a few feet on either side. Nothing like this," he replied. "Michaw has lovely neighborhoods, too, but I've never seen a house made out of that material. It's beautiful. You called it rusticated?"

Doro followed his gaze. "That's what some people call it. The material is cement block made to look like cut stone. A local man has a company that produces it. My grandparents built the house in 1910. It was exciting when they moved in because it's so different. Most houses in Michaw are older and either brick or frame."

Ev got out and came around to open Doro's door. "The stone is pretty, and I love the big porch."

"So do I," Doro murmured as she exited the automobile. "I especially like the white wicker furniture. We had some in my childhood home. On the front and back porches. Gramma is storing it in the attic for me."

Seconds of silence passed before Ev spoke again. "You can use it in your own home."

Something in his tone made Doro study his expression. Again, she saw an emotion akin to longing. Her heart raced. How soon would they go from stepping out to courting? How soon did she want to make the change? Unsure, Doro smiled. "That's the idea."

"It's a good one."

Before they could say more, Gramma Rose stepped on to the porch and greeted them. "I'm glad you two came early." She moved to the front stairs and smiled at Ev. "You must be Everett Mallow. I've heard so much about you. All good."

Faint color crept into his tanned face. "I am Ev Mallow, ma'am, and thank you for inviting me."

"It's our pleasure to have you. Please sit down." She gestured to the group of chairs behind her.

"Thank you, ma'am," he replied before following Doro on to the porch. After both women were seated, Ev took the chair beside Doro.

The older woman's gaze went to his left arm. "Is your wound healing well?"

The pink in Ev's cheeks intensified. "Yes, ma'am. It was only a graze, and it's fine now."

Gramma Rose's expression indicated disbelief, which Doro shared. Although she had driven carefully, he had winced every time the car hit a rut. Because contradicting Ev would only embarrass him more, she moved to another topic. "It was nice of you to have us come early."

"From what you and Aggie told me when you visited the other day, Officer Mallow hasn't had a break for the past three weeks. With classes starting soon, I thought some quiet time relaxing on the porch would be pleasant for both of you," Gramma Rose replied. "Besides, someone needs to make ice cream. My housekeeper and I have a marble cake in the oven, but using the churn is laborious. Too much for either of us these days."

"My favorite cake," Doro said with unbridled enthusiasm. "Chocolate and white with chocolate frosting. Yum."

"It sounds fantastic." Ev grinned. "What kind of ice cream?"

"Vanilla goes well with the cake," Gramma Rose replied.

"Does the person who churns also get to taste test?" Ev's tone held a note of amusement.

"Of course," the older lady said. "But I won't put either of you to work until you have lemonade and cookies, Officer Mallow. Or can I call you Ev?"

"Ev is good," he told her.

"Ev, sit down and relax while Doro and I get refreshments. We won't be but a moment."

After following her grandmother into the kitchen, Doro greeted the housekeeper. Mrs. Ogilvie welcomed her with open arms. "Happy birthday," the lady said, stepping back and scanning Doro. "You look more and more like your mother with every passing year. Hair the color of milk chocolate and eyes like the sea. Those eyes are sparkling now. Glad to see that. I know you miss your folks on special occasions like today."

In a reflexive action, Doro touched the gold locket at her throat. Given to Doro's mother from her father years ago, the treasure had been passed down when Julia McLaren Banyon had left Michaw for a Colorado sanitorium. The jewelry served as a precious link to her family, so Doro wore it every day. "Thank you," she murmured. "Mother is so pretty."

"And you are, too, my dear," the housekeeper assured her. "In fact, I've never seen you look lovelier. Does it have something to do with your beau?"

Heat scorched Doro's cheeks. Ev was not really hers, but he might be in the future. That prospect kept her from objecting to the observation, although she did not directly address it. "Ev and I are going to make the ice cream. Since dinner is at six o'clock, we should do that after refreshments. We want it to be ready for dessert." She sniffed the air where hints of vanilla and chocolate lingered. "The cake smells wonderful."

"Your favorite," the housekeeper said. "Dinner will be, too. Fried chicken, cole slaw, baked beans, fresh tomatoes from my garden, and biscuits."

"What a wonderful meal," Doro replied.

Laughter rumbled out of the housekeeper. "You could pick up a few pounds. Now, let me make up a tray, and I'll carry it out. I'd like to meet your beau."

"I'd like you to meet him, too," Doro said without bothering to correct the woman.

After introducing the housekeeper and Ev, Doro spent a pleasant interlude with him and her grandmother drinking lemonade and eating cookies. "This is lovely," she murmured.

"It is," Ev agreed, "but as good as your shortbread is, I don't want to spoil my dinner."

"I hope you'll forgive an old lady for being impertinent, but you look a bit thin, my boy," Gramma Rose said.

Ev flushed. "I've lost a little weight lately."

Doro thought he had dropped more than a few pounds but did not comment. A young lady did not discuss a young man's physique. "I'm sure Mrs. Ogilvie made far more than enough, so you can take some home."

"You certainly can," her grandmother agreed.

Ev murmured his thanks.

"I'd like to take some cookies back with us," Doro said. "I promised the Waggoner girls a treat when I went again, but we headed there before I had a chance to get something, and I've been busy ever since."

"How thoughtful," her grandmother said. "Mrs. Ogilvie always bakes far more than we can eat, so I'll have her box up a couple of dozen."

"Wonderful," Doro said with a grin. "We'll go out tomorrow."

A smile wreathed Gramma Rose's face. "The two of you are spending time together, which is lovely." She turned to Ev. "I'll confess that I've wanted to meet you."

When another flush rose in Ev's lean cheeks, Doro felt a knot of apprehension. The housekeeper had referred to him as her beau. Doro did not mind, as long as Ev didn't hear it. "Yes, well. You have."

Her grandmother shot her an odd look before turning to Ev again. "I'm dying to know more about your last case. Doro has only had time to share the basics."

After Ev turned to Doro, she shrugged. "Gramma knows I went to a speakeasy, so you don't have to hide any details."

A chuckle left Rose McLaren. "I've been wondering about those places, and my granddaughter satisfied my curiosity. But I love whodunits, and I read them often, so the investigation is of great interest."

"Doro told me about you helping to solve the murder on your train trip home," Ev observed.

A satisfied smile lifted Gramma Rose's lips. "I enjoyed almost every minute." She cast a solemn glance at Doro. "Except for when Doro was missing."

"She has a penchant for taking risks," Ev said, his expression serious.

Doro put up one hand. "Just give Gramma Rose a summary of the case."

Ev chuckled. "Yes, ma'am." He took a long drink of lemonade before continuing. "You know we had a wide range of suspects at the start."

Gramma Rose nodded. "That made it a more troublesome case, didn't it?"

"It did," he agreed. "Anyone from either the Zee-Yarrow gang or the Kesler brothers' boys could've been responsible. We considered Jug Barnes, since he was a small-time customer of the Fultons and a sometimes delivery man for others. Then, there was Alf Waggoner, who was an errand boy, and even Mrs. Fulton."

"Because she wasn't honest with Aggie and me," Doro added. "It turned out to be for good reason, but we didn't know that until very late."

"But you eliminated Mr. Barnes and Alf earlier?" Gramma Rose asked.

"Not really," Ev replied. "We put all three down our list and kept them there until almost the end."

The older woman nodded. "You went undercover with the Zee-Yarrow gang because they were top suspects."

"Cal Zee wouldn't dirty his hands, but Cutter Yarrow would and did. I wasn't convinced he and Patrick Sweebe, one of their men, were involved until the night we went to the diner. All along, Phil Kesler seemed like a strong suspect, and I wondered about Mrs. Fulton's friends. Abe and Beatrice Jacoby weren't involved, but he was hedging his bets by not completely cutting ties with Zee and Yarrow, which his wife knew, but Mrs. Fulton didn't." Ev winked at Doro. "Your granddaughter kept saying something was odd about how the waitress acted when she and Aggie met Mrs. Fulton in the diner. And she was right, because it was Mrs. Jacoby."

Doro could not repress a pleased grin. "It was just a feeling."

"Those are important in detective work," Ev said. "Anyhow, we'd narrowed our suspects down to Yarrow and two others from his gang. He was the killer. According to Sweebe, Yarrow meant to get rid of Fulton, which isn't surprising, since he stole more booze from them than from the Keslers. A lot more."

Doro was glad Ev didn't share the ugly details about how Fulton was killed. Her grandmother need not know that.

Gramma Rose put her glass aside. "Doro mentioned the youngest Kesler going to the Fulton place after the murder."

"Yep," Ev agreed. "He and Jacoby were planning to pick up liquor. They were surprised to find Fulton dead. Phil Kesler can be a tough customer, but he was good enough to help Abe Jacoby get Mrs. Fulton to safety."

"But not for altruistic reasons," Doro pointed out.

"No. He was hoping to draw Yarrow and others from the gang into a shootout or put them under suspicion for murder, which he did," Ev said.

"I'm glad you were with Doro," Gramma Rose said.

Ev's silver gaze took on a warm glow. "I wouldn't have had it any other way."

Emotion clogged Doro's throat, and she swallowed hard before speaking. "Me, either." For a long moment silence reigned.

Gramma Rose chuckled. "You made a number of arrests, and not only in conjunction with the murder. Right?"

"That's right," Ev concurred. "The Bureau even found Cal Zee as he was about to head to Canada. That won't end bootlegging in the area, but four speakeasies are closed and two gangs are shut down."

"What about Mrs. Fulton? Where will she go?" Gramma Rose asked.

"She's staying in Toledo for now. Abe Jacoby is in jail, but his wife is free. I'm not sure any charges will be pressed against her. She invited Mrs. Fulton to stay with her at the diner apartment," Ev said. "After the trials, the widow will probably go to California, where a relative lives."

Surprise flickered across Gramma Rose's face. "Really? Mrs. Fulton is staying with the friend who took off and left to fend for herself? I'd think she'd be upset."

"Abe Jacoby forced his wife to leave that night, when Sweebe and the other two brought Mrs. Fulton to the diner. He feared being killed, and I'm surprised he wasn't," Doro put in.

"Patrick isn't as blood-thirsty as Cutter," Ev observed.

"Lucky for the Jacobys. Mrs. Jacoby and Mrs. Fulton have been friends since childhood, so I hope it works out."

"As do I," her grandmother said. She turned to Ev. "And you've helped young Alf and his family."

"They're better off with Ev's sister and her family," Doro added.

"And you're going to correspond with Charlotte, which will help her," Ev said.

Gramma Rose turned to Doro. "You mentioned her when we spoke on the telephone yesterday. I'm glad you'll stay in touch. She sounds like a bright young lady."

"She is," Doro agreed. "Aggie and I are heading a scholarship committee, and we plan to work on getting more funds for girls. It may take time, but we should be able to offer one to Charlotte by the time she finished high school."

Her grandmother clapped her hands together. "How wonderful. But what about their home? Surely, they didn't simply abandon it."

Ev's countenance grew solemn again. "No, they were able to close out the mortgage on the Waggoner place. Since they only owned the house, not any acreage, they got a small amount of cash. It was an enormous relief to Mrs. Waggoner."

"I imagine so," Gramma Rose said. "Overall, the family will be better off."

Ev nodded. "With the gangsters in jail, I agree. A fresh start should be good for them."

"Very astute observation," Gramma Rose said. "What about Jug Barnes?"

"He was only a small-time customer of the Fultons. He shouldn't have been at the house with Alf after the murder, but they thought some liquor might be left in one of the sheds. There wasn't," Ev responded. "This case may cure him of wanting a nip every night."

"I should think so," Rose said. "All-in-all, it ended well."

"It did," Doro agreed. "Agent Canton even found out about the agent who was on the take."

Her grandmother smiled. "You and Aggie mentioned that. I'm glad to know he's been found out."

"So was Lowery Canton," Ev added. "He hadn't been with the Bureau long, but he'll be in jail for a time."

Gramma Rose looked from Ev to Doro. "I hope this will be your last case for a while."

"I hope so, too. Classes start on Wednesday, and I have plenty to do," Doro said.

Her grandmother got to her feet. "I want to check on the table and the meal. We'll get the churn and ingredients ready, so be prepared to make ice cream in about a half-hour."

"Yes, ma'am," Ev replied. "I'm looking forward to it."

"Doro will help you," Gramma Rose said, before stepping inside.

⁂

Thirty minutes later, Doro and Ev were on the back porch. After assembling the ingredients, she began to make the sweet concoction.

After a couple of minutes, Ev spoke. "I can churn for a while."

Doubt assailed Doro. "Are you sure? I mean, I don't want you doing more damage to your arm."

"It's fine now," he assured her.

Doro's brows rose. "So, you keep saying, but you winced every time the car hit a rut on the way here."

A sliver of silence pierced the conversation. "It gives me a little trouble, but not nearly as much as it did," Ev admitted with a rueful smile. Before Doro could comment, he hurried on. "Step away and let me have a try. I've never made ice cream, so this will be fun. Besides, the birthday girl shouldn't do work on her special day."

Doro moved back. "Have at it."

After rolling up his sleeves, Ev took over. "Did you make ice cream often as a child? We never did."

"For special occasions," Doro replied. "At least we did until the candy shop in Michaw started making and selling it. Then, my dad bought a quart for our birthdays and such."

"The place near the theaters on the Main Street right in Sylvania has good ice cream."

After dinner and a movie, they had stopped there. The memory sent warmth through her. That had been such a wonderful evening, despite its end. Surely, they would have more dates like that one. They had not yet, but only a few days had passed since the Fulton murder case was cracked. Maybe this was a date. Or maybe not. Surely, Ev would ask her to step out again. As much as she wanted to know exactly when, Doro kept to the current topic. "Theirs is excellent, but my grandmother thinks it's more special to make it fresh, and I agree. Fresh-baked birthday cake and fresh-churned ice cream. There couldn't be a better dessert."

"Both sound terrific," Ev continued to work on the concoction.

"We'll celebrate your birthday with dinner. What kind of cake do you like? We're having marble today. Aggie could make one, but Gramma Rose and the housekeeper wanted her to have a break, so they made mine."

Ev nodded. "You, Aggie, and I will be busy in another week. I want to greet students, especially the new ones. The campus security officer should be approachable, not stern." He paused in his task. "Last year, I managed to keep my time as a Prohibition agent secret from the students and most of the staff. Now, I'm not sure I can."

"It shouldn't matter. I don't know of anyone on campus being involved in rumrunning, although some may buy bootlegged booze or go to speakeasies."

"I'm not digging into that, but people may think I am," he replied.

"If anyone at the college asks, I'll say we were investigating Mr. Fulton's murder, but not that you were undercover with the Bureau. Aggie and Wade won't mention anything different, and neither will Colleen. Wade has already asked her to keep quiet."

For a long moment, the sound of the churn was the only noise. Finally, Ev responded. "All right, because I don't want folks thinking I'm still working for it or ever will again."

His tone and expression underscored the statement, which removed the last of Doro's worry. "I'm glad to hear that because you seemed comfortable being undercover. Adept, too. I was impressed at how calm you were. If I hadn't already known you, I would've believed you were really part of the gang."

Some indefinable emotion flickered in his gaze. "I don't know if that's a compliment or a complaint."

"Neither," she replied. "Just an observation."

Something akin to relief eased his expression. "I can play a role, but it doesn't mean I like doing it or really feel at ease. I prefer being myself." He stopped churning the ice cream and focused completely on Doro. "I prefer being a campus security officer and deputy constable, just like I love living in Michaw and I plan to stay."

Doro smiled. "Good. So do I." The emotion simmering between them was palpable. She wanted him to act on it, but her grandmother's back porch was not the right place. "Let's talk about your birthday."

After returning to his task, Ev took up the thread of conversation. "All right. Since my birthday falls on a Sunday, we won't have to juggle work with dinner. Could we invite Aggie, Wade, and his children?"

The mention of her friend and the town constable reminded Doro of her note to Aggie's brother. Had he received it yet? What would be his response? Would Aggie be upset at Doro's interference? But she was not really meddling. She was helping pave the way for Aggie and Wade to wed. Briefly, she considered telling Ev, but dismissed the idea. Perhaps she would after hearing from her friend's brother. Doro picked up the thread of conversation.

"That's good because Gramma suggested having your party here. We can invite Aggie, Wade, his children, and whoever else you want. Gram and Mrs. Ogilive will whip everything up, including cake. White, marble, spice, banana, chocolate? What sounds good?"

A rueful smile touched his lips. "You know I have a serious sweet tooth, so any of them would be delicious. But I'm partial to chocolate."

"Chocolate cake with chocolate frosting and vanilla ice cream?" she asked.

"My mouth is watering," he replied with a laugh.

Hers was, too, but not for ice cream and cake. No, not at all.

Thank you!

Thank you for reading The Bottled Bootlegger! *I hope you enjoyed it. If you have time, please rate or review it. Comments from readers are helpful and appreciated. I am on Goodreads and BookBub. Most retailers also accept reviews. If you purchased from my website, there is a review option.*

https://www.goodreads.com/author/show/21325652.D_S_Lang

https://www.bookbub.com/profile/d-s-lang

For more information, please go to my website or Facebook page.

https://dslangbooks.com

https://www.facebook.com/profile.php?id=100064024056297

You can sign up for my newsletter on my website. I share other authors' work, news about my books, a peek into the writing life, historical tidbits, and more. Your email will never be shared, and you can unsubscribe at any time!

About the Author

D.S. Lang, a retired educator, started making up stories to entertain herself as an only child, and she is still making them up. Now, she puts them in writing. She is an avid storyteller and reader, with a To Be Read stack that is overflowing. In her free time, D.S. enjoys swimming, reading (of course), spending time with family and friends, and walking with her dog, Izzy.

A lover of language, D.S. has published over 10 books, with more on tap. Her aim is to write novels that blend history and mystery with dashes of drama, splashes of humor, and touches of romance to create charming stories with authentic details. When you finish one of her books, she hopes you have a smile on your face!

Set during the post-Great War period in small-town Ohio, the books welcome readers into an exciting period of American history, when women were navigating new roles, and the country was dealing with Prohibition and the aftermath of war. Living through those times required spunk, which her amateur sleuths have in spades.

Author's Series Notes

At one time, there actually was a Mitchaw, Ohio (sometimes called Mitchaw Corners). It was the birthplace of many of my relatives, including my dad. At its height, Mitchaw was an unincorporated village surrounded by farms. Like many other small, rural communities, it has disappeared as a separate entity. Now, it is part of Sylvania Township, and subdivisions have replaced most farms.

The town never had a college, nor was it as large and bustling as the Michaw in the Doro books. That is a big reason I dropped the "t" to change the spelling. However, Sylvania is a very real city. It is my hometown and where I still live. Since the 1920s, when this book is set, it has gone from a small village of around 2000 to a small city of 19,000. The township's population is approximately 50,000.

Doro Banyon Cozy Historical Mystery series

The Doro Banyon series has a cozier tone than the Arabella Stewart books. History and mystery still mesh as amateur sleuth Doro solves whodunits with a team of colorful characters in smalltown America during the 1920s. Travel back in time to a college campus and crack cases with them!

Book 5-<u>The Bottled Bootlegger</u>

Book 6-<u>The Doomed Doctor</u> (coming in April 2025)

If you want to know what happens with Doro and Ev between books 5 and 6, download "The Vintage Valentine," a Doro Banyon short story. Doro and Ev take a break from detective work as they plan to attend Michaw College's Sweetheart Ball. When a snowstorm hits the area, their special evening is in jeopardy. Can a family heirloom and a vintage card work their magic and bring the pair together? To get this free tale, scan the QR code or click on the link!

The story is not a mystery, but paranormal and suspense touches highlight this tale.

https://dl.bookfunnel.com/oxouyzca9y

Arabella Stewart Historical Mystery series

The Arabella Stewart Historical Mystery series is set in small-town Ohio after the Great War. Bella returns home from serving as a U.S. Army Signal Corps operator to find her family resort and hometown in dire straits, and the murder of a neighbor adds to the trouble. Much to the dismay of Constable Jax Hastings, an Army veteran, Bella turns amateur sleuth to solve the case. As the series continues, Bella and Jax vanquish the shadows of the war, while solving a series of whodunits with a team of colorful characters. Love and laughter occur along the way. If you love history and mystery mixed with touches of humor, romance, and drama, this series is for you!

Book One-A Precarious Homecoming
Book Two-A Lingering Shadow
Book Three-A Lethal Arrogance
Book Four-A Baffling Absence
Book Five-A Fatal Reunion
Book Six-A Surreptitious Undertaking
Book Seven-A Treacherous Accusation
Book Eight-An Uncertain Ceremony

Menu for Doro's Birthday Dinner (and a few recipes)

Recipes for items with an asterisk follow.

Sliced garden freshtomatoes
Creamy cole slaw*
Baked beans*
Fried Chicken
Biscuits with butter
Marble cake*
Home-churned vanilla ice cream

Baked Beans

1 two-pound can of pork and beans

1 small onion-grated

2 T brown sugar

¼ cup molasses

1 t white vinegar

3 strips of bacon

½ cup ketchup

Salt and pepper

Fry bacon. Put all other ingredients in a baking dish and mix well. Top with bacon.

Bake at 300 degrees for 1 ½ to 2 hours.

My mom made delicious baked beans for every summer holiday and event. She had a wonderful old brown baking crock for them.

Creamy Cole Slaw

1 large head of cabbage (about 4-5 cups) shredded. OR a 28-30 ounce package of cole slaw mix.

1 cup mayonnaise

¼ cup sugar

1 t celery salt

1 ½ t lemon juice

½ t onion powder

Salt and pepper to tase.

Combine mayo, sugar, lemon juice, onion powder, celery salt,salt and pepper in a large mixing bowl. Let sit until sugar is dissolved.

Shred cabbage. Then, fold it into the above mixture.

Taste test and adjust seasonings accordingly.

Cover and refrigerate for an hour before serving.

My paternal grandmother made creamy cole slaw every summer for the Cherry family reunion. I was ten before I knew there was another kind! I loved to help her, and we always tasted the concoction and adjusted the ingredients until it was just right.

Marble Cake

Marble cake was my favorite choice for my birthday when I was growing up. We had a wonderful bakery in town (Seitz's Bakery), and my mom (who was a marvelous cook) always ordered a special treat from there. Needless to say, it was baked from scratch. Mrs. Ogilvie, Gramma Rose's housekeeper,would also have made this yummy cake from scratch. Today, we have quick and easy options, so I've included a recipe using cake mixes.

Ingredients:

One box white (or yellow) cake mix. Use instructions on box and add ingredients accordingly.

One box chocolate (or Devil's food) cake mix. Use instructions on box and add ingredients accordingly.

Directions:

Prepare two baking pans. Grease and flour or use baking spray. Remember you have two complete cake mixes, so the pans need to be large. Or you can use four pans. Pans should be no more than 2/3 full when you put them into the oven.

Preheat oven to 375 degrees.

In a large mixing bowl, make white cake batter according to box directions.

In a separate bowl, do the same with chocolate cake mix.

Pour batter into pans, bit-by-bit. You can do this by alternating dollops of mix—white before chocolate, white before chocolate. Then, swirl a little but not too much! You want to have a marble effect.

Bake for 40-45 minutes or until a toothpick comes out clean. Baking times vary according to your oven, the weather, and altitude so, check after 20 minutes.

Let cake pans cool on rack for 10-15 minutes. Carefully remove cake from pans and allow to cool fully.

Frost with chocolate or white icing. For an extra easy final step, you can buy buttercream frosting!

For the simplest marble cake, buy a box mix and canned frosting! No matter what kind you use, it's a lovely cake.

Book Notes

Vehicles play important roles in this mystery. I've loved cars since I was a little girl, so it is fun to research vintage automobiles. In 1929, a number of cars had push-button starters, so keys were not necessary. That is the case with most of the vehicles in the book.

In my area, Northwest Ohio, bootlegging was common during Prohibition. Gangsters and speakeasies abounded in Toledo, so there is a lot of local lore about the topic. Prohibition agents like Lowery Canton had their hands full trying to corral violence between rival gangs and stop the flow of illegal liquor.

Ohio "went dry" before the Volstead Act prohibited the manufacture, sale, and distribution of alcohol. Prohibition was finally repealed nationwide in 1933, although some counties did not fall in line. The latest estimate suggests that 80 counties in the United States remain dry.